THE
CHIP SHOP WAR

Terry Sanderson

First Published in 2021

Copyright © Terry Sanderson

otherway@dircon.co.uk

*The author asserts his moral right under the
Copyright, Designs and Patent Act, 1988
to be identified as the author of this work.*

*CIP catalogue record for this title is available
from the British Library.*

For Keith – my strength and support

**The following story is set in an alternative
and totally imaginary Rotherham.
All characters are fictitious
and any resemblance to any person living or dead
is purely coincidental and unintended.
All incidents described are imagined
and not based on any actual events**

.

INTRODUCTION

by Terry Sanderson

Perhaps, before we embark on this storm-tossed voyage, I should say a few words of introduction about Doreen Potts and her family. They were childhood neighbours of mine when, in my youth, I lived in Rotherham, an ancient town which is situated in what was once the industrial heartland of South Yorkshire.

The closure of the coal mines and disappearance of the steel industry had somewhat impoverished the town. Doreen, her husband Derek, and their family had, like so many others, become impoverished with it.

Doreen was a matriarch even then, but she was a good friend to my mother and always made me welcome when I went to their house to play Monopoly with her son, Gary.

Gary was in my class at school, and we were good mates. I wasn't quite so friendly with Doreen's daughter, Sylvia. She was a bit too wayward for my taste. She matured early and knew the sort of things that girls of her age don't generally know.

Then there was Derek's mother, Iris, who was never a welcome visitor at their house. Whenever Iris called on them, there was invariably a very loud argument, which we could hear through the wall (and sometimes down the street). Despite Doreen's hostility towards Iris, husband Derek remained loyal to his mother and, as intolerable as Doreen found her, Iris was never actually forbidden to visit the house.

That is, until Sylvia brought disaster on them after she got involved in a religious cult that, through a long and convoluted series of events, got Doreen sent to prison. Although she was eventually cleared of all charges and released, she blamed Iris for her misfortune (not without reason) and banished her to the outer reaches of geriatric care.

But that's another story and was recounted in Doreen's previous book, *The Potts Papers*.

The present scenario finds the family at their home in the posher part of Rotherham, in the upmarket Evergreen Close. How such a family came to live in this four-bedroomed detached house in such a salubrious and leafy area is probably best not gone into.

1

It may have had something to do with the aforementioned religious cult and its attendant scam, or it might have been the result of a lucky five horse accumulator that Derek managed to land at the bookmakers. We'd best leave it at that.

When I moved to London, Doreen kept in touch by letter and email. She was forever grateful for the help I gave her when Gary came out as gay. She imagined that because I was also gay, that I had all the answers. I think she found that writing down her experiences was a kind of therapy. She said that the diaries were her way of saving her sanity, she said, a counsellor that you didn't have to pay for. And so, I was kept abreast of the continuing disaster that was Doreen's life.

In the end, I thought Doreen's story deserved a wider audience, so I asked if I could reproduce her letters and emails with the intention that anyone in doubt could hear her side of the tale. She was happy with that and, in fact, she also provided me with her extensive diaries to flesh it out.

So, when I put the letters, emails and diaries together to make a semi-coherent record of what had happened, she gave me permission to make small alterations to render it more readable. I corrected the more glaring spelling errors and added a bit of punctuation, something Doreen had found mostly unnecessary. But I didn't want to lose the unique sound of Doreen's voice and her very personal mode of expression. I'd heard enough of it when I was a child, to get the particular lilt. She spent hours in my mother's house chattering endlessly about the things that concerned her (mainly the goings-on at the Housewives Register and the ongoing feud with her "friend" Marje Bickerstaffe).

So, when she embarked on another adventure, I asked if I could repeat the exercise. She was amenable and, with her Christmas card that year, she enclosed her diary for 2001.

It is that unselfconscious diary that forms the basis of what follows. My contribution has been merely to remove the endless musings on such topics as the comparative merits of a Ewbank over a Hoover and put it all in some kind of order.

I've added just enough to fill in the blanks, and enough translation to make Doreen's take on the English language comprehensible to the casual reader.

Excerpts from Doreen's Diary, 2001

It was over Christmas dinner that I made the prediction to my husband.

"Derek," I said. "I'm going to achieve something this year. I can feel it in my water."

"This sounds bad," he said. "What exactly are you going to achieve?"

"Something new and challenging. Something that will change my life going forward."

"Oh God," he said. "Whenever you get the urge to do something new and challenging, Doreen, disaster nearly always follows."

"You'll not put me off with your negative thinking," I said. "I need to throw in the towel to myself. I'm going to have to find some focus for my energy. I need an enterprise."

"There's no need for you to have an enterprise. You've got everything you want here—this house, your family, a bit put by in the bank. What's the point of taking risks when everything's hunky dory?"

"That's the problem," I said. "Hunky dory will no longer cut it. I'm dessicating through lack of stimulation.".

"Well, get a job, then," he suggested.

"That's all very well for you to say, but who the hell is going to employ me? Not only am I the wrong side of fifty, but besides washing, hoovering and wielding a tin opener, I can't do nothing. I'm not qualified in anything. I've got no certificates."

"Well, get some. I did. I got my certificate in fork lift truck driving. You can go to night school. There are courses you can do."

He loves patting himself on the back with his certificate. You'd think it was the No Bell prize instead of a bit of paper saying he's safe to be in charge of a dangerous vehicle. I could crown him with it sometimes.

He's not interested any more. Now he's got his job at the depot he couldn't give a monkey's about me. As long as there's something to eat on the table when he gets home, that's all he's bothered about.

But fate can play funny ticks can't it? It can give you a little jolt. And that's just what happened when I went down to Deans's fish and chip shop to get our dinner today. I said to Mrs Deans, as she wrapped my order, I said: "You've been at this game an awful long time haven't you, Alice? I'll bet you could get in the Guinness Book of Records, the number of fish you've fried and chips you've wrapped over the years."

"You might be right there, Doreen. We've been here thirty-seven years, but it can't go on much longer. We're getting on, you know. We're going to have to pack it up soon."

Mr Deans nodded sadly in the background as he battered a couple of haddock in the time-honoured way—one drag to the right, one drag to the left, a half drag to the right and lift it out. "All good things must come to an end," he said.

I must say, they looked knackered. Mr Deans's shoulders are all hunched, and his hair is snowy white. Hers is, too. I hadn't noticed how white their hair was before. You take people like that for granted, don't you? You don't notice them getting old when you see them regular.

I've been going to that shop every few days since I was a lass, and it's always been owned by Mr and Mrs Deans. Lovely couple. You never see them apart. They're like a pair of them Sudanese twins—joined at the hip, metaphysically speaking. They live together and work together, and they have done since I can remember. And they never row or shout at each other. They always seem happy. Lord and Lady Echo I used to call them. They never contradicted one another not like my mam and dad used to.

My mam and dad did nothing but contradict one another.

I actually worked in Deans's chip shop once, many moons ago, as an insistant. It was just for the first year after I was married. It gave us that bit of extra money you need when you're getting started. I quite enjoyed my time there, actually.

I remember Derek and me did a lot of our courting outside that shop, as well. We'd go there about seven in the evening. He'd have rock salmon and chips and I'd have cod with mushy peas. We'd feed each other the scraps at the bottom of the packet—little bits of batter that had come off the fish—then we'd go up the alley and have a snog. I remember our lips were all greasy and salty. Ever since then I've thought of Deans's fish and chip shop in an erotic kind of way. Same as some folk think of dirty weekends in Brighton.

At that time, when we were a couple of teenagers just getting started, Derek considered it his manly duty to try to get his hand in my blouse. It was the done thing. But he didn't succeed very often.

4

You didn't allow it in them days. It was like an undeclared war between lads and lasses—lads would try it on, lasses would thwart them. Sometimes you'd have to wrestle with them or smack them really hard in the face when they persisted, but it was all good natured.

When I was a teenager, I had a job in the peanut factory. It was the only work you could get round here in them days. All the lasses would get together at tea break and discuss how far we'd let our boyfriends go that weekend. We'd sit giggling in the canteen saying: "Have you let him have a feel?" "Has he had your brassiere off?" "Has he tried to go up your skirt?" "Did his doo-da go hard?"

It was great having all that power over lads. You'd snog them for a bit, let their hands start wandering, and just when they thought they were well in, you'd push them off and say: "Stop that, you dirty bugger. You ought to be ashamed of yourself." Then next time you'd let them go a bit further, and push them even harder, and call them worse names.

But you never went the whole way. You'd sit on their lap and wiggle about and what not, you know, just to give them a thrill, and just when they were enjoying themselves and starting to breath heavy, you'd jump up and say: "That's filthy!"

But God help any lass who let her boyfriend "go all the way". Word would soon get round and they'd get called all sorts, slags, whores, the lot. We was very innocent then. I recall Peggy Ainsworth being sent to Coventry because she admitted to going to a dance without any knickers on.

Nowadays lasses get called names if they aren't carrying three-packs of condoms in their handbags.

The Deans's always had the knack of frying excellent fish suppers. It isn't a gift given to everyone—as those who are forced to patronise the Chips & More! down Elvington Road know very well. Traditional chips have to be cut to a certain thickness. I can't be doing with the ones you get at these fast-food takeaways—them so-called French fries. Horrible. Like eating a packet of dry twigs with salt on.

Deans's chips were just the right thickness—big enough to be able to bite into a couple of times, but not so big that they lose their flavour. They insisted on using Maris Pipers whenever they could. They're the best taters for chips. Them Chinese takeaways can't make chips. Too thick and soggy. They want to stick to what they're good at—chicken chow main and special fried rice and that.

And they've no idea about chips abroad on the continent. We went on a day trip to Belgium once, and we had some chips off a stall. Revolting. Apparently, they fry them twice, and then pour mayonnaise over them. Have you ever heard anything like it?

I said to Mrs Deans as she stirred the fryer with her wire scoop: "I don't know how we're going to manage when you jack it in, love. These are the only decent fish and chips for miles. I'm going to get a petition up to ensure that it stays as a fish and chip shop after you've gone. We don't want it turning into another burger joint—we've got enough of that rubbish as it is."

"Well, it's nice to feel you've been appreciated, and your life's work hasn't been in vain," she said, lowering the battered fish into the fryer, causing the oil to bubble and hiss. "A lot of people have said the same. We'll try not to sell it to anybody who's not going to carry on the tradition, although there's only so long we can hold out before we're took to the great chip shop in the sky—and we want to have a bit of retirement before then."

"Well, of course you do," I said sadly, looking round the old chippy, perhaps for the last time.

"Do you know anybody who might be interested in taking over, Doreen?" Mrs Deans said.

"I don't, love," I said. "But I'll put word about."

"What about giving it a go yourself, duck? I remember you used to be lovely with the customers when you worked here. You'd be able to make a go of it if anybody could." She turned to her husband. "I say Doreen'd be able to make a go of it, wouldn't she Dad?"

"Yes, she'd make a smashing go of it would Doreen, no problem," Mr Deans echoed.

"Me?" I laughed. "I don't know nothing about running a fish and chip shop, Mrs Deans. All I can do is wrap them up and hand them over. I even had trouble adding up if you recall."

"We've got tills for that now, duck. Does all the adding up and taking away for you," says Mrs Deans.

"That's right," said Mr Deans. "Adding up, taking away. The till does it all for you these days."

"I'm no businesswoman," I said. "I haven't any experience."

"Well, neither did we have when we first inherited the shop from me mam and dad, did we Dad? Complete novices we were.."

"Aye we were. New starters."

"There's not a great deal to it. You can go on courses. Read books," said Mrs Deans. "And if you've got a bit of go in you, there's plenty of scope for improvements. Isn't there, Dad?"

"There is that. You could make improvements certainly. If you had a bit of go in you."

"And we're not asking the earth for it, are we Dad?" Mrs Deans says. "We're robbing ourselves to be honest. It's going for a song actually."

"Aye, that's right. A knock-down price."

"And it's well-established. We're charging nothing for the good will."

"Nothing. Not a penny for the good will."

"I'll think about it," I laughed. "But don't wait for me."

I walked to the door and turned back and said: "But if Ronald McDonald puts in a bid, don't let him have it."

As I came home with my fish and chips twice and a carton of mushy peas, I felt quite nostalgic.

Everything changes, I thought. Nothing stays the same.

Then I got to thinking.

If I wanted the chip shop to stay open, why didn't I take Mrs Deans up on her offer? I could take it over. Maybe this was the opportunity I'd been looking for. A new career as the queen of the fish and chip shop. I could just see myself wielding the scoop and giving a few extras to under-nourished kiddies. I could introduce new innovations like salmon fish cakes.

The more I thought about the idea, the more it was turning from being a non-starter into something quite exciting. I started thinking how much the Deans's were going to want for a smashing little business like that.

And whether what we had in the bank would cover it.

* * *

I didn't sleep too well last night. I couldn't give over thinking about the fish shop. Derek knew something was on my mind, but I didn't say anything over breakfast. I needed time to see whether the idea grew on me or whether it withered on the vine.

No sooner was he out of the house and gone to work than the phone rings. Sheffield Social Services Department on the line. Mr Allinson, social worker assigned to Mrs Potts senior.

Iris.

My heart sank. Iris is my mother-in-law. The woman whose name is not mentioned in this house without crossing yourself or spitting, but preferably not at all. A woman whose existence I would like to forget, but who has caused me such grief that she is branded into my memory for ever. It was like telepathy—if I was feeling good or excited or pleased about something, if the sun was shining in my life, Iris had this uncanny knack of sending a cloud to put it into the shade.

"I wonder if it would be possible to pop round and see you and your husband at some stage in the near future," this social worker was saying. "It's about your mother-in-law, Iris."

"Is she dead?" I said hopefully.

He sounded a bit shocked and said: "No."

"Is she in terrible pain and agony, then?" I said.

"No, not really."

"Oh," I said, and the tone of disappointment in my voice seemed to make him even further appalled.

"But she isn't very well. I think the time's coming for us to have a little chat about her future."

"I don't see why," I said. "She's nothing further to do with us. We've abandoned her and you can't force us to take responsibility—I've looked into it. She'll have to be put into one of them homes. And it'll be one with a poor reputation if there's any justice."

"I get the impression you don't get on with your mother-in-law," this Mr Allinson says.

"Very perspective of you," I said with a sarky tone of voice.

"Well, I wondered if we could make an appointment for me to pop round, anyway. I've got my statutory duty to do, Mrs Potts. And perhaps your husband will feel differently about it when he hears what's been happening. When would it be convenient to call in?"

We made an appointment for the following Monday evening, after Derek got in from the depot.

But when Derek got home that night, I told him straight, I said: "Your mother is not coming here, I don't care what state she's in.

8

And that's final. They'll have to make other arrangements. Is that clear?"

He looked at the carpet. "Is it?" I repeated, determined he wasn't going to plead ignorance at a later date.

He just bit his lip and looked worried.

* * *

I've thought about little else other than the chip shop for the last two days, and eventually I rang Mrs Deans and asked if she would be prepared to hold her horses for a week as regards putting it on the market, while I worked on Derek. He'd take some persuading, I said.

"I understand, love. Men don't like change, do they? They often have to be coaxed, even when it's in their own best interests. You butter him up, love, and we won't go the estate agent until the middle of next week. We quite like the idea of you having the shop..."

(In the background I could hear Mr Deans saying "Aye, we do.")

"...it makes us feel comfortable knowing that it won't fall into the wrong hands."

Now I'm all at odds with myself. One half of me head is crazy with excitement over the chippy, the other is mad with worry about where this Iris business is leading.

I was walking about the house, dusting, polishing, rearranging my knick-knacks, and generally being hyper. "Look," I said to myself. "Count your blessings and stop mithering. Whatever will be will be, kay sara, sara." Then I thought: bugger that, I'm not waiting for bloody Doris Day to run my life. I'm going to be pro-active. *I'm* going to make things happen.

Eventually I decided to occupy myself at the shops. There's nothing like a bit of shopping for calming the nerves. So, I decided to hit the town (as our Sylvia calls it), with the intention of wearing the embossing off me credit card.

There's plenty still in the bank as a result of that newspaper pay-out we had last year. Tens of thousands, in fact. Not that I'd want to repeat the experiences that brought the money into our hands. What happened was that my daughter Sylvia became embroiled in an unfortunate religious scandal that took the nation's fancy, and the newspapers were queuing up to pay us for the details.

9

That period of our lives comes under the heading "least said soonest mended". Iris—miss clever-clogs, know-all herself—thought she could get away with murder. The upshot was, I ended up in jail on trumped up charges and it took several weeks of nightmare incarceration before I was found innocent and released. We've turned over a new leaf since then, which includes abandoning Iris to the geriatric care industry. But it has left us flushed, cash-wise.

Anyway, I was getting my coat on ready for the fray (town gets ever so crowded on the first day of the sales, but I love all that argy-bargy, it makes you feel alive), when our Sylvia comes in, carrying her baby.

I should explain that my daughter is living here with us at Evergreen Close at the moment. She is a single unmarried mother. Last year she gave birth to a baby, Charmaine Bernadette. Despite the unfortunate parentage of the kiddy (which is something else I don't want to dwell on), that child is a smasher and the apple of my eye. She's so gorgeous that sometimes I just can't stop looking at her. I get so excited I have to fettle the stairs to calm meself down (I'm off the tablets now, with the help of that support group).

Charmaine Bernadette has got a great mop of gorgeous jet-black hair, and she's always laughing. I love kiddies when they're that age, don't you? I could put her between two slices of bread and eat her for me tea, she's that lovely.

Anyway, our Sylvia comes in and sees me with me coat on. She says: "Where are you going, Mam?"

"I'm off to town," I says. "Is there owt you want fetching back?"

"No, but if you hang on a minute, I'll come with you. We could do with a bit of an outing, me and the babby."

I says, "You're not coming out with me in that state."

"What do you mean?" she says. "What's up with me?"

"Well, for a kick-off, your hair looks a bugger. When did you last do anything to it?"

"Do anything? Like what?"

"Like comb it. And them clothes. Have you ironed that skirt?"

"I haven't had time," she says.

"It wouldn't take long," I said. "There's not much of it. I'm surprised you don't freeze to death wearing such short skirts in this weather."

Mind you, they're all at it, aren't they, these young lasses? Dressing themselves up like street walkers. I wish the fashion would change to something a bit smarter.

I picked me handbag up and turned on her again. "You're neglecting yourself, Sylvia. Since you had that babby you've gone downhill faster than a runaway truck. You want to shape yourself."

She looked in the mirror over the mantelpiece, flinched, and then looked away.

"I'm not that bad," she says. "You're bound to be a bit under weather when you've just given birth. Everybody is."

"It's twelve months since that babby popped out. She's nearly walking and you're still claiming to be suffering the after-effects. I'm not kidding, you look like you've just been discharged from the TB clinic and walked straight out into a hurricane."

Her bottom lip trembled. "I've lost interest in everything, except our Charmaine Bernadette," she says.

"Well, you want to pull your socks up. Or your tights. What's wrong with you? A young woman like you should take a pride in her appearance. It's not as if we're poor. You don't have to dress in all that cheap tack. And that black nail polish you've put on your toes— you look like you've got gangrene in your feet. I've not seen nothing like it since me grandad's diabetes got the better of him."

Her lip trembled even faster. "I've got post-natal depression," she wailed and then starts crying. "Oh, Mam, I feel that unattractive. I just feel as though no man is ever going to look at me again. All me friends are married, and here's me, still living with me Mam and Dad, changing nappies and getting titty bottles ready all day. Life's passing me by and I'm only 23."

She slumped on to the settee and started sobbing.

I couldn't help feeling sorry for her, sitting there with her short skirt on, trying to make her dumpy little legs look like something special. She's all out of proportion, you see. Short legs, wide hips and the most enormous bosom for a girl of her size. One minute she's trying to hide them with billowy blouses, the next she's got these tight jumpers on looking like something out of the Sunday Sport. And her hair! She's had that many chemicals on it over the years that it now looks as if it needs a pitchfork rather than a comb.

But she's not had an easy time, poor lass. Now she's lumbered with our Charmaine Bernadette, even though she's nowt but a kid herself.

11

"I just want a bit of a laugh. Is that too much to ask?" our Sylvia was sobbing.

"Just think on," I says. "It were a bit of a laugh that landed you in this state in the first place. If you hadn't been so fond of bits of laughs you might be in with a chance."

"Men run a mile when they see me coming. The instant they clap eyes on that pushchair, they're off. I used to have men galore at one bit."

"Well, perhaps you should learn a lesson. It's quality you want to go for now, not quantity. Anybody can find themselves a dickhead to marry, Sylvia. I can personally testify to that myself. But you ought to aim a bit higher. Demand something better."

I sat beside her and held her hand. "Look, love. I know how you're feeling. At your age you've still got hormones. Sometimes they're more trouble than they're worth, are hormones, but there's not much you can do about them when they're raging. You've got to learn that the type of men that you've been knocking about with are not exactly long-term prospects. They might be good-looking (although I have to say, not many of them have been), but you need somebody who can provide for you and the kiddy. And I don't mean provide stolen goods, neither."

"I understand that, Mam, but it's not easy to be sensible when your body's crying out for a man's touch. Love me, it's saying. I need loving. I'm a loving sort of person. It's got to find expression or I'll go round the twist."

"As I say, sex. Hormones. manking about. Whilst ever you're in thrall to your hormones there's no talking to you. Take my advice, when you have the change of life, don't go on that hormone replacement lark. When you get to my age, you don't want your hormones replacing, you're glad to be shut of them. When you've got them, all they say is sex, sex, sex."

"No," she says. "Mine aren't saying sex, Mam, they're saying love. I just want a bit of affection and reassurance. I just want a man to cuddle me and hold me. I'm not bothered about the mucky part, just the romance and kissing."

"Aye, well men's priorities tend to be the other way round. They like to start with the slimy bits, and they'll think about kissing and cuddling afterwards. That's if they can stay awake long enough."

There's no doubt she doesn't seem right. She's got this listless look, pale but not interesting. No colour in her cheeks. Eyes sunk in. My heart goes out to her.

"Look," I said. "Go and comb your rat tails, change into some decent clothes—a skirt that goes below your navel and doesn't smell of baby sick—and then we'll go and get you a tonic from the chemist. You're not eating properly, neither. Not enough vitamins. We'll go to Burger King and get you a decent meal, my treat. That should set you up. And after that, I'll take you to Maison Tracey's and get your hair rescued. You'll look a new lass with them split ends cut off and all that gel got rid of. I'll ring Darryl now to see if he can fit you in. It'll buck you up. I'll pay."

She pulled a face and said: "I can't be bothered, Mam. I haven't got the energy."

"Can't be bothered?" I says, dragging her to her feet. "Go and get ready. Today is the first day of your new life. I'll see to that. And get a bottle ready for our Charmaine, we're going to be out a long time."

Well, we were. Town was even more crowded this year than ever. There were that many people you could hardly move.

I have to say that the pushchair was handy at the sales. When I got to John Lewis's department store I cut a swathe through the crowd with it, ramming it into the backs of people's legs.

I chose our Sylvia's outfit for her (red top, black midi-length skirt, lovely jacket, reasonable knee boots) because I know what would have happened if I'd given her a free hand—more tiny skirts and tight tops, more ripped jeans and bovver boots. She said she didn't like what I'd picked for her, but I said take it or leave it, so she took it.

I dropped her off at the hairdresser's, Maison Tracey's, after we'd had our dinner. Our Gary's old school friend, Darryl, works there. I think he must get staff discount because he changes the colour of his hair every other week. I said to him, I said: "I want her transforming, Darryl. Made-over sort of thing, like they do on the telly. Be radical but be soft. I don't want her looking like something from a motorbike gang. Think in terms of Audrey Hepburn. You know—elfin."

He looked doubtful about that, but he said: "I'll let my creative urges run riot, Mrs Potts, don't you worry about that."

Well, it mithered me when he said that. I thought back to that time when his creative urges was put to work on a perm he gave me. I ended up in casualty with third degree burns to my scalp.

I took Tracey (of Maison Tracey fame) to one side and asked her quietly if she'd mind seeing to our Sylvia personally herself. "A hair styling disaster at this point in her life might tip her over the edge," I whispered. Tracey said she understood. Nice woman, if a bit over-fond of the make-up.

So, while our Sylvia was being creatively titivated, I took our Charmaine Bernadette round to her uncle Gary's. His new flat is just round the corner from Maison Tracey's.

Now I should tell those persons who don't know my family that my son Gary lives with his friend Bill. Them as can read between the lines will have realised that Gary is not as other mothers' sons. He is a homosexual gay person, a fact that I apologise for having to mention, but it's no use trying to brush it under the bed. I always get it out of the way as soon as possible when I meet new people, so that I can stop thinking about it at the first opportunity. Don't get me wrong—I have no problem with my son's unusual predications. After all, if Elton John's mother can cope with it, so can I. I love my son just as much as any mother, and I tell him all the time that he's to be proud of himself, to be dignified, and not to worry about the shame he's brought on the family.

We've known his 'little secret' for many years now, and have completely come to terms with it, in many ways. Nowadays it is a non-issue. Except for the nights I lay awake tossing and turning and thinking about the daughter-in-law I shall never have, and the grandkiddies that will for ever be denied to me.

Anyway, our Gary and his 'husband' Bill (a lovely lad in some ways, although I wouldn't trust him as far as I could throw him. He works as a nurse at the Northern General) have got themselves this new flat on Inglewood Street. Beautiful inside. Two bedrooms, gorgeous living room and separate kitchenette. Lots more space than they had at their previous flat, and quite a reasonable rent, given they're both working at good jobs. However, they're on the second floor which is a bugger when you've got a push chair.

"Are you keeping your lavs nice?" I said to him, as he brought me a cup of tea.

"Yes, mother. And thank you for the year's supply of Domestos. A very thoughtful Christmas gift."

"Well, I could have brought you Old Spice as usual, but you wouldn't have thanked me for it. Don't think I don't notice it's never on your bathroom shelf, even though I've been buying you a big bottle every year since you started shaving."

He quickly changed the subject. "How's Gran getting on these days?" he says.

Well, that did it. I turned on him. "Gary! No sooner am I through the door than you mention the forbidden person. I've told you not to utter that woman's name in my presence again. Now change the subject."

"I only asked. Only I didn't see her over Christmas this year. She never even called, and she wasn't in when I rang her."

"She's a person non grata as far as I'm concerned. She ceased to exist for me after that terrible trick she pulled. You more than anybody should know what she did and what she's capable of."

"I know, Mam, but that's all past and gone. Family feuds are a waste of time," he says. "You only end up hurting yourself."

"I'm warning you—if you keep talking about her, I'm going."

I tell you, that woman has some kind of psychotic connection to my brain. Whenever I manage to shove her out of my mind for a minute or two she somehow manages to shove herself back in again. There's no escape. Iris is 75 now and living in—or should I say domineering—a sheltered accommodation block in Sheffield. This is her second one.

Iris and I have what is called an unhappy history. We do not get on. That's putting it mildly. She hates my guts and the feeling is mutual as regards me hating hers. When we get together it's like a re-run of the Vietnam war. I say that quite deliberately, because if I had napalm, I'd use it on her. And I'm not kidding.

We now avoid each other as much as possible. She's not going to get the opportunity to bring any more misery down on us with her scheming. Not if I can help it.

She used to come over to us and spend Christmas at one time. That was before the disaster. She's banned from the house now. I won't even speak to her on the phone. She had the cheek to send me a Christmas present via Derek. A face cloth gift pack with matching talcum powder. Packed by deaf people in Wilmslow, apparently. I sent it straight down to the Oxfam shop for recycling. I refuse to perfume myself with her leftovers.

But Derek doesn't feel he can abandon her, what with her being his mother. He feels a bounden duty to keep in touch, so we can't cut off contacts completely, much as I'd like to. He goes over to the sheltered housing complex to see her from time to time, particularly at holidays. I wait outside in the car. I say, "Look, Derek, I am not going in there. Not without garlic and a wooden stake. You do your duty as you see fit, and then we'll go home."

The next time I go to an event where she is present it will be at her funeral, but then only to dance on her grave. Well, that's enough about her. It's making me depressed just thinking about her.

The next shock came when I went to collect our Sylvia from Maison Tracey's. I couldn't believe my eyes. She'd had her hair dyed purple and cut really short, a crew cut sort of thing with little spikes—as though somebody on drugs had run riot with the pinking shears. I nearly dropped the babby when I saw it.

"God almighty!" I said. "What the bloody hell have you done to her, Tracey? She looks as though she's fallen head-first into the waste disposal."

"I tried to stop her, Mrs Potts," says Tracey, "but she made me do it. She's very strong-willed is your Sylvia."

"Made you do it? Did she hold a gun to your head?" I shouted. "I could have you up for this. It's patent neglect."

"Don't blame us," Darryl said. "She kicked up something chronic. We had to do what she wanted. After all, she is over 21. She can do what she likes with her own hair. We couldn't force her to have an Audrey Hepburn."

I got hold of our Sylvia's arm and gave her a shake. "Put a scarf on and get in the taxi," I said. "You're going to frighten this babby to death looking like that. What on earth was you thinking about?"

"It's what I wanted. I felt like a change," she says, all defiant, thrusting her bottom lip out. "You can stick Audrey Hepburn up your arse. Who is she, anyroad?"

"Well I'll tell you this for nothing, lady, you are not stepping out of the house till your hair's grown back. There's folk locked up for less than what you've done."

I stormed out of Maison Tracey's without leaving a tip and threatening never to go back again. They didn't seem all that bothered.

* * *

16

I'm not kidding, I'll swing for our Sylvia. She only went and got the receipts for them new clothes out of my purse and took them back to the shop for a refund. Then she went up to the second-hand motorbike gear place and bought herself a semi-worn out leather jacket and a pair of jeans with rips in the knees. I wouldn't mind but she hasn't even got a motorbike. I said to her, I said, "What the hell are you thinking about? You haven't even got a motorbike."

"It's the image I'm going for, slightly dikey" she says. "I feel tons better with these clothes on. I feel human again."

* * *

Our Sylvia was parading about the house in that bloody leather coat of hers. It stinks to high heaven. God knows who owned it before, but it looks as if a visit to the VD clinic wouldn't do it any harm.

I told her, I said: "Look, lady, we've got a social worker coming to visit after tea about your Granny Iris, so you'd better make yourself scarce. If he sees you prancing about dressed like that, he'll start instituting enquiries about our Charmaine Bernadette. Get off over to our Gary's for the evening and take the babby with you."

She were off like a shot. Even though she's got a clean sheet as regards illegal or antisocial activity at the moment, she's not fond of social workers, isn't our Sylvia. She's got a long and unhappy history, you see.

Well, true to his word this Mr Allinson turns up just after we'd finished our beans on toast with a poached egg. Typical social worker, all brief case and scuffed shoes. Patches sewn on the elbows of his jacket. I knew he was a bearer of bad tidings as soon as I saw him. He got this folder out of his case containing lots of important-looking papers. That's always a bad sign with social workers, when they get folders out. They try to put the wind up you with forms. But I could see that as he sat on the settee, he was weighing us up, seeing which of us to work on.

"Now," said this Allinson chap to Derek, "I'm going to have to be honest with you, Mr Potts. I'm afraid your mother isn't doing too well at the moment. In fact, she's deteriorating rather rapidly. Her health isn't all it could be."

"Deteriorating?" Derek said, suddenly looking worried and perching on the edge of his armchair. "In what way, Mr Allinson? She seemed perfectly all right last time I saw her just before

Christmas. She were a bit mardy, but that's not unusual with me mother. She's always complaining about her health."

"Well, the decline is physical *and* mental, I'm afraid. I've got the doctor's report here, if you'd like to see it. You'll find full particulars in that." He shuffled papers and handed something over to Derek. "As you'll see, her mind seems to be going. A form of dementia the doctor was saying. There's nothing much we can do about it, and it's likely to be progressive."

I could see straight away where all this doom and gloom was leading and decided I'd put my foot down early doors. "She's not coming here," I said, as firmly as I could.

"But what about this sheltered housing she's in?" Derek was saying. "They'll look after her there, won't they?"

"Well, you see, that's where we hit problems," says Mr Allinson. "One of the main conditions for staying in these sheltered housing units is that residents retain a degree of independence. They've got to be able to cope on a day-to-day basis. Now, because of funding cuts, I'm afraid our wardens' hours have been reduced from twenty-four to twelve. We just can't afford the night shift any more. And that's when your mother tends to be most active."

"I know what's coming next," I said. "And she's not coming here."

Mr Allinson tried to ignore me and continued to talk directly at Derek. "Last week Iris tried to make a fire in the fireplace of her flat. She put paper and sticks and some coal in the grate and lit it. As you know, these fireplaces are only ornamental. They're non-functional as regards being of any use. They're there just to act as surrounds for the electric fires that we use to heat the units. There isn't even a chimney."

"She's harking back, you see," says Derek. "She were raised in a coal-mining town. Her husband was a miner and they always had a coal fire burning in the grate. She got up every morning for forty years during her married life and made a fire just like you're describing."

"As you can imagine, Mr Potts, it's rather dangerous to be lighting fires in such circumstances—especially as she was using a can of petrol to get it going. Anything could have happened. There could have been a tragic conflagration if Mrs Dalton, the lady next door, hadn't had her daughter visiting. Andrea saw what was happening through the window and raised the alarm. Otherwise, I dread to think."

"She's not coming here, Derek," I said. "We can't have an arsonist running riot on the premises. We've a kiddy to think of."

Derek shushed me and says to this social worker, "So what are you saying, Mr Allinson?"

"Well, it's clear that your mother can't stay in her present accommodation. It isn't safe."

"She's not coming..."

"Oh, shut it, Doreen," Derek shouted. "I'm trying to talk sensible to Mr Allinson. So, what do you suggest, then, Mr Allinson? Have you got a residential home for people like her, then? Can she be put in a place with other old people who've lost their marbles?"

"At the moment, Mr Potts, I'm afraid we don't have any beds, as such. There's an increasing demand for this kind of accommodation, and we just don't have the money to fund it."

"Where is she now, then? Have you put her somewhere safe?"

"At present she's in St Joseph's. In a geriatric ward."

"That's perfect," I said, breathing a sigh of relief. "That's the right place for her—locked up at last in the lunatic asylum. It's long overdue is that."

"We can't leave her there," Derek was wailing. "It's Victorian."

"They take beautiful care of them in St Joseph's," I said. "You should know, you've been in there yourself." I turned to Mr Allinson. "Only as a temporary measure, you understand. Mental health runs in the family. Mr Potts had a bit of a bad do last year and had to be committed."

"*Admitted...*" corrected Derek. "I was *admitted*, not committed. I went in voluntary."

"Well," said Mr Allinson, "I'm afraid it can only be a temporary measure for your mother. She only got a place there because she was regarded as an acute case after the incident last week. They don't have the facilities for keeping people over the longer term any more at St Joseph's. In fact, going forward, they're talking in terms of closing it down altogether. Turning it into luxury flats."

"So where *can* she go?" asked Derek.

"The options are few these days, Mr Potts, I'm sorry to say. Economic restraints have meant a lot of the care we might have offered in the past is now no longer available. It's all private and very expensive. What the council can contribute would depend very much on individual circumstances."

"Her circumstances are easy enough to assess," I said. "She's got nowt. She's technically a pauper. She hasn't got no income nor no savings that we know of. Nothing of that nature at all. And as I said before, we've abandoned her. We're certainly not volunteering to have our savings dibbed into to support her. She's not eating up our nest egg in nursing home costs."

"Just a minute, Doreen..." says Derek.

"Never mind just a minute," I said. "I can feel her drawing closer to this house with every sentence that is spoke. *She is not coming here*. Can you hear me, Derek? SHE IS NOT COMING HERE!"

Mr Allinson shifted in his place so that his back was to me and he was facing Derek. Body language, you see. I've read about in my *Woman's Own*.

"I have to say, Mr Potts, that the future looks bleak for your mother," he said. He'd spotted the crack in Derek's defences and he was straight in there to prise it open. Standing between us, he was trying to create what is called in body language circles a symbolic chasm.

"Don't lay it on," I said. "I can see what you're up to. You're trying to sow doubts in his mind, aren't you?"

Mr Allinson ignored my challenge, and said, "The truth is, Mr Potts—can I call you Derek?—the truth is Derek, that your mother is in a very unenviable situation. Unable to make decisions for herself, she is going to end up with the absolute minimum standards of care. Life can be hard for those without an advocate. There's no money, you see. It's all been cut. Chop, chop, chop."

"Not all of it," I said.

Derek looked even more worried and rubbed his chin. "Let me think about it," he says. "How long can she stop at St Joseph's?"

"Her bed there is secure until next Wednesday. After that, I'm afraid she'll be cast adrift. We'll have to do the best we can for her, but that won't be much."

"Just a minute," I said. "She's worked all her life, paid her stamps—and so did her husband, until he were fatally killed on his sixty-fifth birthday. He never saw a penny of his pension. Where did all that money go? What happened to the welfare state?"

"That's a question many of us are asking," said Mr Allinson, sighing and packing the papers back into his briefcase. "I'll be in

20

touch with you before we make any decisions, Derek. I'm sure you'll want to know what's happening to your mother."

"No he doesn't," I said. "We've washed our hands of her."

Mr Allinson ignored me again and turned to Derek. "Mr Potts?" he says.

Derek hesitated, and then said: "Aye, you keep me informed, lad. Let me know what's going off, and I'll see what's to be done."

Mr Allinson smiled in a triumphant kind of way, shook hands with Derek, and went out without so much as a tarra to me.

As soon as he was out of the door, I set about Derek.

"You must think I'm dim. I can see what's going through your head, Derek, and you can forget about it. You know what your mother did to me. She nearly put me away for good. Have you forgotten that?"

"It weren't her fault."

"It were entirely her fault," I said. "I nearly got a life sentence because of her. Now you're thinking about bringing her back into our home and imposing another life sentence on me. I can hardly believe it. Where's your loyalty to me?"

"You heard the man. She's nowt but a shadow, waiting for the valley of death. A woman facing the abbess. We can't leave her to face it alone."

"I don't care who she's facing, I'm not having it. If she comes here, I'm moving out."

He looked at me.

"I mean it, Derek. I'll bugger off, and then see how you manage."

"Where're you going to bugger off to?" he says.

I was temporarily silenced at that point. At first I was going to say that I'd go to our Gary's, but Derek knows I would be as welcome there as dog muck on the bottom of a shoe.

Actually, I got a bit of a shock through me stomach when I realised there weren't anywhere I could go in an emergency. My own mother and father are dead, my only brother is in Australia, and I haven't heard from him for twenty years. For all I know, he could have succumbed as well. I think Derek must have realised that I was at his mercy.

"It doesn't sound as though she's got much longer to go, anyway," he says. "We could manage to help her in her final days, surely, Doreen? You're a compassionate and generous woman."

21

"Generally I would agree with you, but my compassion and generosity runs out when it comes to people like Joseph Stalin and your mother. In fact, I wouldn't give her the snot off me nose let alone a place at me table," I said. "If she comes here, I'll not raise a finger to help her. You'll have to give up your job and see to her yourself. I want to do something filfulling with my life, not become a slave to your mother's madness."

"You pretend to be hard, Doreen, but it isn't you. Let's sleep on it and talk about it in the morning. See if we can think of a solution that would satisfy us both."

Sleep on it, he says! Sleep on it! I never closed my eyes the whole night for thinking about it. Just when I hoped my life was opening up with possibilities, it suddenly has the shadow of Iris looming over it again.

I'm fed up.

* * *

Derek went to see his mother this morning and came back all tearful. "It's terrible what's happened to her," he says. "She can't be more than three stone in weight. She's like one of them apoplectics that spew all their food up."

"I've heard that before," I said. "She's pulled that one in the past—cracking on she's done for and then staging a miracle recovery."

"You wouldn't think it was put on if you saw her now. She's nowt but skin and bone."

"Skin and bone and craftiness," I said.

"Well, you can be as hard as you like, Doreen, but she is my mother when done and said all. And she's the best mother I ever had. I feel responsible for her. She raised me at her knee from early childhood and I owe her something in her hour of need."

"I've given you fair warning, Derek. I am not going to devote my life to caring for her here. Why should I after the stunt she pulled last time? If you decide to bring her to this house, I shall neglect her something terrible. So, on your own head be it. I won't lift a finger."

"We can make some arrangements. We've got money in the bank. We could have a nurse in, somebody to see to her functions in a dignified manner."

"Do what you want, but I will not assist. The day that nurse goes down with flu you'll be looking to me to step into the breach, won't you? Well, you can forget it. I shall absent myself away." I was working myself into a right old paddy. "And don't forget that most of the money we've got in the bank belongs to me. I will not have it poured down the plug hole of your mother's decline. If she wants to drag out her final days to several years, that's up to her, but she's not indulging herself on my money. So now then."

With that I got me coat on ready to go to the shops. But he caught me by the arm.

"Doreen, have a bit of pity. She can't last very long, not in that state. Come and see her and you'll realise how bad it is."

"Go and see her?" I snorted. "Go and see her! I'd rather have my eyes poked out with red hot knitting needles."

"Well, if you don't come with me, I shall have to make decisions by myself. I shall have to arrange the arrangements without consulting you. You may not like the final verdict."

He had a point. At least if I was there, I could put my two penn'orth in.

"They're having a case conference about her at St Joseph's on Tuesday. I'd like you to come. All the decisions will be made there. Given that it might affect you, I think you ought to be there."

"Right then, I will. But my purpose in going is only to protect my own and my family's interests. This is not an official visit to her, as such. There won't be no distressed sitting by bedsides on my part. If I should see her, it will only be by coincidental accident. After all, we've a baby in the house and one set of incontinent bowels is quite enough to be going on with. In addition, we don't want germs fetching from that hospital."

He obviously thinks that when I see her in her pitiful state I'll crumble and change my mind. But I won't. I've made my decision in advance not to.

* * *

I got a phone call from our Gary complaining about our Sylvia making a nuisance of herself. You see, Gary and Bill have decided to have their flat redecorated and fully refashioned in a Scandinavian style. I don't care for it myself, but it's their business how uncomfortable they want to make their home. From the

23

pictures I've seen, it looks like a station waiting room. I said to our Gary, "Them chairs look right uncomfortable, all tubular steel and wood. You'll never be able to settle down for an evening's televiewing in them. You'd have aggravated piles within a week. And where are you supposed to put all your stuff? Your coffee table and that? The place in that picture looks empty."

Anyway, they've got this interior decorator in and our Sylvia has taken a shine to him. Matt he's called. Our Gary says he's a 'big, butch, blond lad' and our Sylvia is now a daily visitor to the flat while this Matt is trying to work.

"She's throwing herself at him," our Gary says. "She's tormenting him and trying to distract him from his business. It'll never be finished if she doesn't give over. She knows we're paying him by the hour but she just keeps stopping him working."

I said, "It isn't that you're jealous, is it? Have you got your eye on him for yourself?"

"Well, he is very attractive, Mam, but I don't think our Sylvia is in the same league as him. It's pathetic to see her making such a fool of herself. He's showing no interest—in fact, he looks quite embarrassed about it."

"I'll have a word with her," I said.

So when she got back I told her what our Gary had said. "Oh, he thinks every man's like him. But I don't think Matt is one of them. He's ever so gorgeous and he's got this curly blond hair, I just want to run my fingers through it."

"You're not making a show of yourself, are you?" I said to her.

"I just want a boyfriend mam. If I could have somebody like Matt in my life, I wouldn't ask for anything else."

"Look, you're just inviting more disappointment. You've got to stop getting crushes on unobtainable fellers that you can't have."

She stamped her foot and let out a little scream of frustration. "What's wrong with me?" she said. Why can't I have what other women have?"

* * *

We arrived at St Joseph's just after dinner to attend this case conference affair. St Joseph's has been modernised a bit, but it is still very much an old-fashioned mental asylum. The Government won't let them touch the outside because it's a listed Grade B building or summat. When you walk down the driveway towards it, it's like walking into Dracula's castle. Then, when you get inside there's all these corridors. Miles of them. The sooner they shut it down the better.

Anyway, after we'd walked for ages, following signs and asking directions from folks dressed up in nurses' uniforms, we found Primrose Ward.

I whispered to Derek, "Primrose Ward? It's more like Stalag 49."

Apparently, the ward was painted yellow once—hence Primrose—but there's been so much cigarette smoke it's gone brown. I thought *I* was obsessed by fags, but this whole place revolves around them. Nobody seems to talk about nothing else. "Have you got a cig? Have you got a light? Have you got any Rizlas?" that's all we got from the inmates from walking through the door to going home.

The sister on this ward comes up to query us. When she found out who we was, she showed us into this room and then the social worker arrived, that Mr Allinson. All smiles he was, although I notice he had the same shirt on again. We sat and chatted for a few minutes, then he said: "Would you like to come and see Iris, Doreen? She's on the ward at the moment, sitting in her chair."

"No thank you," I said, dead severe. "If we could just get this over and done with and we'll be on our way."

After a bit, the psychiatrist that's been assigned to her case arrived. Doctor Calloway. Pretty young woman she was. You'd think she could find herself a better job than this. Then a nurse came, and we all sat round in a circle and introduced ourselves.

"Now, as you know, we're here to decide what to do for Mrs Potts senior," said Mr Allinson. "Perhaps I'd better start by telling you what I've managed to discover from my department, in the way of options." He gets his clip board out.

"Now, I'm afraid there is little prospect of Iris going back to her previous accommodation in the sheltered housing unit. I met with the management committee and they were adamant that they couldn't cope with Iris in her current state. Indeed, they were having problems with her even before she became ill."

"That's a surprise," I sneered.

"Well, anyway, I did a quick ring round of the nursing homes we have in the area," says Mr Allinson, "and I'm afraid we could only find one that was willing to take her at the moment. Oak Dene." He shuffled in his seat and coughed. "Now, I'll have to be straight with you, Mr and Mrs Potts. Oak Dene is currently subject to an inquiry and we were hoping not to have to admit anyone until our investigations are completed. I'm sure the allegations will prove groundless but, all the same, we'd prefer to wait and see. The problem is that no-one else has any space just now."

"What exactly is the allegations?" says Derek.

"Well, I'm not really at liberty to discuss it," says Mr Allinson, all shifty. "It wouldn't be fair to the company that owns it to make any comments before the inquiry is completed. But you may have read about it in the newspaper."

"No," says Derek.

"Well," says Mr Allinson, reaching into his brief case and pulling out this bit he'd cut out of the *Advertiser*. "I suppose this much is in the public domain, so I can't be criticised for showing you what the press has had to say."

It was a story about how this woman reporter had posed as a care assistant and sneaked a hidden camera into Oak Dene and took photographs of the old folk tied to their chairs with washing lines. One old lady had had a glass of cold water chucked over her, and another had been dragged round the floor by her suspenders. The food was like something you read about in an African famine.

"It's shocking," I said, when I'd read it. "I don't understand how they get away with it. How come the people who run this place haven't been had up?"

"I'm sure there will be appropriate action taken if it is deemed necessary," said Mr Allinson. "But proper procedures have to be gone through. It's only fair on everyone concerned that no precipitous action is taken."

"Fair on everyone?" I said. "What about these old folk who have to endure it—is it fair on them?"

"I'm afraid you've got the wrong person if you want a political argument, Mrs Potts. My hands are tied," said Mr Allinson.

"Yes, and so were poor old Mrs Bentley's in that home. I wouldn't send a dog there."

"Well, that's all we have on offer at the moment, Mrs Potts," he said, snapping his brief case shut. "If you aren't prepared to come up with some suggestions of your own, the council will have no alternative but to take up the place at Oak Dene on Mrs Potts senior's behalf."

Derek looked at me crestfallen and kept casting his eyes down to this newspaper cutting.

They well and truly had me in a corner and I was furious.

"What about her condition, Dr Calloway?" I said to this psychiatrist. "Because she's a bugger for swinging the lead, you know. She's conned top specialists with her supposed ailments. You're only a slip of a lass. She's a professional hospital-fooler."

"Not this time," says Dr Calloway. "She's suffering from a form of progressive dementia. I expect you've heard of it?"

"Of course I have. I know what it is. When old folk can't remember and start trying to mow the lawn with the vacuum cleaner."

"It's slightly more than that, Mrs Potts. It's a degenerative disease that will eventually lead to Iris's death." She turned to Derek and patted his hand. "Sorry to be so blunt, Mr Potts, but I think it's best to be fully armed with the facts."

Derek let out a little sob and put his hands over his face.

"Now, people with dementia can be very difficult to manage, as I'm sure you're aware. If you decide to take her home, you'll need some support."

"Derek's going to look after her," I said. "I'm not doing it. My husband reckons he's going to get some professional help in. Pay for a nurse, kind of thing."

"So you *have* discussed it," said Mr Allinson, brightening up.

"Don't get excited," I said to him. "I haven't said yes, and I haven't said no."

"Well, I'm proposing to bring Iris into this conference," says Dr Calloway. "So that she can participate. We're very much into empowering our patients here. Then you can all make up your minds up together."

She nodded to this nurse, who went out to get her.

They were backing me further and further into the corner. For all my determination not to see her, here I was now having to sit in the same room. After a couple of minutes, the nurse fetched Iris in.

What a shambling wreck she was, dressed in this floor-length candlewick dressing gown with food all down the front. It just swallowed her up, and you could just about see her head poking out, perched on a tiny neck. Her hands had disappeared up the sleeves. Her hair consisted of these out-of-control thin white wisps, and she

27

had her dentures out and her mouth lolling open. It shocked me, I'll be honest.

"Hello, Iris," shouts Dr. Calloway. "How are you today?"

Iris looked at her as though she were an alien from outer space.

"Are you going to sit down and join us?" the doctor bawls, doing these right exaggerated lip movements.

Iris has this puzzled look on her face. The nurse sits her down.

"Your son is here to see you," Dr Calloway says to her. "Can you see him?"

Iris looked round the room with this frightened expression on her face. She looked straight past me and Derek.

"Do you see Derek, Iris?" the doctor repeated.

This croaky little voice came out of her, "I haven't got a son. How could I have a son when I'm not married? Where's me mother? She said she was coming to take me home. Have I to put me shoes on?"

"Get her a cup of tea, nurse," said doctor Calloway, and then she turned to us. "Now, you see, Mr and Mrs Potts, her short-term memory has almost entirely gone. She can still remember things that happened many years ago, but not things that happened yesterday."

"Is there any chance that she'll get better?" I said.

Doctor Calloway bit her lip and shook her head. "We can give her some drugs that might stabilise her. They work for some people. Help them recover a few of their lost memories. But generally, it's downhill all the way from here, I'm afraid."

Iris had found her hand, somewhere up her sleeve, and was picking away at this bit of loose cotton on her dressing gown.

Derek was trying not to cry, but the tears were welling up, and the corners of his mouth had turned down.

"Oh, Mam," he says. "What a terrible thing to happen to you. What have you done to deserve this?"

He knelt down in front of her and laid his head in her lap and sobbed. She looked down and put her hand on his head. "What're you scriking for lad? Have you been naughty? Has your Mam given you a clout?"

This just set him off again. It were quite pathetic to see, and I felt myself filling up as well. I went over and put my arms round his shoulder. "Come and sit down, love," I said. "We'll not let her go to Oak Dene."

He sat back on his chair and blew his nose. After he'd composed himself, we got down to the business of fetching her home. Dr. Calloway said that Iris would be kept in the hospital for another fortnight to try to build up her physical strength and to give this new drug an opportunity to work. After that, she would be all ours.

Mr Allinson was ever so grateful, and he whispered in my ear: "You've done the right thing, Doreen. I wouldn't have wanted to send my worst enemy to Oak Dene. You've took a big load off my mind."

"I've taken it off your mind and put it straight on to mine," I said.

We got up to go, and Derek went to give his mother a kiss goodbye.

"We'll soon have you home, Mam," he was saying.

"Have you seen me skipping rope?" she says. "Some lads have pinched it."

I didn't think there was much point in saying owt to her, given she didn't know me from Adam, so I was just going to leave when Dr Calloway says, "Would you like to take your mother back on to the ward, Mr Potts? You might as well get used to having her around, she's going to be a big part of your life for the time being."

She might as well have tied a sack of coal on my back when she said that. I suddenly felt terribly burdened.

Derek took Iris by the arm. "Come on then, mam, let's have you back to bed," he said.

While he was taking her back to the ward, Dr Calloway took me to one side.

"Are you convinced now that your mother-in-law is not faking it?" the doctor said to me.

"Well, I'll admit she's putting on a good show. But I've seen it before," I said.

"This is ridiculous. You heard what the social services said yesterday—she'll have to move into Oak Dene if you won't take her."

"Look, Dr Calloway," I said, leaning closer to her. "Can I be honest with you?"

She indicated for me to go on.

"Iris has got nothing to look forward to, has she?"

"Well, her quality of life won't improve much if that's what you mean. But it will certainly get worse if she has to go to an institution."

"Well, what do you think about voluntary euthanasia or even insisted dying? Don't you think that might be the best thing all round?"

"You mean kill her?" Dr Calloway said.

"Basically, yes—but all legal and above board and in her best interests."

She started gathering her papers together. "I'm afraid that's one service that is not available on the National Health Service."

"Well," I asked, "could we go private?".

"I hope you're joking, Mrs Potts," she said. "And even if you are, it's in very poor taste if I might say so. She got up, looked at me severely and said "Good afternoon." Then she walked out.

I went into the ward to find Derek. Iris's name was hanging on a clipboard at the bottom of her bed. "Iris Potts (Mrs)". It seemed sad somehow because, to all intents and purposes, Iris Pott (Mrs) no longer existed.

I helped her in to the bed and tucked up the sheets. All that hatred I had for her had suddenly evaporated in the face of this sorry, slobbering sight, with her nose running and her eyes all red.

"We're off, then," I said.

I bent over to pick my bag up, when I suddenly thought I heard that quavery voice of hers say: "See you on Thursday, then, Doreen."

I nearly jumped out of my skin, it were like hearing a ghost. But when I stood up and looked at her, she were fast on, snoring.

I shivered, it was that strange.

"Did you hear her say anything just then?" I said to Derek.

"No," says Derek. "Like what?"

I looked at her again. Her eyes were closed, but I was certain there was a hint of a smile on her face that hadn't been there before.

But perhaps it's just me.

* * *

Derek continued to visit Iris every couple of days to see her progress. Doctor Calloway had put her on this new miracle drug, Gerontosil, it's called. It's supposed to help people with dementia to recover some of their memory and to stop the slide into bolivian.

Derek was saying she looks a lot perkier, and is showing an interest in her grub again, although she still doesn't recognise him.

Apparently, she was asking him to fasten her shoelaces yesterday, because she said she was only a little girl and she hadn't learned how to do it yet.

He's calmed down a bit, though, since the threat of her immediate passing over has passed over.

* * *

I've got myself right worked up about this fish shop lark. The more I think about it, the more I like it. Not only would it give us another source of income it would give me a purpose in life, something to nurture and care for.

It's funny, isn't it, how things work out? Only a few weeks ago I was maundering about having no purpose, and now this turns up like magic.

It was like destiny had put it in front of me and said: 'here you are, Doreen, opportunity knocks. Take it or leave it. But if you leave it, I shan't be putting too many more chances your way. You're not getting any younger and I've got to share the opportunities out among the young folk—that's only fair.'

I was waiting for the right moment to broach the idea with Derek, but all he seems interested in is his mother. He keeps trying to persuade me to visit her. I said, what for? He says to see the progress she's making. This drug, apparently, is having a marvellous effect on her. Last time she saw Derek she said to him, "I know you, don't I, young man? You've got the look of a relative about you. What's your favourite colour Smartie?"

But I thought I'd better face the consequences and admit to him what I had in mind. Or at least let him know that there was an express train coming down the track.

"I'm thinking about getting involved in a bit of an investment opportunity. I'll give you full particulars when I've instituted the necessary enquiries."

* * *

We've had a right old how-do-you-do over the last couple of weeks—there's been so much happening I haven't really had the time to keep my diary up to date. But I've got a few minutes now, so I'll fill in the missing particulars.

31

Well, to start with, Iris came home. You've never seen nothing like it. She was brought from the hospital in an ambulance, wearing her dressing gown and having to be carried into the living room in a special chair. I was tempted to put the Queen of Sheba music on the record player. Talk about laying it on with a trowel!

She tried to look pathetic, gasping for air and holding her head and that, but once again, there was something not quite right about the whole performance. She looked about fifty times better than the last time I saw her. She'd put weight on, her complexion had lost that waxy, embalmed look—in fact I'd go as far as to say she had roses in her cheeks. Her hair isn't as wild and scruffy as it was in the hospital. Last time I saw her, she looked as though she'd just shampooed in chip fat and lost the comb.

Actually, she looked healthier than me. She had a sparkle in her eye.

I said to Derek: "That miracle drug they're giving her—can you get some for me? I don't know about a month in the bin, she looks as though she's been on a fortnight's holiday to Skegness."

"Now don't start, Doreen," he said. "You promised you'd give her every consideration as regards not harassing her. Let's try and make her feel welcome. She may look champion in comparison to what she looked like before, but she's still far from well."

"Do you want to go to your room, Iris?" I said to her. "The bed's all ready."

Derek glared at me as if to say, she's no sooner through the door than you're shoving her out of sight at the first opportunity.

It didn't seem to matter to Iris. She stared at me with this puzzled look on her face, as though I were talking Chinese. Her whole expression looked put on, a really poor acting job. In fact, my pearl necklace looks more genuine than her attempts at gaining sympathy.

"I've got to go to work now," Derek says, putting his coat on. "I'll leave you two girls to get on with it, shall I?"

"Er... excuse me. There's only so much 'getting on with' that I'll be doing," I reminded Derek. "If that nurse doesn't turn up at nine, I'll be fetching your mother round to that warehouse of yours and you can drive her about in your forklift truck all day."

He smiled nervously and said: "Tara then, Mam. It's nice to have you back with us. I'll see you tonight when I get home from work." He kissed her on the forehead and went to the door. He turned round and mimimoked at me to be nice to his mother. I turned away from him, and he went off.

"He's a nice lad, in't he?" Iris said. "Is he something to do with insurance?"

I gave her the severest look I could muster, one that said, 'I'm not impressed with your play-acting so knock it off'. She raised her eyebrows and looked back. "Do I know you, love?" she says. "Have you come to read the gas meter?"

"That's enough, Iris," I said. "I'm not going along with it. I can see what you're up to and you can save yourself the trouble. You can't kid me with your phony-baloney."

"A bit of polony?" she says. "Is that what we're having for us tea? Yes, I like a bit of polony."

I decided to be brisk rather than sympathetic, so I said, "I'm going to make myself a cup of tea, do you want one?"

"Cup of tea, love?" she says. "Does the gas board provide cups of tea now?"

"Pack it up, Iris, can't you? You've got what you wanted, you're back in the house. Let's get on with it like adults."

"I've got me tablets to take," she says, rummaging in her handbag. "I'm poorly, you know. You always know you're poorly when you've got tablets to take. Is it a cold I've got? Will it mean I can stop off school?"

"I'm seeing about getting you out to a day centre from nine to four," I said. "I'm not having you here all day talking like a six-year old."

"A day centre?"

"For old ladies. Sewing and knitting, playing bingo and that. Having their constipation seen to."

"Old ladies?"

"Yes, old ladies. Like you."

"But I'm only seven. I had my birthday last week. Me daddy gave me a dolly that says mama when you squeeze it's belly."

"Did your daddy tell you what *you'll* be saying when I squeeze your neck?" I said and went into the kitchen to put the kettle on.

While I was waiting for it to boil, I thought I'd have a go at catching her out. So, I went out the back door and tip-toed round to the living room window and peeped in. I wanted to see what she got up to while she thought nobody was watching.

She sat holding her hand up in front of her, twiddling her fingers, looking at them as if they were the most interesting thing in the world. A normal person wouldn't do that, I thought. Maybe she really is bonkers.

I brought her the cup of tea. She started to drink it and then said. "There's no sugar in it, Mrs. I can't drink it without sugar."

Then she drank it straight down in two gulps.

After a bit she said, "Don't I know you? You look familiar."

"You know me all right," I said. "I'm Doreen. Your daughter-in-law. Derek's wife."

"Oh, that's right. Derek's wife." Then after a pause she said: "Derek who, love?"

"I'll ring the social services to see when you can start at that centre," I said. "I'll try and get it brought forward to tomorrow. Or this afternoon, perhaps."

I was on my way to the phone when the doorbell rang. It was the nurse, Mrs Ibbotson. She looked efficient enough. Middle aged, hair tied back in a bun, back ramrod straight. She looked a bit severe. Face like a wet Tuesday.

I showed her through to the living room.

"This is Iris," I said. "Actually, she's only just arrived. They've just delivered her from the hospital."

"Well, I'll give you a few minutes to settle in, then, Iris," says Nurse Ibbotson, taking her gloves off. "While I have a word with your daughter-in-law." She turned to me and pursed her lips. "Now then, Mrs Potts," she says. "I'll just make clear the terms of my engagement so that we know where we stand."

She took her coat off and hung it behind the door. "It's very warm in here. I'm not sure I can stand the central heating up this high." She was wearing a nurse's uniform with one of them wide belts and a watch that hangs upside down off her breast.

I started to say something, when she interrupted. "Now, your husband has engaged me from eight a.m. to six at night. I shall return at eight in the evening to get your mother-in-law ready for bed and get her tucked in. As soon as that's done, you'll not see me for dust. Those are my hours and that's what I'll be working. I don't do overtime. I'll walk in through that door on the dot of eight and I shall walk back out of it at the stroke of six. There's no room for negotiation on the matter, so please don't ask."

"I..." I began, but she wasn't to be stopped.

"And by the way, if you've anything to say about me, I'd prefer you to say it to my face. I don't want private conversations out of earshot regarding my performance. If there is any comment you want to make, I don't want it whispered. If there's so much as a whiff of talking behind my back, I shall be off like a shot. Is that clear?" She started unloading this leather bag she'd fetched with her.

"Are you the nit nurse?" Iris says.

"No. I'm Nurse Ibbotson," she says. She turned to me: "I make allowances for the demented, but not for anyone else."

"You're a bit on the tetchy side," I said, taking up her offer to say it to her face. "I've hardly opened my mouth and you're down my throat."

She got up and started putting her gloves on. "If my performance isn't satisfactory, then there's plenty of other work at the agency. I don't have to stay where I'm not wanted. I'm fully qualified and heavily experienced."

"Hold on a minute, love," I said to her. "Far be it from me to question your abilities. I want you to know that I'm a great admirer of those with certificates. Especially medical ones. I've got a semi-son-in-law who's a nurse, so I know what I'm talking about. Angels, that's what you are, angels. And I think it's a scandal that the government won't pay you a proper wage. I'm sorry if I gave offence, it certainly wasn't intended. Can we try and get off to a better start?"

She turned to me with a savage eye. "I'm here to do my duty by your mother-in-law. My services have been bought and paid for and I shall execute them with my usual professionalism. You'll have no cause for complaint, and if you have, you'll make your complaint directly to me, not in a huddle after I've gone. Or by phone or letter to the agency."

"Yes, that's fair enough," I said. I felt like giving her a smack in the gob, but I had to hold my temper. I needed her. We could see about getting a replacement tomorrow, but I didn't want leaving on my own with Iris on that particular day. I had other fish to fry.

Iris broke the spell when she pipes up: "Don't expect tea in here, nursey. I've been here two weeks and they haven't offered me a cup yet. Am I in to have my in-growing toenails seen to?"

"She's a bit... y'know..." I said, doing screwy signs against my forehead by way of explanation.

35

"Don't worry, Mrs Potts. I've been fully briefed by the hospital. I know exactly what state she's in. Now," she said to Iris in a loud, bossy voice, "after you've had your tea, we'll have a nice warm bath and then we'll do our exercises."

"Exercises?" I said. "She's hardly able to stand up. You're not having her doing that Zumba are you?"

Nurse Ibbotson turned on me with an almost murderous look. "Are you questioning my professionalism, Mrs Potts? Are you saying I don't know what I'm doing?"

She picked her gloves up again in that threatening kind of way.

I cringed and said: "No, no. I was just wondering. Put your gloves down, love."

"I was referring to her memory exercises. They go with the drugs. We're trying to help her regain her lost memory. I'll just ask her a few questions, prompt her to remember things in the past. Now, am I going to be able to get on, or are you going to query everything I say?"

"No, you carry on. I'll say no more. But now you're here, I'm going to pop out for a while. I've got a few enquiries to institute as regards a business proposition."

Out of the corner of my eye I saw Iris suddenly perk up. All at once she was all ears. I thought, yes, you crafty old crow, the mention of business has got your curiosity galloping.

"I shan't be long," I said. "You see, me and my husband are thinking of setting up a business."

I paused to see the effect that had on Iris. Her ears were almost flapping, and there was definitely a look of concentration on her face. Now, I thought, I've caught her. I'll just push this a bit further.

I lowered my voice and whispered into the nurse's ear, "I don't want to upset Iris with the details, you see. I'll keep it away from her so as not to stress her out."

"That's entirely up to you," said the nurse.

"Come into the kitchen a moment, would you, Nurse Ibbotson, and I'll just give you a bit of background."

The nurse got up from the settee and followed me into the kitchen. I whispered a few things to her, just loud enough for Iris to be able to hear that something was being said. Then I raised my voice a little: "Now you won't tell any of this to Iris, will you?"

"Of course not," said Nurse Ibbotson. "Confidentiality is second nature to a nurse. Your business is private as far as I'm concerned. I'm indifferent to it so long as it's not illegal."

Then I lowered my voice again so that Iris wouldn't be able to make out what I was saying. I kept it up for a few seconds and then I crept to the kitchen door. I suddenly pushed it open and, as expected, it came into contact with the side of Iris's head. There was a crash as it hit her on the ear and she fell over.

Iris was sprawled out on the floor on the other side of the door, looking annoyed.

"Oh dear, what's happened?" said the nurse, running to examine her.

"I don't think you need look for broken bones," I said. "The most she'll be suffering from is a cauliflower ear."

I could see Iris scowling at me as the nurse helped her to her feet and got her back on the settee.

"Now remember, Nurse, not a word..." And with that I went out before she could give me a roasting for daring to suggest I knew better than she did.

I was actually on my way to see the Deans's about the chip shop. I went to the door at the side of the shop and rang the bell. Mrs Deans unlocked and unbolted the street door, which had been lined with metal and reinforced with wooden bars, and took me up the stairs to their little flat above. It didn't seem to have changed in the years since I was last there. They hadn't changed the dark colour scheme or the furniture, and it looked like what it was—the abode of old folks. Cosy, though, and spotless clean. You could see from the worn-out look of the rug and the threadbare appearance of the upholstery that she hadn't stinted on her duties with the hoover.

I sat myself down and Alice made a cup of tea.

"I've been thinking about what you were saying, Mrs Deans," I said. "You know, about me taking over this place. I'm definitely interested if we can reach a satisfactory conclusion about the price."

"Ah well, you see, Doreen, there's been a bit of a complication since last time we spoke," she said.

"Aye, it's a complication all right," said Mr Deans, sitting in his favourite chair and shaking his head.

"You see, love, we've had another offer."

"Who from?" I said.

"A firm," she said.

Here we go, I thought. Gazumping. Or worse still, trying to up the price with unsubstantiated threats of competition. I'd thought better of the Deans's. I'd always considered them to be of the old school who meant everything they said and who you could have trusted with your last penny.

"I've only got limited cash resources," I said. "It isn't a bottomless pit, our bank account, I can tell you that."

"Oh, don't get the wrong idea," says Mrs Deans, taking hold of my hand. "I wouldn't try to diddle you, Doreen. I hope that's not what you're thinking."

"I hope it's not, neither," echoed Mr Deans. "We don't want you thinking that."

"Well, what's it about, then?" I asked.

Mrs Deans went over to the mantelpiece and took this letter from behind the clock. She handed it to me.

I read it out, "From the legal and property department, Arnold Addison Fast Food Outlets Ltd. Dear Mr and Mrs Deans. The Arnold Addison company is looking for new properties to accommodate our extensive expansion programme. We feel that your own property would be a suitable addition and wonder whether you had considered selling? The Arnold Addison company is prepared to make an offer which I am sure you will find very generous. We are prepared to offer the full value of your shop—as determined by an independent assessor—plus ten per cent. We will also absorb all costs involved in the sale. If you receive other offers for the property in excess of this, we would advise you that we are prepared to negotiate further. Please telephone the above number as soon as possible to arrange a convenient time for our representative to call and discuss this matter. We look forward to hearing from you in early course, yours sincerely, Mortimer Hackett, properties acquisitions department."

I put the letter down, puzzled. "I don't understand," I said.

"No, neither do we," Mrs Deans said. "They've made this offer without so much as looking round the place."

"Who are they, anyway?" I said.

"Arnold Addison? They own that chain of chip shops—Chips & More! I think they're called," said Mrs Deans.

"Aye, that's it," said Mr Deans. "Chips & More!"

"Oh God," I said. "They're horrible. You can't tell the chips from the polystyrene cups that they serve them in. And the fish!"

"Frozen," said Mrs Deans. "Everything they sell is frozen. Chips, peas, pies, fishcakes, the lot. They distribute it from a central factory in Hackenthorpe."

"That's the one. That one in Hackenthorpe," Mr Deans crooned.

"They must have forty or fifty fish shops in Yorkshire now," continued Mrs Deans. "They're all over the place—and spreading like the plague. The problem is, they're rubbish. They're changing the nature of the product. Young folk are growing up thinking that fish and chips are a foodstuff without flavour. What they serve at these Chips & More! shops are all sloppy and slimy, and you have to put a right lot of salt and vinegar on them. Youngsters'll never know what the real thing tasted like if Arnold Addison has his way. Genuine fish and chips will become a distant memory."

"That's right," said Mr Deans. "Tradition will go out of the window. It'll be that Addison muck that rules the trade soon."

"Well," I said, picking the letter up. "I can't compete with this, Mrs Deans. I can't enter into no bidding contest with a conglomerate. They sound pretty desperate to get their hands on it."

"That's what we can't fathom," said Mrs Deans. "Why are they so anxious to get hold of this place when it's on its last legs?"

"How do you mean?" I said.

Mrs Deans looked a bit shifty, then said: "We shall have to come clean with you, Doreen. The place is running at a loss. There's not much passing trade, you see, love. Not like there used to be in the olden days of the steel works and the factories. It's a waste land round here."

I looked out of the window, across the road to the new housing estate that's just about finished with all the for sale notices up. Then it occurred to me.

"It's this," I said, pointing to the hundreds of new houses just about ready to be sold. "This here estate. Once that gets going it'll be a different story."

"Yes, but when will that be, love?" said Mrs Deans. "We've been hanging on for years on the assumption that the place will be buzzing again once them houses are occupied. But somehow they never get finished. There's been a lot of money lost over that place. The firm that started it went out of business, and then another one took it over and they went bust as well. Now there's another one working on it. It's a pink elephant."

"Well, maybe Addison's know something we don't know."

"You mean, that the place is going to be put to some use after all?"

"Well, of course it is. They don't just abandon brand new housing estates, love. Stands to reason," I said. "That's the only way they'd be offering you unlimited cash." I turned back to them "Well, you must get yourselves a decent solicitor and get the best deal you can. Screw every last penny out of them. This place will be a gold mine once them houses are up and running, and Addison how's-yer-father knows it."

"All them kiddies from that estate eating Addison's fish and chips. It's a shame that they'll be so culturally disadvantaged," Mrs Deans lamented.

"Disadvantaged is the word," moaned Mr Deans. "Imagine it, a great tradition like this being destroyed so that some fat businessman can make more profit."

"It's obscene," said Mrs Deans with passion.

"Utterly obscene," added Mr Deans, with equal, if not more, emotion.

"You can't stop progress, love," I said, trying to comfort them. "Although I'm not sure progress is quite the right word for it."

"But we *can* stop it!" said Mrs Deans, suddenly smiling. "We can! At least on our own patch."

"Can we love?" queried Mr Deans. "Have you come up with an idea?"

"Yes, I have," she said. "We can sell to Doreen, here. That would spike their guns. And I know she'd carry on a grand and honourable tradition. She's got the same feel for it as what we have."

Mr Deans was warming to the idea. "She has that. Their guns would be well and truly spiked if we sold to Doreen."

Mrs Deans said, "After all, you're a traditionalist, Doreen. You'll ensure that this establishment continues to produce chips and fish in the way they were intended to be produced. This great British dish will not be sacrificed on the altar of profit."

"Although a profit isn't to be sniffed at, of course," added Mr Deans. "You can't live on fresh air."

"But I can't match them moneywise," I said. "I can give you the asking price and no more."

"That'll suit me, Doreen," said Mrs Deans. "What about you, dad? What's your opinion?"

"It'll suit me down to the ground," Mr Deans smiled.

"I can't let you," I said. "You've your retirement to think of. You'll want as big a lump sum as you can get. Old age and poverty aren't good partners."

"Don't you worry about us, Doreen. We've been sensible over the years. We've provided for our old age, haven't we, dad?"

"Oh, we've been sensible all right. We've got pension and insurance plans coming out of our ears," he said.

"And not only that. We've got a bungalow in Mablethorpe waiting for us. We've had it for yonks, but we've never been able to use it properly due to the demands of the fish and chip trade. Isn't that right, dad?"

"Aye, it is, mother. Mablethorpe is our dream destination. We've had it in mind for many moons. Now it's becoming a reality."

"If you're absolutely sure, the two of you. If you're absolutely certain, then I'm going straight round to the solicitors and putting wheels in motion."

They turned and smiled at each other, and then they smiled at me.

"We shall be able to greet Harbour Lights with renewed pleasure," said Mrs Deans.

"Harbour Lights?" I said.

"The bungalow. That's what we've called it. Harbour Lights."

"That's lovely," I said. "Quite romantic."

I didn't say any more, because my memories of Mablethorpe do not include a harbour nor are they romantic. I didn't want to pour cold water on their dream.

* * *

Once more a long gap between entries in my diary, but once again a bit of time to get it up to date.

The reason I've been so busy is because of the chip shop. That's a tale and a half. It started when I had to tell Derek what I was planning. At first he was dead against it. "You're not spending all our savings on a barmy scheme like that," he said. "The money's in the building society and that's where it's stopping."

"Oh no it's not. You've got to speculate before you can get an accumulator up. Even you should know that."

When I explained to him about the housing estate and the offer from Arnold Addison he got more interested.

"We might be able to turn this into a nice little earner," he said. "If we buy it off them Deans's at a knock down price and then sell it on to that Addison crowd, we could be quids in. Even the bank manager would approve of that little bit of speculation."

"That's not the idea," I said. "The idea is to keep the tradition going."

"Bugger the tradition, Doreen. If we play our cards right we could end up with enough to buy ourselves a proper car rather than that clapped out pile of junk I'm driving at the moment."

"This is not wheeling and dealing, Derek. I'm playing fair by the Deans's. They've been straight by me and I'm going to keep my word to them."

"Now, Doreen, are you sure about this?" he said. "It's a big thing taking on a business. It means commitment. You'll be on duty at all times. Folk expect regular hours from a chip shop—unexpected closures can cause riots. And you'll have to employ people. Yes, think about that. Being a boss is fraught with potential heartache and catastrophe."

"I don't know how you make that out. How can creating jobs be a cause for heartache? Especially when the jobs you are creating are for your own family."

"What? You're not talking in terms of our Sylvia, are you? She's never done a hands turn in her life. I don't see what use she could be to you."

"She can assist. After all, shovelling fish and chips into paper and wrapping them up doesn't exactly require a master's decree, does it? This could be the making of her, her opportunity to get a career under her belt. After all, she could be heir to this business if she's canny. One day it could all be hers. That might act as an incentive."

"Our Sylvia doesn't have an incentive in her body."

"We'll see."

Iris was sitting in the corner in her bedroom slippers, pretending to knit but dropping stitches left right and centre. I could see that she was craning her neck to make sure she heard everything. Anyway, when Derek had gone out to the Trades and Labour Club, and our Sylvia had took our Charmaine Bernadette for a walk over to our Gary's, I went and sat with Iris. I was determined I was going to trip her up and catch her out.

"Aren't you finding it difficult to keep this up, Iris?" I said.

She looked at me vacant as an unoccupied toilet.

42

"I mean, what's the point now you're back here living with us? I don't understand why this play acting has to go on. It must be very boring for you."

"Can I have a stick of lickerish?" she said.

"You're probably doing this in the hope of wearing me down. Well, you're not going to. Now that we've got that nurse coming round, I don't have to worry about you."

I waited a few seconds and then I said: "She's a bit on the severe side, isn't she, that nurse Ibbotson? A bit sergeant major-ish. I don't expect it's very pleasant having to be seen to by a person like that. She's not what you'd call the soul of compassion. Not exactly from the Florence Nightingale school of nursing, is she? More the Myra Hindley type."

I waited for a response. I could see her eyes narrowing as she struggled to keep her trap shut.

"I told Derek that Nurse Ibbotson was highly satisfactory. He's extended her contract for another month, so you'd better get used to her. I've told her you don't object to enemas. Nurse Ibbotson says that's her speciality. She's going to give you a good old clear-out tomorrow, and I said, make it a strong one. She's bunged up, I said. I don't think it's going to be pleasant."

Her face was going red as she struggled to keep her peace. She waited for me to say something else.

"Only things are changing, you see," I said. "We're on the move, as I'm sure you're fully aware. There's a business proposition that I'm pursuing. Deans's fish shop."

She looked at her skirt and picked at a loose thread, trying to keep control.

"We're sinking nearly all our life's savings into this business. Anything could happen. We could end up poor again."

She lifted her head up and her face looked as though it was going to explode. She could stand it no longer.

"What the hell do you know about fish and chips, Doreen Potts?" she said, letting it all gush out like a bursting dam. "That business could be a goldmine in the right hands, and them hands aren't yours."

I let out a little shriek and clapped my hands. I couldn't resist it, I just got up and had a little dance round the room.

"Got you, you chuffing old fraud! I knew you couldn't keep it up for ever. I knew you wouldn't be able to resist when there's an opportunity to interfere."

Realising that she'd lost control of her normally iron will, she suddenly held her forehead and slumped back into the settee. "Oh, what's happened to me?" she says. "I feel as though I'm coming round from a long sleep. Have I been in a coma?"

"No, but if I had my way you'd be going into one. A permanent one," I said.

I could have happily cracked her skull and laughed about it. She was making a right performance about how dizzy she felt.

"Oh pack it in, Iris," I said. "You can pull the wool over some of the people all of the time, but you never fooled me. I never thought for a minute it was real."

"It must be the medication," she wails. "I must have had amnesia and these drugs have brought me round."

"Amnesia my aunt fanny," I said.

"Well, that's my story and I'm sticking to it," she said. "The doctor will back me up."

"She'll have no option but to back you up. She'll look like a real fool if she admits you've been playing her along. I never believed it, though. Oh no. Not for a minute. Don't forget, I've seen it all before."

"Miss clever clogs, aren't you?" she sneered "Well, we'll see. My chuffing back's killing me sitting down here all day. I'll be glad to be up and about again. I'm dying to get to the shops."

"You're evil, Iris, do you know that? Truly evil. If I knew a vicar I'd have you exercised."

She thrust her face into mine and pulled her tongue out. Then she said: "Have you got any beer in? I've got this hankering for a bottle of light ale. I've denied myself for too long."

"Derek will never forgive you," I said. "The stress you've put that man through is shocking."

She was totally unconcerned. "Only you could pop down to the beer-off if you've got none in the fridge. Get the money out of my handbag."

"He'll be horrified when he finds out you've been deceiving him like this. It's nothing short of cruel what you've been doing."

"Oh give it a rest, Doreen. I know how to handle Derek. He's putty in my hands. If I tell him I've been in a state of amnesia, he'll believe me. He'll just be glad I'm back."

The awful thing is that she's right. She'll play the suffering mother for all it's worth and he won't see it as a heartless deception, just as another miracle recovery.

"I'm prone to this sort of thing," she says, winking at me. "As you know, it's happened before. It must be a chronic condition. You never know when it might strike."

"Cow," I said, but it was frustration really. I knew there was nothing I could do. Everybody would believe her, and I'd be shouting my accusations into empty space.

"And as for that nurse," she said. "If you think I'm letting her shove hose-pipes up my backside you've got another think coming—enema indeed! You can get on the phone and give her the heave-ho right now. Services no longer required. Just put some All-Bran on the shopping list."

The chip shop negotiations are going ahead nicely. There are no complications with the survey, so the solicitors really only have to do the paperwork. I'm doing a shift in the shop every night now so as to learn the business, and next week I'm going on a course about food hygiene and the law. It's all very strict these days. They come inspecting you every five minutes apparently, demanding that you wash your hands all the time and get rid of undesirable insect life. I got my training in cockroach-squashing and mouse-trapping when I lived in that awful council flat on the Vaughan Williams Estate. Oh yes, there was more wildlife in that flat than there is in the Serengeti. But I learned to get the better of them—no rodent could outrun my shovel, and no six-legged scuttler ever retained its three-dimensional form when I'd finished with it. Dirty little buggers. I can't be doing with vermin of any description.

There's none of that problem with the chip shop. The Deans's have kept the place immaculate, and they've never had no problem with the authorities on that score. It didn't matter how many unannounced visits the health department sprang on them, they was never caught out. Five out of five was their score. I hope I can keep the record unbroken.

45

However, vermin doesn't always come in creepy crawly form. Sometimes it walks on two legs. When I came into the shop this afternoon, the big plate glass window had been smashed and was boarded up. It looked a right sight.

It's become a regular occurrence recently, according to the Deans's, the smashing of this big window. It's a rough area, but that should change when the estate gets into gear. The vagrants and yobbos and dope-heads will be driven out. I hope.

I said to Mrs Deans, I said: "Why don't you get one of them metal grills that you can wind down at night. They'll not be able to smash your windows then."

"We've thought about it, Doreen," said Mrs Deans, "but it's a dear do making your property into a fortress. It's not a tuppence ha'penny job installing all that lot. But if you want to go ahead and do it, you'd probably find it in your best interests. If we was stopping here we'd certainly have it put in."

Another expense. This is turning out to be not quite the bargain I'd thought and the money is gradually being swallowed up. Still, it should be a good investment once all them houses are fully occupied. Folk are beginning to move in, so it shouldn't be long before we see an upturn.

However, I'm being abducted into the trade, and Mr Deans is explaining every angle of the fish and chip business to me. I'm having to learn fast because they're planning to be out in a fortnight and off to Harbour Lights.

Although it's hard work, I'm glad to get away from home. Iris's "miraculous" recovery has thrilled Derek to bits, just as she predicted it would. Every time he comes in from work he goes over and kisses her and tells her how relieved he is that she's on the mend. "I thought I'd never hear you complaining about your bad feet again, Mam," he'll say, as she tells him all kinds of tales about how I've been abusing her. If only I dare do it!

I try not to speak to her unless I have to and treat her with the utmost contempt she deserves.

Nevertheless, she's anxious to interfere with my project and she drops regular hints that she'd like to put her oar in. I just tell her to mind her own business.

"You'll need all the help you can get," she keeps saying. "You've no business acumen, no idea what's involved. You'll be in queer street within a month and all that money down the drain."

"I'm not listening, Iris. I've got as much business vacuuming as you have. You don't exactly have to be a genius to run a chuffing fish and chip shop. And what there is to know I'm being taught by lifelong experts, Mr and Mrs Deans. I've become a member of the National Federation of Fish Friers and have a subscription to the Fish Friers Review, so I'm now a complete professional."

Me and Iris were in the house on our own—our Sylvia seems to be spending a lot of time round at our Gary's lately for some reason, probably that lad she's got her eye on—and so it's bicker, bicker, bicker all day long. It's difficult to ignore Iris, you see, because she can always find your weak spot, the thing that sets you off.

However, Iris's flow of unwanted advice was interrupted by a knock at door. It was this tall, thin old chap wearing an expensive-looking black wool coat. He had a pencil moustache and sunken eyes. He looked just like an undertaker. I thought: If he's come to measure Iris up for her pine overcoat, he's welcome. I'll hold her down while he does it.

"I'm looking for Mrs Doreen Potts," he says. His voice matched his face, deep and slow. He could have been doing a Boris Karloff impression.

"That's me," I said, stepping back a bit and wishing I'd put the chain on the door.

"Ah, Mrs Potts. My name is Mortimer Hackett, I'm representing Arnold Addison and company. I wonder if I could have a private word?"

"Arnold Addison?" I says. "That's that Chips & More! carry on, isn't it?"

"Yes, that's our trading name." He flashed his business card.

"Come in, Mr Hackett."

I led him into the living room where Iris was sitting, earholing as usual.

"You'll have to excuse my mother-in-law, Mr Hackett. I've been trying for some time to get rid of her, but she's become something of a limpet."

"Ah well, we all have our problems, Mrs Potts." He sat himself down. "Now I'm sure you know why I'm here. It's in connection with the Deans's enterprise."

"Oh aye," says Iris, getting all interested. "What's your angle, then?"

47

"This has nowt to do with you, Iris," I said. "Excuse me Mr Hackett while I get shut of her. It won't take a moment to lock her in her room."

I took Iris by the arm and bustled her up the stairs.

"This could be important, Doreen," she was saying. "You could make yourself a small fortune if you handle this right. You don't want to do it on your own with a negotiation like that. I can help you."

I opened her bedroom door and shoved her in and closed it. Then I locked it.

"You're barmy, Doreen," she was saying from the other side of the door. "They'll take you for a ride. Let me out. Can't you see they've sent an expert to rip you off."

I went back downstairs and smiled at Mr Hackett, even though he did have a rather creepy air about him. His cheeks were hollow and his face bony, like a skeleton. His own smile, which revealed a row of tombstone teeth, was permanently fixed on his face. It made my flesh crawl just looking at him.

"Sorry about that little exhibition, Mr Hackett. My mother-in-law is something of nuisance as regards poking her nose in. Now, how can I help you?"

"Well, Mrs Potts, as you know, we're very interested in the Deans's shop ourselves and we've been trying to enter into negotiations with them over it. But apparently they prefer to sell to you."

"That's right."

This horrible grin grew even bigger and it made him look more poorly and malnourished than ever, but from deep in his sockets, his eyes were gleaming. "Well, Mr Addison has set his heart on this shop," he said. "He'd like to add it to the chain."

"Would he? Would he really? In a strategic position is it, sort of thing?"

"Well, I wouldn't go as far as to say that. It's just that we are trying to establish ourselves as a major player in the fast-food industry, and it's a matter of logistics—being accessible to more people. There's a small hole in our coverage in that area. It would be convenient for us to fill that hole."

"The thing is, you see, Mr Hackett, the thing is, I'm quite looking forward to setting up in business myself. I'm all siked up to it, as my son would say. I'm undergoing intensive training at this very moment and have become a registered fish frier."

"I understand that, Mrs Potts. Entrepreneurial activity is the backbone of our economy and the Arnold Addison Corporation doesn't wish to discourage it. But there are other businesses you could go into. No end of opportunities, especially if you have the capital to finance it. And that's where we come in."

"Oh aye," I says, dead non-committal "And what exactly are you suggesting?"

"Well, we would be prepared to buy the Deans's shop from you—ensuring of course that you would walk away from such a deal well satisfied with the outcome."

"Oh aye?"

"Yes indeed, Mr Addison himself has authorised me to be generous in our negotiation." As the smile got wider, the eyes got smaller and more dead looking, and even more tombstone teeth were put on show.

"The only fly in the soup," I said, "is that I don't want to sell. And I'm not going to sell. I've got a purpose in taking over this chip shop, a noble purpose, and I'm going to see it through."

"You haven't heard what terms we're prepared to offer, Mrs Potts. I think you might want to reconsider your position when you've heard what we're proposing."

"I have reconsidered it. And I've re-reconsidered it. And I'm going to carry on. It's about more than money, is this. I want a purpose in life, and I've found one with this shop. I'm afraid Mr Addison can't buy me a purpose in life. So, he'll have to put that in his pipe and smoke it."

The smile disappeared from Mr Hackett's face instantly. The gravestone teeth were once more veiled by these thin, very red, lips. "I think you are being very foolish, Mrs Potts, if I might say so. You haven't even heard our terms yet."

"I told you, money is not the issue at issue here."

"Look, I've written down the amount we are prepared to pay for this shop. It's in this envelope. I suggest you look at it, and then discuss it with your family."

His complexion was that of a corpse, pasty with crinkly skin like screwed up paper. I began to wonder whether he should be out in daylight, or whether he risked turning into a pile of dust if the sun shone on him.

"I'm sorry you've turned out for nothing, Mr Hackett. You could have rung from the cemetery and I'd have said you were wasting your time disinterring yourself."

"I should warn you, Mrs Potts, that Arnold Addison is not a man to get on the wrong side of. He has influence. He's a powerful man."

"You mean he's got money and a few chip shops. Well, I'm not impressed. And I'm not frightened neither." And, to emphasise the point, I ripped the envelope up and threw the pieces in the bin without even opening it.

"Well," he said, getting up. "Don't say I didn't warn you, Mrs Potts. I'll give you a couple of days to think over the offer, then I'll call you again."

"Save yourself the trouble, love," I said. "This lady's not for turning."

He looked at me with this hateful stare, then shook his head and went out.

But for all my bravado I was trembling. Mr Hackett was a scary man. It was like having a visit from Dracula.

Upstairs I could hear Iris knocking on the door to be let out. Much as I regret saying this, I could really have done with some advice from her. I went up and released her from captivity.

"How much did he offer?" she said. "Have you agreed terms yet?"

"There are no terms to be agreed," I said grandly. "I'm not interested in their offer. I want to open my fish shop. I have consigned his offer to the bin."

"You're a fool, Doreen. An absolute fool," she said reclaiming the bits of the torn envelope from the waste basket and piecing them together. When she'd put it together, she gasped, "Have you seen how much they're prepared to pay?" she said.

I said nothing, pretending not to be interested in the amount, but secretly noting where she put the pieces so I could have a look later.

"But there's no harm done yet," she said. "In fact, playing hard to get might cause them to up the anti. Money's nothing to these multi-national conglomerates. They spend millions and never think twice about it. You could have your share if you play you cards right."

"I don't think you're listening to me, Iris. I'm not selling and there's an end to it. Doreen's Traditional Fish and Chip Emporium will be opening on schedule, I hope, and that's more important to me than any amount of cash."

"Silly tart," Iris said. "Derek will go mad when he hears about this. He'll have your guts for garters if you've chucked away thousands of quid for the sake of some back street chip shop."

"The matter is closed, Iris," I said regally.

"Aye, and it's about time your gob was closed, an'all," she said.

I wasn't listening. I was worrying.

* * *

Now that the big day is approaching, Iris is at me every time I come through the door. "You want to have a big opening offer—free chips with every haddock ordered on the first day. You ought to put an advert in the local paper. You should be stuffing leaflets through people's letter-boxes—you can get kids to do it for you for fifty pence an hour. Why don't you..."

"Why don't *you* shut your cakehole and mind your own business!" I said.

"That's a bit harsh, Doreen," Derek says, looking over his paper. "She's only trying to help. Aren't you, Mam? You're only trying to help."

"That's all I'm trying to do, Derek, love, help. And look at how I'm treated. Called from a pig to a dog just for trying to help."

"If you want to help, Iris," I said. "Just keep your trap shut. That would be most helpful indeed."

"You'll want an extra hand on your opening night. There'll be teething problems. You can't depend on our Sylvia, she's too flighty. She'll probably end up dropping the baby in the deep fat frier," Iris said.

"Our Sylvia can manage. I've given her very intense instruction in wrapping fish and chips, and she's mastered it. It won't be long before she can operate the till, just a few more months practice. She'll cope."

"Yes, but an extra hand wouldn't go amiss just until you're up and running," Iris said. "Even if it's only to make cups of tea."

"You—make cups of tea? That'll be the day. I know precisely what will happen if I let you behind that counter—you'll try to take over. Attempt a cooder tat."

51

"No, Doreen, I won't. I just want to make sure that this venture is a success. I want to do my share for the family business."

"You can't say fairer than that, Doreen," Derek says, entering his plea on her behalf. "It's in all our interests for this chip shop to succeed."

I looked Derek straight in the eye and said, ever so slowly: "Let me put this as plain as I can. *She's not bleeding well coming into my shop. Not now. Not ever. And that's the end of it.* I'm not having her anywhere near me. She'll have me banged up in jail again in no time, just like before."

Iris snivelled and wiped her nose on the back of her hand. This got just the response she wanted from Derek. He put his arm round her and gave her his handkerchief. "Never mind, Mam. You've made your offer, and she's rejected it. You've nothing to chastise yourself for if she comes a cropper."

"Oh, Derek," she says, clinging on to his lapels and crying into his chest, "What have I done to deserve this kind of treatment? She must think I'm completely without feelings. She's kicking me down while I'm out."

I'd have gladly kicked her from one end of Evergreen Close to the other, only I was interrupted by a knock on the door. I looked out of the window and saw a large car parked by the gate. A Rolls Royce Silver Shadow.

Our Sylvia came rushing downstairs, having spotted the car from her window. "Have you seen that car?" she said. "It must be somebody posh coming."

"This can only mean one thing," I said. "Arnold Addison is here in person."

Iris recovered instantly. "This is your chance, Doreen. This could be our lucky day. Let me handle it for you. I'll squeeze him for a good deal."

"See?" I said to Derek. "She's at it again, muscling in."

"She's right, though, Doreen. He must be serious if he's personally here in person. Let's think about it."

I went to the door and there he was, Arnold Addison himself. I recognised him off them adverts on the telly. "The Original Chips & More! Chips Chipperson says come on down and enjoy the great British tradition of fish and chips at its best."

Fat sod he were, about six foot two, and with a waistline to match. He obviously enjoyed his own products a little too much because his expensive-looking camel coat was straining at the buttons. He was looming over me in the doorway. That's the only way to describe it—looming.

"Doreen, int'it?" he said with a big smile and pushing his hand out for me to shake. I took hold and he squeezed my fingers so hard I heard the bones crack. "I know it's you from the description old Mortimer gave me."

His voice was as big as his frame, loud and carrying.

"You'll be Mr Addison," I said, rubbing my hand to get rid of the pain.

"Mr Addison be buggered," he said. "Arnold to you, lass. I won't have no formality, I'm against it, all bar with juniors. You call me Arnold and I'll call you Doreen. Then we're equals in the business game."

He turned back to the car and shouted, "Ainsley! Where are you! Come here!"

From the other side of the car a young lad, difficult to tell his age, emerged. Small, thin, hunched over.

"Well, come on then!" Arnold ordered. "We haven't got all day."

The lad walked reluctantly up to the door, looking at the ground.

"This is my lad, Ainsley," Arnold said. "I'm showing him the ropes for the time when he takes over."

Ainsley was having problems making eye contact.

"Say hello, Ainsley," Arnold ordered. A weedy little voice could be heard saying: "Hello".

"He's a bit on shy side," said Arnold, "but we'll soon knock that out of him."

He walked past me and into the living room, followed by Ainsley. The lad sat in a chair, staring mostly at the floor, but occasionally glancing at our Sylvia, who was wearing one of her very tight jumper and short skirt ensembles.

Arnold slipped his gloves off and then his hat. "Very salubrious area you're living in, Doreen. Evergreen Close. I considered a house here myself at one bit. But Irene—that's the wife—she insisted on something even more upmarket when the business took off. She's got ideas beyond her station, that woman. I keep warning her. Irene, lass, I say to her, you forget your roots at your peril. Her mother were a laundress and her father a farmhand. She's on about having a four-poster bed now. Have you ever heard the like?"

He went over to Derek and gave him a handshake, too. Derek winced as his fingers were crushed together.

"You're Derek, if I'm not mistaken," said Arnold. "The hubby of this talented lady. Right?"

"Aye," said Derek.

"And this gorgeous creature?" he said, turning to Iris.

"Mrs Potts senior," said Iris, rather sternly.

"Oh, the famous Iris, is it?" he shouted.

"Not to you," Iris scowled. "To you I'm the famous Mrs Potts senior. And I'm not deaf."

Arnold let out this really loud belly laugh. But there wasn't much mirth in it. It was a bit frightening actually. Although there was a smile on his lips, his eyes were like a shark's, no expression. "Sorry, Iris, love. I always assume the golden oldies are hard of hearing unless I'm told the contrary."

He turned to me: "You've done well for yourself, Doreen. You come from modest stock, like me. I started with nowt and now I've got summat. I've got a substantial summat, actually. But it didn't come out of thin air. I've grafted for every ha'penny of that brass. Grafted night and day. It's only when you've had nowt that you appreciate having summat. In't that right?"

Derek was mesmerised by this great big barrage balloon of a man filling up the room, and he nodded.

"We've got a lot in common, you and me, Doreen, believe it or not," barked Arnold.

"Like what, for instance?" I said.

"Like wanting to have our own way—for instance. We both like that."

I said nowt and waited.

"Are we having a cup of tea, then, mother?" he said to Iris, as he took off his overcoat. His jacket was unbuttoned, and this grotesque stomach stuck out from under it. He was wearing these great big trousers, held up by a pair of cheap braces. They'd obviously been specially made to contain the mound of flesh he was carrying in front of him. The trouser bottoms rode up well past his ankles, revealing a pair of blinding red and green socks. His legs were thin and bandy, giving him the look of humpty-dumpty.

Iris stared daggers at him and didn't move, but Derek indicated to her to make the tea. She reluctantly went into the kitchen.

"It's nice to have aged parents around, but they can become a bit of a burden at times, can't they? I know, I had to have mine put in a home. A very nice home. One of my own, in fact. We're diversifying, you see, Doreen. Moving the business into other areas. It's a nice little side-line is looking after the old folk. They're very lucrative these days, what with the council closing its own premises down. Oh aye, I'm a great believer in rest homes for the aged. Satisfactory for all concerned—you get shut and they get looked after."

He sat on the settee without being asked. There wasn't room for anyone else.

"That Oak Dene wasn't one of your homes was it? That one that was in the paper recently," I said.

He shuffled in his seat and grunted. "Aye, well, that were most unfortunate were that, Doreen. I blame it on the staff. You do your best to get good people, but you end up with sadists. I've personally set about sorting that out. There'll be no repeat of that. Oh no. We're instituting new procedures that will cover our tracks much more effectively in future. Had a very adverse effect on the business did that little episode. But as I've found in the past, these things are soon forgotten. Make a few scapegoats amongst your workers and then its business as usual."

"Sit yourself, down, the pair of you," he said, as though *we* were the guests in *his* house. We did as we were bidden and sat in the chairs. "My mother was a right pain. Yack, yack, yack. You couldn't shut her up. I thank the Lord I had a rest home to send her to."

I could hear Iris in the kitchen, banging things about in fury.

"Nah then, Doreen, lass," Arnold says. "Old Mortimer tells me you've got some tomfool idea about hanging on to that run-down chip shop on Balaclava Street."

"That's right, although I don't see what's tomfool about it."

"Nay, lass, after the offer he made you? We're not talking peanuts here, you know. This is not chicken feed we're on about. It's way above its true value. Your surveyor must have told you that. It's no place for a lady, in't Balaclava Street. It's all hooligans and rapists."

"And housing estates," I added.

"Oh, I see," he said. "You imagine that this here new housing estate is going to make your fortune, do you? I shouldn't set much

55

store by that development, Doreen, duck. They're not the fish and chip types. Young upwardly mobile yuppies mostly. They go for that frog and eyetie muck."

"We'll see," I said. "And anyway, did that ghoul of yours tell you *why* I wasn't selling?"

Arnold burst out laughing again, and his huge belly wobbled obscenely. "Ghoul!" he bellowed. "That's a good one. Old Mortimer is a bit of a fright when you think about it. Kiddies run off screaming when he walks down the street."

"Well, what I told him, I'll tell you," I said, my ears ringing from the volume of his not-very-amusing guffaws. "I'm opening that shop on my own account and I'm not selling it. Not to you, nor nobody else neither."

"Aye, lass, that's very commendable," he said, as though he didn't believe a word I was saying. "The spirit of free enterprise is a wonderful thing, but it has to be moderated with common sense. After all, profit is what it's all about. Making brass."

"He's right about that at least, Doreen," says Iris, coming in with a tray of tea.

"See?" says Arnold. "Even the old dear knows that much about business."

Iris slammed the tray down so hard that the tea splashed up all over the table.

"Now look, Doreen," he says, all coaxing, "be reasonable." He turned to Iris and bawled: "This is not that semi-skimmed milk, is it, mother? Have you not got any of the real kind?"

Iris glared at him. "I'm not your chuffing mother," she growled through clenched dentures.

He picked his own cup up, put six spoonfuls of sugar in it and stirred it for about five minutes. "I love old folk," he was saying. "They think they know it all, don't they? How does that saying go? With age comes wisdom. I don't think so. It's a lot of tripe is that. With age comes senility. In my opinion, pensioners should be seen and not heard. And preferably not even seen if I'm honest."

Iris was crimson with fury.

Then Arnold turned to Derek. "Go on then, Derek, you tell her. Talk some sense into that wife of yours."

Derek was still in a trance, totally overpowered by Arnold's presence. He said nothing, but his mother wasn't intimidated. "How much are you upping the offer by?" she said.

Arnold's stomach wobbled again in amusement. "She's a case this one, isn't she? They don't make 'em like that anymore. She's like my mother. Only mine's in a home. Best place for 'em."

"She's got a point though," I said. "What are we talking in terms of?"

"Ho, ho!" grinned Arnold, "Do I see signs of your capitalist nature emerging, Doreen? Is the money beginning to erode your principles? Quite right, lass, so it should."

He slurped his tea and when he'd done, he put the cup down.

"Right, well, I haven't come all the way from Chesterfield to sit here exchanging pleasantries. Let's get down to business," he said.

There was a film of sweat on his face, and wet patches were appearing on his shirt under the armpits. "I shan't insult you with daft attempts to get you to take less. I'll just put my best offer on the table, take it or leave it."

He put his hand into his trouser pocket and brought out a cheque book. Then he took out a pen and wrote down "Pay Doreen Potts £121,500". He tore the cheque out with a flourish and waved it in front of my face.

"Now then, I'll bet that's made your nickers wet, hasn't it, lass?"

"I'm unmoved," I said.

Derek's head was going from side to side as though he were at a tennis match, following the cheque as it was wafted in front of him. His mouth had fallen open like some idiot, and I half expected him to drool.

Arnold noticed the effect his cheque was having. "See, Doreen? Your husband has made his mind up. A straight £10,000 profit and never had to lift a finger for it. Never had to get your hands mucky. There's not many opportunities like that going to come your way in a lifetime."

"Take it Doreen," Derek said. "Snatch his hand off."

I hesitated, and Arnold could see I was in two minds. "He's giving you good advice, Doreen. This is a once-only offer. I shan't be back tomorrow."

My hand was itching to take hold of that cheque.

"No, I want my shop," I heard myself saying, but my voice was less convincing than before.

"Now look, Doreen. I've told you I can't increase the cash offer any further, and I mean it. But what about another little incentive? Think about this..." he leaned closer to me and there was suddenly an acrid smell of sweat in my nose. I tried not to react, but it must have shown on my face. "There are vacancies in my homes for the elderly. I could make one available at your disposal for the old 'un here. Dear old Iris. Get her off your back. You'll find it a great relief, and she'll be well looked after." He paused, then said: "That'll be in addition to, and as well as, the cheque, of course."

I looked at Iris, then at the cheque and then at Derek.

"You'll be able to pursue the career of your choice, with a bit of capital to do it, and no responsibilities for broken down relatives," Arnold was coaxing.

But then Iris suddenly said: "Tell him to stick it up his arse, Doreen. Tell him to take his smelly fat tits out of the house and bugger off."

"Y'what?" I said.

"He's revolting," said Iris. "A great, wobbling tub of grease. Don't have nothing to do with him. Show him the door."

"Now then, steady on," says Arnold. "I'll stand for a lot from the old folk, but common fishwifery I won't tolerate Your mother's a bit of a shrew, isn't she Derek? You want to keep her on a tight rein or she could damage your family's interests."

"She's right, though," I said to him. "You are horrible. And I'm not selling the shop, so you can stick your cheque where Iris suggested."

"Look," said Arnold, suddenly losing the bonhomie. "I've had enough of this messing about. Let me put my cards on the table, Doreen. I want that shop, and I'm going to have it. You don't honestly think you can stand in my way do you? I've got resources at my disposal. Major resources."

"I don't care how much you offer. I'm not interested, and that's final."

Derek was going to say something, but I raised my hand to stop him. "I said final and I meant final."

"I shan't increase the offer if that's what you're after," Arnold bellowed. "I thought when I offered you a generous settlement we could dispense with all this taradiddle. You're a fool to yourself, Doreen, if you let me go through that door with this cheque still in my possession. You'll not get another chance. I'm not going to humiliate myself on the altar of your greed, lady." He put his gloves on, then his coat. "Not that there's anything wrong with greed. I'm all for it. But there are limits, Doreen, and this is the limit to what

I'm prepared to offer for that shop. Once I'm out of this house I shan't come back..."

"Thank God for that," Iris muttered.

"But you won't have heard the last of me. Oh no. I shan't be leaving it at that. There are other avenues, other ways of reaching the conclusion that I want."

"And what's that supposed to mean?" I said.

"You'll see if you don't take this cheque, madam."

He waved the cheque once more. Then he stood and waited.

I said nowt.

"Very well, Doreen. On your own head be it. You people don't know what's good for you."

He opened the door and stomped down the garden path.

"Fat arse," Iris shouted after him as he got into his car.

Ainsley was still sitting in the chair, apparently oblivious to his father's temper and was staring at our Sylvia, who was clearly doing her best to incite him. She was crossing and uncrossing her legs and I wasn't at all certain that she was wearing nickers. Ainsley seemed hypnotised by the performance.

Then Arnold arrived back at the door and shouted: "Ainsley! Shift yourself!"

Ainsley was startled back to attention and followed his father to the car.

When they were gone, Derek said to me: "What the hell did you think you were doing? That's money we could have done with."

"Not everything's to do with money," I said.

He turned to his mother. "And as for you, I'm ashamed of you. Talking to a guest like that."

"Revolting lump," she said. "I wouldn't give him the time of day. You've done the right thing, Doreen."

Derek was frustrated: "I can't believe that he was trying to stuff £10,000 clear profit into your pocket, and you sent him packing."

"Doreen's got a dream, Derek, can't you see that?" says Iris "It's something that you've never had. She wants to create something that's all hers. If I'd been a man, I'd have done something like this myself instead of doing what I did do. Wasting my life being a bleeding housewife. I could have been something worthwhile if I hadn't been held back."

"Mother!" said Derek, shocked. "What are you saying? That you regret marrying me dad and having me?"

"I'm just saying..." Iris was biting her tongue.

Derek's voice cracked a little bit. "You've hurt me, mother. Cut me to the quick."

I said: "Every man thinks he's the apple of his mother's eye, when all the time he's the pip stuck in her gullet."

"Well, it's charming is that," says Derek, all emotional. "Told by my own mother that I wasn't wanted."

"That's not what I said," Iris corrected. "All I'm saying is that if I'd been born into a later generation, I could have had you *and* a satisfying career. You might have been the son of a powerful woman now if I'd been able to filful my potential. As it is, I'm just an insignificant old biddy who everybody wants to put away."

Then she started crying. They fell into each other's arms sobbing and apologising. It makes me sick to see how easily Iris winds the great sentimental idiot round her little finger.

I took our Sylvia to one side this morning, after she'd seen to the babby and I said: "Now look, lady, I want a bit more commitment from you. You're hardly ever at home these days, you're always over at our Gary's. I don't know what the attraction is over there, but I want to know that you're going to take this job at the chip shop seriously. I can't have you being unpredictable. I need reliable staff that won't let me down."

"I said I'd do it, didn't I? It's just that I'm suffering a bit of emotional turmoil at the moment. I've got something on my mind."

"I know what you've got on your mind—same as you've always got. Lads. Well, I want your full attention, never mind turmoil. I want them fish and chips properly wrapped from day one. Opening night is only two weeks away, and I want it to be special. So concentrate. I want a first-class, A1 job doing as regards the packaging of our product and the handing out of change."

"It's only a bleeding fish and chip shop, Mam."

"Only? Only?" I said. "Arnold Addison started out with 'only' a fish and chip shop and now he's got a conglomerated empire plc. Wouldn't you like to achieve something like that?"

She sighed and shrugged her shoulders.

I was at a loss as to how to motivate her. Then I hit on the very idea.

"You know Mr and Mrs Deans will be moving out next week? Well, their flat over the shop will be vacant."

Her eyes lit up and she suddenly stopped looking sullen.

"A flat?" She ran over to me and linked arms. "Can I have it, Mam?"

"You've changed your tune all of a sudden."

"It'd be great. My own flat. And right in town. Can I Mam? It's just what I need to buck me up."

"You can have it so long as you're my insistant in the shop. The flat goes with the job. Is that clear? It's a tied cottage. If you let me down, you'll be out, and no messing about."

"Oh, Mam!" she gave me a great big kiss. "I won't let you down."

That sounded familiar, but having her right there on the premises meant there'd be no feeble excuses for not coming into work, and I'd get to see our Charmaine Bernadette every day as well. I shall just have to make sure she doesn't turn it into a meeting place for the Hell's Angels.

* * *

I went into the shop for my shift today as usual, but Mrs Deans was a bit on the quiet side. So was Mr Deans.

I served a few customers, then, when it was quiet, I said: "Is something up, Mrs Deans? You don't seem your usual chatty self today."

"It's nothing love. Don't you worry about it."

"It's not to do with the move is it? Has something gone wrong?"

"Oh no, we're all set for that, Doreen. Got the removal van booked and everything. No, it isn't that."

I served a couple more customers, then I turned to Mr Deans.

"You're looking a bit under the weather as well," I said. "Are you sure there isn't something I can do?"

"Why don't you tell her, mother?" he said.

"Have I to tell her?" she replied.

"I think it would be best," he said.

She turned to me. "It's just that we've been having these phone calls, Doreen. Late at night."

"Phone calls?"

"Not nice," she said.

"Not very pleasant at all," Mr Deans echoed.

"What—like mucky phone calls? Heavy breathing and that?"

"Oh no, Doreen, nothing like that."

"No, don't get that idea," the faithful husband says.

"Well," I said, stirring the chips in the fryer, "You can either tell me or we can go on playing twenty questions all night until I guess the answer."

"It's that firm. That Addison and company," she said. "They keep demanding that we gazump you. They want us to withdraw from our agreement, offering us more and more money."

"A small fortune they've offered us."

"And what have you said?"

"Well, we have to keep turning them down, don't we? We won't go back on our deal with you, Doreen. We're on the verge of exchanging contracts. It wouldn't be right to go back on our word now."

Mr Deans battered a piece of rock salmon and said: "No we won't. Nothing would make us renegade on our word."

"The thing is," says Mrs Deans, lowering her voice and looking round as though we were being eavesdropped on, "They make these threats."

"Threats?" I said.

"Veiled threats," she said.

"That's the kind of threats they are—veiled," Mr Deans said.

"Like what?" I said.

"They've...They've threatened..." she was breathing hard, as though she couldn't bring herself to say it. "They've threatened to... make life difficult for us."

"Make life difficult? In what way?"

"They said they could... cause inconvenience."

"Cause inconvenience?" I said, trying to work it out.

"They said there might be... a disturbance."

"Well, that's veiled alright. What do you think they mean?"

"I don't know, but it's the way they say it, you see."

"Aye, it's the tone of voice," Mr Deans added.

"But what have they said they'd do?"

"Well, nothing pacific. Nothing you can put your finger on, but when a total stranger rings you up at gone midnight and talks about hubbubs, it makes your hair stand on end."

"It does, it makes your hair stand on end," said Mr Deans, even though he's completely bald on top. "I haven't slept for a week thinking about these hubbubs."

"Don't let them intimidate you, love," I said. "In a couple of weeks you'll be gone to Harbour Lights and well out of it. Just try and stick it out until then. Take your phone off the hook when you go to bed and take no notice of them."

They still looked worried. Anyway, a bit later on, these two youths came into the shop. I didn't like the look of them at all. A right shifty pair, and up to no good. Mr and Mrs Deans have this baseball bat under the counter just for such occasions, and I checked with my foot that it was still there.

One of them hovered by the door while the other one came up to the counter.

"Just to remind you," I said, "That we have video surveillance installed and we won't hesitate to put it on Crimewatch if necessary. Now, how can I help you?"

"You haven't got no video surveillance," he said, dead arrogant.

"Yes, we have. It's discreetly hidden on the premises. You may not be able to see the camera, but it can see you."

All lies, of course, but if people can put "Beware of the Dog" signs up, when all they've got is a miniature poodle, then why shouldn't I crack on about video surveillance?

"Are you the new owner?" he says.

"What's it to you? We're here to sell fish and chips, not discuss our financial arrangements with total strangers."

"Cod and large chips twice," he said. "Open."

As I was wrapping his order, Mrs Deans comes over and takes fifty quid out of the till and hands it over to him. This youth counted it and signalled to his mate who was standing by the door.

"Thanks, Ma," he said. "Make sure this lady knows the score, will you? I don't think she's quite got the picture."

They strolled out without the fish and chips.

"What was that all about?" I said.

Mrs Deans looked sheepish.

"And what were you paying for?"

"Well, Doreen, it's our insurance premium. We were going to tell you."

"Insurance? Shouldn't he have issued a receipt for cash?"

"They don't issue receipts for that kind of insurance, duck," said Mr Deans, also looking shamefaced.

"Who's operating this here insurance company?" I said, "the Mutual Threats and Menaces Corporation?"

"Oh no, it's Mr Warren. It's his patch round here. Syd Warren. Lovely man."

"You're paying protection money to somebody and you call him a lovely man?"

"Well, he's seen us all right, hasn't he Dad?" said Mrs Deans.

"Yes, we've been all right under Mr Warren," confirmed Mr Deans. "Until recently."

"This is shocking. I'm surprised at you. How long has it been going on?"

"Well, we've been paying for nearly three years now, haven't we, Dad— and we've been OK. He's been seeing off the worst of the hooligans. Then, when we put the place on the market, all this persecution started."

"So, in effect you're paying for nothing?"

They looked at the floor, biting their lips.

"And you never said nothing to me?" I chided.

"We're sorry, but we assumed everybody knew that there were these kinds of expenses."

"Protection money? Gangsters? You should have said something. It never occurred to me that Al Capone was alive and well and living in Rotherham. What else has he got, a speakeasy over the wool and knitting shop? A house of ill-repute behind the Trades and Labour Club? How much are you paying for this so-called insurance?"

"Well, fifty pounds every fortnight." said Mrs Deans.

I gasped, but she said: "It's not all that much in the scheme of things, and it really has been a boon while the area's been so run-down. Everybody knows this is Syd Warren's patch. They leave us alone because they know what will happen if they don't."

"I'm speechless," I said.

"Do you want us to go back to that Addison firm and say we've re-thought the matter over again?" Mrs Deans said. "We could do that. We could take his offer and save a lot of problems."

"No, hold your horses," I said. "I'm going to see what can be done about this. I'm not going to hand over my hard-earned profits to no hoodlum."

"Oh, don't talk like that, Doreen," Mrs Deans begged. "Be sensible. They don't like being messed about with."

"No, and neither do I. This has got to stop, and I'm going to get it stopped."

* * *

I went round to the police station this morning and asked to see somebody in charge of organised crime and corruption. The man on the desk looked at me gone out and asked if it was in connection with the spate of stolen mountain bikes on the estate. I said, no, it's about gangsterism. He said he'd get Sergeant Hagley to have a word. "Who shall I say is calling?" he said.

"You shall say Doreen Potts is calling, that's who you shall say."

When the sergeant arrived, we went into this room and I said: "There are racketeers operating in this town, taking protection money from innocent old people who can't afford it and who just want a quiet life in their chip shop."

He looked bewildered. "Hold on a minute, Mrs Potts. Can we start at the beginning?"

I told him what was happening and he made some notes in his book. Then he looked at me and said: "Organised crime is a serious business, Mrs Potts. It's certainly something we shall have to look into. Leave it with me, I'll see what's to be done."

"And make sure you do," I said. "And remember the name of public enemy number one—Syd Warren."

After that I went to see Mrs Chakrabarti who keeps the newsagents next door to the fish shop. She was behind the counter, dressed in her sari, filling the shelves with cigarettes and bottles of vodka and other spirits. I introduced myself, telling her I was her perspective new neighbour and she seemed pleased. "Why don't you come in the back for a cup of tea, luv," she said. "We'll get to know each other. We fellow traders have got to work together, haven't we?"

She sent one of her sons out to look after the shop while she entertained me.

It was strange seeing this little Indian woman talking like a native Rotherhamite. Her accent was broader than mine, and that's going some. She had a nice little sitting room in the back, with a stove, a sink and a couple of armchairs.

"Tell me Mrs Chakrabarti..." I said, sipping the tea.

"Oh, call me Kulvinder, love," she said. "And I'll call you Doreen."

"Kulvinder?" I said, "That's a nice name. Tell me, Kulvinder, are you being troubled by lads demanding money? You know what I mean—protection money?"

Her friendly attitude suddenly evaporated. "No," she said, looking at the floor and becoming evasive. "I don't know what you mean, love. We keep ourselves to ourselves, me and me husband. We don't go looking for bother."

"I know you don't. None of us do. But bother sometimes comes looking for us, and we've no option but to face up to it. Now, Mr and Mrs Deans next door have told me that you're paying the same money as they are to Syd Warren and his crowd. It's no good denying it, they've seen the lads coming in here to collect."

"Them lads come to buy their cigs from us, that's all—and their Sun."

"Don't come it, Kulvinder, I know all about it. Everybody on this parade of shops is paying."

"We don't want any repercussions. When they first came here I was like you—on my high horse. I told them to get lost. I said, I'm not paying money for nowt to silly kids like you. If you don't fling your hooks, I'll tell your mother to smack your legs. I thought that was the end of it, but then the damage started. Fireworks and dog muck through the letterbox, graffiti all over the shop—Pakis go home, that sort of stuff. We'd never had that before. We tried to stick it out, but it just got worse and worse until every time we showed ourselves on the doorstep there'd be kids throwing bricks at us and spitting at the customers as they came out. Folk stopped coming to the shop. They were buying their stuff elsewhere. Our turnover plummeted. We had no option in the end. I said to my husband, we've a lot to lose if we don't get on the right side of this lot, we'll have to give them what they want."

"And have you had any trouble since you started paying?"

"Oh no, love. That's one thing about it, you see. If you keep your payments up, they leave you alone. And so do all the other little buggers in the area. If any kids start their tricks, Mr Warren sees to it that they get a bloody good hiding. Nobody dares to step out of line now Mr Warren's in charge. Before we started paying him to look after us, we used to be under attack all the time."

"You've seen what's been happening to Mr and Mrs Deans's shop?"

"Shocking. Breaking their windows like that. I know they're old and defenceless, but they ought to keep up their payments. It's the only way."

"But it's not the only way, Kulvinder. You shouldn't have to be shovelling your livelihood into the pockets of them no-goods. They want stopping."

She shuffled in her seat and looked uncomfortable.

"Don't you think so?" I said.

She looked away, and then she said, without conviction: "Oh yes. It isn't right. But..."

"But what? We can stop them if we stick together and co-operate with the police. The bobbies can clear them out. After all, that's what they're there for."

"You're new round here, aren't you, duck?"

"Well, yes."

"You wouldn't be talking like that if you'd been through what we've been through. You wouldn't be talking in terms of bobbies, love. See my little Sandeep through there? We went on us holidays once and left him in charge for a week. He was so proud. Said it made him feel like a grown up. Trouble is, we forgot to tell him to pay the money. When we come back, they'd knocked hell out of him. Blacked both his eyes and kicked two teeth out. The police wasn't interested."

"They shouldn't be able to terrorise folk like that. They've got to be stopped."

She looked around to make sure no one was overhearing, and then she lowered her voice: "Take a tip from me, love—pay up and shut up. Forget about the police. If you value your business, just get on with it."

"But it can't be right, Kulvinder, love. Twenty-five quid a week is a lot to a small business like mine."

"That twenty-five quid is the best investment you'll make. Live with it, Doreen."

"Suppose the police did try to do something about it, would you help them?"

"I know nothing, love." She picked up the teacups and took them to the sink. "Don't expect no help from the folk round here. Not from the Everything-for-a-Pound shop or from Mrs Kirk's quality home furnishings, three doors down. They value their necks too much. And don't involve me with no police. It's took us twenty years to build up this business, and it's all we've got."

I was disheartened, but I went next door to the Deans's ready to open up for the dinnertime trade.

* * *

When I got into the shop this morning, the big window was broken again. But there was worse. Mr and Mrs Deans were mopping the floor inside. There was a horrible smell, like a sewerage pipe had burst.

"What's happened?" I said, trying not to gag.

"It were like this when we came down this morning. Somebody broke the window and poured this... muck all over the floor. Gallons of it. Tons of it. We've been clearing up for two hours and we still haven't got rid of it."

She wasn't exaggerating. They'd spread gallons of excrement and urine all over the shop. They must have been collecting it for ages—and somebody must have had diarrhoea along the way. Even though Mr and Mrs Deans had cleaned a lot of it up, the stink was overwhelming.

The old folks were near to tears. I felt that sorry for them I started to fill up meself.

"Go on up to your flat and have a bath and a cup of tea, the pair of you." I said. "You've done enough, I'll finish this off. I'll go round to the supermarket and get a crate of bleach and some air freshener."

"If word gets round that this has happened, I don't know what we'll do," said Mrs Deans, with her bottom lip wobbling. No sooner were the words out of her mouth, than the door opens and this man with a clip board comes in.

"Environmental health," he said, but as soon as he took his first breath, he started to gag. He made a quick exit back on to the pavement. When I went out to him, he was holding his hanky over his face.

"You were quick off the mark," I said.

"We had an anonymous phone call that you had an environmental disaster that needed urgent attention," he said.

"I suppose it's fair to call a hundredweight of shite an environmental disaster. That's if you measure shite by weight and not volume," I said.

I explained what had happened.

"In all the years I've done this job, this is the most disgusting thing I've ever seen," he said. "I'm afraid I'm going to have to close you down, Mrs Potts. I can't allow you to serve food in there at this present moment in time. Not with that... that..."

"Shite?" I suggested.

"Quite. Not with that... all over everything."

"I'm going to get cracking on it now. Get the strongest cleaning agents I can find. It'll be more steriler than an operating theatre when I've finished with it. I shan't stop till I've cleaned every speck of it."

"This is unprecedented, Mrs Potts. I'm afraid ordinary cleaning won't be sufficient. There'll have to be tests. We'll need to fetch instruments down here to measure the bacteria. After all, there's nothing like... like..."

"Shite?"

"...for spreading diseases. Have you sent for the police?"

"I'll do that now. But I don't think it's fingerprints they're going to be looking for."

So, I went up to the flat and broke the news to the Deans's who were both having a little weep. "This is the end is it then, Doreen?" Mrs Deans moaned. "We won't blame you if you want to pull out now. We can't expect you to put up with this."

"Not at all," I said, trying to sound defiant, but underneath it all I just wanted to run away and forget the whole thing. "I won't let them beat me. I'm going to fight back. We can't have the town run by hooligans like this. The police have just got to step in and interfere. If they don't, I'll take it to the government."

"That's if you live long enough to do it," said Mrs Deans. "You can't stand up to this lot on your own, love. They're too powerful. They're violent."

"They are, duck, they're very violent," confirmed Mr Deans, blowing his nose.

"I'm not on my own, though, am I? I've got the full might of the law on my side. Speaking of which I'm going to ring them now."

I went to the phone and called Sergeant Hagley. He said he'd send someone down to investigate. He didn't sound particularly enthusiastic about doing it, though.

Anyway, about half an hour later this young constable arrives. I said to him: "You're not on work experience, are you? You don't look more than fourteen."

"I'm twenty-two actually, and fully trained."

"Where's the big guns?" I said: "They can't have sent a lad like you to investigate a full-blown, mafia-style criminal conspiracy can they?"

"I thought it were vandalism," he said.

"Well, on the face of it, it is," I said. "But it's who's done the vandalism that matters and why. This isn't the work of school kids or teenage tearaways. This is real criminality in action. This is punishment from a protection racket."

"Do you realise how many complaints we get about vandalism round here?" he said, wrinkling his nose at the lingering whiff. "If we sent the flying squad out to all of them our budget would be finished in about three days."

"This isn't ordinary vandalism," I said. "This is a gang that's extorting money from the businesspeople in this area, for so-called protection."

"What, and you've refused to pay?"

"No, on the contrary, the people who own this shop are fully up to date. It's just pure spite."

"But why would they attack you if you're paying your dues?"

I was outraged. "To start with, they are not dues. Dues are what you owe, and we don't owe them nothing, they just terrorise us into paying. And secondly, I don't know why they're persecuting these people. They've done everything they've been asked, and yet still they get treated like this."

"Perhaps they want the contributions increased. Perhaps they're softening you up to pay more."

"Look," I said. "Whose side are you on, exactly? You sound as though you couldn't care less. Fancy sending a lad like you to take on a godfather like Syd Warren. We want the top dogs on this. The CID, MI5 and the FBI. When you get back to that station, put them on full alert. Tell them somebody is going to get fatally killed if they don't tackle this problem soon."

70

"OK," he said, looking about as interested as I do when there's football on the television.

He turned to go. I said: "Aren't you even going to ask for a statement? Write something in your notebook?"

"We've stopped recording minor incidents of vandalism. It creates too much paperwork. The budget won't stand it."

"Budget?" I shouted. "Budget?" But before I could say anything else, he was getting on his bike and riding off.

I went upstairs and called Sergeant Hagley again. "I'll get a full report of your allegations from the constable when he gets back," he said. "Meanwhile, you're going to have to leave it with us. You've got adequate insurance, haven't you?"

"Well, yes, but..."

Before I could say anything else, he'd put the phone down.

Mrs and Mrs Deans were watching and shaking their heads.

"We told you it would be no joy from the police," Mrs Deans said.

"I'm not leaving it there," I said, full of umbrage. "I'll go to his superiors. I'll take it as far as I can, and then further."

They shook their heads again in a hopeless kind of way.

* * *

Derek thinks I'm absolutely nuts to go ahead with the exchange of contracts. He's tried everything to persuade me out of doing it. "Once you've done that you're committed. You can't get out of it."

"They're not going to stop me having my dream," I said.

"Can't you have a dream where everybody else has them—in bed? Why does it have to be in the crime capital of the North?"

I started to feel a bit choked up, and there were tears springing to my eyes. "I want this shop. I've grown fond of it." I know I was being irrational and sentimental, but I'd painted myself into a corner.

"There's others to think of besides yourself," he said. "We'll all be at risk if you start a gang war. They're ruthless, these small-time mobsters."

"You've got to have a gang to conduct a gang war, and I haven't got one. I'll cope on my own."

"Well, you keep me out of it, and the kids and me mother. Don't involve them in no crusade to clean up the streets."

71

I knew he was right, but I was in one of them nobody's-going-to-tell-me-what-to-do moods. So, the exchange of contracts went ahead, and a few days later we paid the Deans's the money, and they ceremoniously handed over the keys. The keys to my little kingdom. Or my kingdom as will be, when I've had the industrial cleaners in and the extra security grilles installed over the windows. As soon as the environmental health have cleared me for total hygiene, we can re-open. That should take about a fortnight. The Deans's have knocked two thousand off the price to compensate me for the lost business, so I don't feel so bad.

We had a little party in the flat over the shop to say farewell to the old couple. I brought in a bottle of prosecco and some beer, and we had a toast to their achievements, and we wished them well for a long and happy retirement at Harbour Lights. Mrs Deans got all excitable and had to be given a sip of brandy. Mr Deans then had a crying do and a similar reviver was given to him.

Our Sylvia, thoughtful and sensitive to the last, was poking about all over the flat saying things like: "God, look at this horrible old sideboard. I'm getting rid of this as soon as I move in."

That set Mrs Deans off again. "That were me mother's sideboard. I'm only leaving it because there's no room for it at Harbour Lights." She sobbed at the prospect of our Sylvia chucking it on the tip at the first opportunity.

"Try to be a bit more considerate of their feelings," I whispered to her. "Their whole lives are tied up in this little flat."

She shrugged and said: "I know but this bleeding wallpaper will have to come down. It's horrible. Makes the place look like a Victorian back parlour."

"We only had the place re-decorated last year," Mrs Deans wept. "That wallpaper cost a lot of money."

I glowered at our Sylvia, but she just continued to take measurements and tut at the carpets and curtains, which the Deans's are kindly leaving. I don't know where she's suddenly got this interest in interior decorating and furniture. Up to now she's been indifferent as to whether she lived in a pig-hole or a palace, it was all the same to her. Paint and wall coverings might as well not have existed. Now, all of a sudden, she's up in anaglypta and current in curtain fabrics. I shouldn't complain, it might be a sign of her getting domesticated.

Anyway, after Mr and Mrs Deans had cried themselves dry, and everybody had personally shook their hands and kissed them, Derek carried their bags down the stairs. We all followed into the street and threw streamers after them as they got into their minicab to take them to Mablethorpe. Everybody waved and promised they'd look them up at Harbour Lights if ever they was on that stretch of the Lincolnshire coast, and off they went.

"It's the end of an era," I says to Derek, starting to choke up again.

"Aye, but the beginning of a new one," he said. "Providing you survive more than a week."

"They were a lovely couple, weren't they?" I said to Derek, feeling all sentimental.

"Have they gone?" our Sylvia shouts from the upstairs window. "Thank Christ for that. Now I can start moving me stuff in."

After we'd cleared up a bit, we went home and I started on the job of trying to think of a name for the shop. I sat with a notepad and pencil and doodled a few ideas. "Doreen's Fish and Chips" told the whole story but didn't seem quite enough for such an important establishment. "Doreen's Fish and Chip Emporium" sounded fancier, but a bit old-fashioned. Then I thought about a seaside theme. The present name "Ocean Breezes" seemed OK until I realised it didn't have my name in it, so I tried "Doreen's Ocean Breezes". Or even "Chez Doreen", but that might give the impression we were serving French fries instead of proper chips.

"You're a bleeding egomaniac," Derek said as he looked over my shoulder at my efforts. "What's wrong with just calling it Balaclava Street Fish and Chip Shop?"

I waved him away and put my thinking cap on again.

Just after tea, the phone rang. It was Mrs Deans from Mablethorpe. She was in a right tizzy.

"Doreen! Doreen!" she was shouting. "They've burned Harbour Lights down."

"Hold on," I said, as a shock went through my stomach. "How do you mean they've burnt it down. Who has?"

"It's just a pile of ruins, a black hole in the ground! What are we going to do? What are we going to do?" She was sobbing and screaming.

"Is Mr Deans there with you, love? Put him on, and I'll see if he can tell me what's happening?"

She handed the phone to Mr Deans.

"What's all this about, Mr Deans?" I said.

"Oh God! Oh God!" he started shouting. "They've burned it down. It's been razed to the ground! Dear Jesus, what are we going to do?"

I felt like telling them to smack each other across the face so I could get some sense out of them.

"Are you saying that there's been an accident at Harbour Lights?" I said. "Have you had a fire?"

"It must have been a conflagration, Doreen, an inferno, a holocaust. Harbour Lights is no more."

"How did it happen?" I said.

Mr Deans composed himself a little, although I could hear his wife wailing something chronic in the background. "It was all over by the time we got here. We arrived to find a pile of ashes. Our dreams have gone up in smoke during the early hours of the morning."

"Was it an accident?" I said.

"The fire brigade and the police are instituting enquiries, but how could it have been an accident? We weren't even connected up to the gas."

"It's terrible news," I said, shedding a little tear. "It's awful. What are you going to do?"

"What *can* we do? We've booked into a boarding house–Cliff Walk, it is—and we'll have to start rebuilding our lives as of tomorrow."

I tried not to, but I couldn't help thinking Cliff Walk was a bit of a funny name for a boarding house in Mablethorpe which is as flat as a pancake.

"You know you can always come back to the flat. I don't want you to be homeless."

"No," he said, very firmly. "Nothing would seduce us to return to that flat. It has too many unhappy memories. We won't be coming back, ever. We shall stay for an intermediate period at the wife's sister's in Heckmondwyke. It's not ideal – neither of us can stick Heckmondwyke—but beggars can't be choosers."

"I can't tell you how sorry I am, Mr Deans," I said.

"And I can't tell you how sorry I am, Doreen, love, that you've been left there with that terrible thing round your neck—you know,

74

a terrible whatsername—a seagull. No, not a seagull, a penguin—no, not a penguin a…"

"Albatross," says, Mrs Deans, briefly interrupting her emotional collapse to help him out.

"Don't you worry about me, Mr Deans, I'm not afraid of Syd Warren and his ilk."

"Well, you should be, Doreen. They're not to be messed about with, as we've just found out to our cost."

"You don't think he's responsible for the Harbour Lights inferno, do you?"

"I'm not saying nothing," said Mr Deans. "But I know what I know. And you want to take every precaution."

With that he bade me a tearful farewell.

I put the phone down all of a quiver. But no sooner had I replaced the receiver than it rang again.

"Hello, is that Mrs Potts?" the deep, slow voice was familiar, but I couldn't quite place it.

"Mortimer Hackett here," he said. My mind was blank.

"Chips & More! Arnold Addison Enterprises?" he prompted.

"Oh, the living dead," I said. "It must be a bit damp underground with all this rain."

His voice was cold. "Mr Addison has asked me to call you with an improved offer."

"No thanks."

"A much-improved offer," he said.

"I'm not selling."

"You're out of your depth, aren't you, Mrs Potts?"

"Am I?" I said.

"We've got our spies. We know what's going on down at Balaclava Street. It doesn't sound very pleasant."

"I can cope."

"There's no need for you to cope. Let Mr Addison do the coping. He's got the resources to fight back against this kind of thing."

"No."

"It won't get any better, you know, Mrs Potts. In fact, knowing the people involved, it can get decidedly worse."

"Oh, shut the lid of your coffin and pipe down," I said and rang off.

Iris was pretending to knit, but I could see she was listening to all this.

I started quivering again.

"What's up, Doreen?" Derek said. "You look as though you've seen a ghost."

"Not seen one, spoke to one," I said.

Iris looked concerned and put her knitting down. "Derek, can't you see she's had bad news of some kind? She looks as white as a sheet. Not one of her own sheets, of course, they're never white. Get her a drink."

She came over and put her arm round me. "What is it, Doreen? Has something awful gone off? Did it involve a fatality" She sat me on the settee and gave me the tot of brandy that Derek had poured.

"It's the Deans's," I said, shaking and shivering. "Harbour Lights has been burnt down. They think it might be arson."

Derek's eyes nearly popped out of his head and he headed back to the brandy bottle to get one for himself. "Is it that Syd Warren?" he said, gulping it down in one go.

"They don't know," I said. "But they've got their suspicions."

"Syd Warren?" Iris said. "What about Syd Warren?"

"Nothing," said Derek. "Nothing for you to get excited about, Mam."

"Never mind that," she said. "I want to know what's going on."

"I don't want you to be worried or excited, Mother," he said. "It's not good for you."

"It's better than chuffing knitting from morning till night. Now come on, Doreen, spill it."

Derek was about to protest further, but his mother silenced him with a loud shush.

So, I told her the whole story.

"This is not Syd Warren's usual M.O.," she said. "He's usually straight with his customers."

"You call a protection racket straight?" I shouted.

"No, give him his due, Doreen," Iris said. "He really does offer protection."

"Yes, and he offers drugs and prostitutes as well, and I don't want to avail meself of either of them, neither."

"That's a rough area round Balaclava Street and Waterloo Way. The folk who live there know they're safe when they sign up with Syd."

"Yes, but safe from what? You have to pay him not to do you over. That's not much of a bargain."

76

"That's not quite right, Doreen," she said. "There was a lot of mindless violence round that area until Syd moved in. It were anarchy. He's brought order."

"You call smashing windows and covering my shop in shite, order?"

"That's what I can't figure out," she said, stroking her chin.

"You call burning down Harbour Lights order?" I shouted at her. "What have the Deans's done to deserve that except line his pockets? He ought to have been giving them a gold watch for the amount they've paid to him over the years, not trashing their shop and torching their house."

"Trashing? Torching?" said Derek. "Where the hell have you learned to talk like that, Doreen? You must be mixing in the wrong company."

"Never mind that," says Iris, "What about Syd Warren."

"What do you know about Syd Warren, anyway, Mother?" asked Derek. "He's a gangster."

"I've known him since he were a lad. I used to go to Bingo with his mother. Lovely woman, barring her cross-eyes. He runs his business fair and square. He isn't into vengeance and persecution, except when he's making sure everybody behaves. I can't understand why he should be carrying on like this with folk who're playing the game. Unless..." She stroked her chin thoughtfully again. "Unless there's somebody else trying to move in on his patch."

"Could you have a word with him, Iris? Appeal to his better instincts—if he's got any. Tell him about this rival gang if that's what it is? He might be able to get it stopped."

"Don't talk ridiculous, Doreen," Derek said. "You're not sending my mother off to mix with bandits and desperados."

"Why not? She's obviously very familiar with that style of life," I said.

"There's a difference between shoplifting due to the balance of her mind being unbalanced and organised extortion rackets," he said.

"Shut it, Derek," Iris said. "You don't know what you're on about." She turned to me. "I could help you out with this, Doreen. Syd Warren is very fond of his mother, and consequently he also has a soft spot for his mother's friends. I could gain access to him like that," she snapped her fingers. "If you tried to see him, you wouldn't get past the front gate of his mansion before the hounds were ripping your throat out. He's got that place of his done up like the Tower of London, nobody gets in and nobody gets out without his say so."

"How do you know all this, Mother?" said Derek, his eyebrows knitted in bewilderment.

"I told you, I used to pal about with his mother, Gracie. He'd do anything for his mother would Syd."

"Well, will you go round there and let him know what's happening? Get him to call his heavies off?" I said.

She sat back in the settee and looked self-satisfied. "Pour me one of them brandies, Derek," she said.

Derek did it and brought it to her.

"So, you want something off me now, do you?" she said, looking at me. "Want a favour."

She sipped the drink and smiled.

"Well, will you?" I asked.

"It's going to cost you, Doreen," she said. "This is valuable work I'm offering to do for you."

I got my purse out. "What? Twenty quid? Thirty? Fifty?"

"Put your purse away, Doreen. Forget the small change. I want something more than cash."

"What? Me soul?" I said.

"Let's think this through, Doreen," she said, savouring her unexpected power.

All of a sudden, she'd changed from being the little old lady knitting a matinee jacket for her grandchild into this hard-faced moll. "If I don't persuade my friend Syd to stop his campaign of terror, you're likely to end up like Mr and Mrs Deans, with a pile of ashes to sweep up rather than a thriving little chip shop."

I thought about our Sylvia and little Charmaine Bernadette living over the top of the shop, with all that danger. Me stomach knotted up and I went to the bottom of the stairs and shouted up to her: "Stop packing, Sylvia, you're not going into that flat."

There was a silence upstairs for a moment and then the door of her room opened.

"Y'what?" our Sylvia says.

"It's not safe to move into Balaclava Street. You and the kiddy are stopping here."

She let out one almighty scream and then shouted: "You wicked cow! I hate you. I hate the chuffing lot of you." And then she ran back into the room screaming and slamming the door.

"There's no guarantee that she'll be safe here, neither," Iris said. "The Deans's were lucky they weren't at home when the fire raisers visited Harbour Lights."

"They wouldn't dare come arsonising on Evergreen Close," I said. "There'd be uproar. They might rule the roost down Balaclava Street and all round there, but even Syd Warren cuts no ice in the nicer parts of town. The police take things seriously round here. They've got to, or there's trouble from the middle classes. And when the middle classes get roused you know about it."

"You're a babe in arms as far as crime is concerned," Iris said. "They don't come riding up on their horses with bandanas round their faces anymore. No, they're a lot more stealthier than that. They can set fires that even the most experienced forensic dicks can't pin on them."

"Dicks?" Derek said, amazed at his mother's crime vocabulary.

"They know all the tricks. They could have this house burning round our ears in no time if they wanted to, and there wouldn't be a clue to be found anywhere. Just a mystery inferno with our charred remains in it."

I shuddered. Derek poured himself a brandy. A big one.

"We'd have to be identified from our dental records," she said, although I'm not sure her ancient dentures would survive the conflagration.

"So, what do you want, then, Iris, if not cash?" I said.

"I want in on the business," she said.

I cleaned out my ear with my little finger. "Say again?"

"I want a partnership in the business. I want to be part of it."

"A job, you mean? An assistant job?"

She looked at me.

I waited.

She said nowt.

"Now look here, Iris," I said. "There are limits. You have no right to come demanding a share of my dream."

"Well, I shan't be demanding a share of your nightmare, and that's what it will be if you don't bring me on board pronto. I can't keep my offer open indefinitely. You'd be a fool not to look this gift horse in the eye."

I appealed to Derek. "Have you heard her?" I said to him. "Can you see what a manipulative old sod you've got for a mother?"

"I must say, Mam," said Derek. "You're being a bit unfair."

"I've told you to shut it," she said, and she looked at him in a way that instantly reduced his age from 55 to seven. It's a skill I've often admired in her. He looked away, sheepish.

"So, there's your choice, Doreen. Either I'm in, or you're burnt out."

"Oh no. I'm not taking your word for anything. Just because you say it's so doesn't make it so. How do I know you're telling the truth about Syd Warren's mother? It could all be fairy tales for all I know."

"You're right to be spectacle, Doreen," she said. "You don't want to trust nobody in business. However, seeing as you need proof..."

She opened her handbag, took out an address book, looked up a telephone number and dialled.

"Hello? Can I speak to Mr Warren, please? Tell him it's Iris Potts in connection with his mother." There was a pause and then she said: "Is that Syd? Hello, love, this is Iris Potts. Is your mother in, love, only I was thinking we might go to the bingo on Friday." She smirked at me. Then she returned to the call. "Oh, is she? On a cruise. That's nice for her. You know how to take care of your mother, Syd. I wish my son would send me on a cruise."

I thought, yes, so do I. On the Titanic preferably.

"What a lovely thing to say, Syd. Well tell her I was asking after her when she gets back, won't you? Tarra, duck."

She put the phone down and looked at me for a reaction.

"So what?" I said. "You could have been ringing the speaking clock for all I know."

"Come here," she said. So, I went over to the phone. "Pick it up and press the redial."

I did.

"Hello, Warren residence," said a man's voice.

I froze. Iris snatched the receiver from my hand and said, in a disguised voice: "Sorry, wrong number," and slammed the phone down.

"Now do you believe me?" She was triumphant.

"I'm going to have to think about this. It's come as something of a shock, being in thrall to you. I might need counselling."

"Aye, and you might need skin grafts an'all if you don't make your mind up."

"I'll come back to you when I've thought it over."

* * *

I went up to the police station today first thing and asked for that Hagley chap. When the desk sergeant rang him up, I heard a voice saying: "Oh Christ, not her again. Tell her I'm out, but enquiries are proceeding."

"He's not in," said the desk sergeant.

"Then I'll see his immediate superior," I said.

"He's not in either."

"You're running the place single handed are you?" I said.

"Why not pop in again tomorrow."

"At which time I expect, he'll not be in again. If I'm any judge of character, he'll not be in for the rest of eternity. I wouldn't be surprised if he hasn't been abducted by aliens."

"Don't be sarky Mrs," he said.

"I'll be more than sarky," I said. "I'm going to take this further. I'm writing to my MP to ask him to bring it to the attention of the Home Secretary. There's something unsavoury about your lack of interest."

"And what's that supposed to mean?"

"Have you ever heard the term backhander?"

He looked at me sharply and said: "I should leave it at that, love, if I were you. I get the distinct impression you're on the verge of saying something that you'll come to regret."

I realised I was going to get nowhere with the bobbies. I was coming to understand what Kulvinder Chakrabarti had been talking about, so I went home. When I got there, our Sylvia was laying on the settee. all listless with red eyes. Our Charmaine Bernadette was asleep at the side of her.

"Are you OK, love?" I said.

She shot me a dirty look and said: "What do you think, after you've gone and ruined my entire life."

"It's only entirely ruined temporarily. You'll get your flat in the end, we've just got a bit of sorting out to do. I don't want you and the babby put at risk."

She shrugged and turned away from me.

81

I noticed that the answering machine was flashing, so I went over to see what it was. "Hello, Mrs Potts, it's Della from Industrial Cleansing and Hygiene Limited. We went to your shop this morning to start work but when we got there, we found the door open. Somebody's broken in, Mrs Potts. I think you ought to get down here as soon as you can. I've sent for the police, but I think you want to come down here yourself. Message timed at 9.27."

It was just gone ten, so I put me coat on and rushed down to the shop. Just as she'd said, the door was wide open, and there was a policeman inside. When I went in, I could hardly believe my eyes. My friers were gone, both of them. The place was empty, except for the counter.

"What the hell's going on?" I said.

"Are you the owner?" this policeman was saying—another youth like the last one.

"Yes, I'm Mrs Potts. What's happened?"

"You've been burglarised, Mrs Potts."

"Who by—Pickfords?" I said. "Where're me friers?"

"Looks like they've been stole," he said. "They must have been at it all night, dismantling them."

"I can't take it in," I was going to sit down, but they'd also taken the two chairs we had for waiting. "Who'd pinch a chip shop's friers?"

"They'll steal anything these days, love. We had a case last week where they took a container-load of emptyings from the campsite's latrine. God knows what they did with that."

"I could tell you," I said, and sighed long and loud.

"The scene of crime officer is on his way, so please don't touch anything."

"Touch anything?" I said. "There's nowt left to touch."

"Anyroad, I've been left to make sure the place is secure."

"Secure?" I scoffed. "It sounds more like a case of bolting the horse after the stable door's been opened."

"I must say, it's a very professional job," he said. "Nobody saw or heard a thing. I've been round all the neighbouring shops and flats."

"You might as well not bother, lad. They all know who's responsible, but you'll get nothing out of them."

"Oh aye? Have you some idea who might have done this, then?"

"If I mention the name Syd Warren, does it mean anything to you?" I said.

"I've heard it mentioned around the station, although I've never come across the man personally."

"No, you're not likely to, neither. I have a feeling Mr Warren has other people doing his dirty work for him. He's determined to put me out of business for some reason—I don't know why. I've offered to pay his protection money."

"Protection money? This sounds serious, Mrs. I'll have a word with my superiors, if you don't mind. I'm a bit out of my depth."

He went outside and started speaking into his walky-talky. After a bit, he came back.

"Well?" I said. "Are they going to fetch him in for questioning?"

"They've got the matter in hand."

"What does that mean?"

"I couldn't say."

I sighed again and suddenly felt very tired and worn out.

"I'd better go home and ring the insurance company. God knows what they're going to make of this."

When I got back Iris was doing her Aerobics for the Aged video. I wish she'd give over. That leotard pulled up between her arse cheeks turns my stomach.

"You win," I said, switching the telly off and plonking myself on the chair.

"What—you mean I'm a partner?"

"On one condition—you get Syd Warren off my back."

I told her what had happened.

"This makes less and less sense," she said. "Look, I'm going to see the solicitor about getting a partnership document drawn up. Then I'll tackle Syd. Shall we say evens-stevens, as regards splitting the shop?"

"No we shan't—seventy-thirty."

"Sixty-forty?"

"Oh, for God's sake, just do something."

She was all smiles as she put her hat and coat on and went to the door. Suddenly she turned back and went over to her chair and took out her knitting. She looked at it, and then chucked it in the waste bin. "I shan't be needing that to pass the time anymore," she said.

* * *

Well, as good as her word, Iris got her solicitor to draw up a document making her a partner in the fish shop. I'm not at all sure I've done the right thing, and my pen hesitated when it was my turn to sign but, in the end, I forced myself—I'm not at all confident I can manage all this argy-bargy myself. I'm not familiar with the workings of the Mob, so I shall need Iris to guide me.

Derek was as pleased as punch when I told him about his mother's new-found place in our lives. "I'm that glad you've made up your differences," he said.

"Don't get the wrong idea," I said to him, "I still hate your mother like poison, but I just happen to need her help, that's all. Needs must, otherwise I wouldn't entertain her."

"I know you don't mean it, Doreen," he said, more in hope than certainty.

"I've got big ideas for that shop," Iris said, as soon as the ink was dry on the contract.

"Have you?" I said. "Well, first of all we've got to wrench it from the clutches of Rotherham's answer to Bugsy Malone."

She went to the phone and dialled. "Hello, is that Syd? Hello, love, this is Iris Potts again. Sorry to trouble you, but it's not about your mother this time, it's about business. Do you think it would be possible to come over and have a little chat with you, duck?" She winked at me. "Well, I'd rather not talk about it over the phone... Yes, love, OK... Have you heard from your Mam, by the way? Is she having a nice time?... Oh, lovely. Right, well. I'll see you this afternoon. And I'm bringing my daughter-in-law, Doreen. You remember her? She used to play with your Evelyn when they were at school together... Yes. See you later, then."

She put the phone down.

Derek was horrified.

"Was that Syd Warren you were arranging to see?" he said.

"And what if it was?" his mother replied.

"I'm not having you consorting with the criminal underclasses, Mother. Nor you, Doreen, neither. What can you be thinking of, mixing with that lot?"

"Syd's a nice lad," Iris said. "And has been since I've known him. Just so long as you don't cross him or get in his way, he's charm itself."

"I don't care if he's Morris Chevalier, you're not getting involved. Don't you realise that people like that will stop at nothing? They've got no scruples."

"Haven't you realised that's why your mother gets on with them so well?" I said to Derek.

He realised he was on to a loser trying to order his mother about, so he stuck his newspaper in front of his face and tutted.

I didn't let on, but I was nervous about the visit myself. All the same, I couldn't see no option but to face up to it and find out what was going on. The alternative didn't bear thinking about.

So, come the appointed hour, we took the bus out to Thrybergh. While we were driving along, I said to Iris: "Tell me something about him, Iris. I've no idea what to expect."

"I've told you he's charm itself—if he likes you. And he likes me."

"But he's got this terrible reputation for violence."

"I don't know why—leaving aside that incident with his first wife, of course."

"What incident?"

"She was found strangled under a hedge by a man walking his dog on a Sunday morning. No-one was ever charged in connection with it. Syd claimed it was suicide, and the coroner agreed with him."

"What, she strangled herself with her own bare hands, did she? That's a bit unusual isn't it? Did Syd have something to do with it?"

"How the hell should I know? I'm not Shylock chuffing Holmes. All I know is that his wife and his mother didn't get on. They were like cat and dog. It was what they call the daughter-in-law syndrome."

"You mean the mother-in-law syndrome?" I said.

"In my experience these fall-outs tend to spring from the daughter-in-law's belligerence. It's just that mother always gets the blame."

"Yes, well my experience tells me the opposite."

"Well, whoever's fault it was, she was strangled and dumped by somebody. It were a big scandal at the time. About twenty years since."

That didn't make me feel any easier.

When we got off the bus, we had about another half mile to walk out into the country. When we got there, we found a big, rambling, stone-built house standing in the middle of a field. It must have belonged to a farm at one time. There were steel fences and razor wire surrounding it, and, at the top of the drive, a big gate with spikes at the top. Iris looked at me and said: "And another thing—be careful what you say about his mother. He's a man obsessed as regards her, so try to stay off the topic if at all possible, which it won't be. Just nod your head and smile." Then she pressed the intercom buzzer.

"Yes?" a man's voice said.

"Iris and Doreen Potts to see Mr Warren," Iris said into the microphone, very business-like, as though it were an everyday occurrence visiting a drug-dealing, extorting, suspected murdering villain.

There was a pause, then the gates started to open by themselves. As we walked in, they closed behind us. My hands were beginning to sweat as we approached the front door. As we got on to the porch, the door opened, also automatically. I could hear big dogs barking somewhere. I stopped and for a minute considered running off, but Iris gave me a push and we walked in.

It was a sizeable entrance hall that we came to first. All marble and gilt, a bit on the vulgar side, I thought. Then another door opens and this man comes out, small he were, but beautifully dressed.

"Come in," he said, beckoning us into another room.

We went in, and there in the middle of another large room, gorgeously furnished and overlooking a big garden, was a tall, spindly man with thinning hair. He was wearing an old cardigan and a pair of corduroy trousers. He turned round as we came in.

"Iris, lovey!" he said, walking over to Iris and kissing her on the cheek. "And this must be Doreen. You're the one who used to pal about with our Evelyn at school, aren't you? Sit yourselves down, ladies."

He must have been about sixty with a shifty look about him, as though he was always on the lookout for, and expecting to find, somebody wanting to do him harm.

"Do you want a cup of tea, either of you?" he said, all smiles.

"I'll have a cuppa, if you're offering," Iris said, calm as you like.

I was scared to have one. My hands were shaking so much I was sure I'd spill it.

He turned to the other chap, who must have been his assistant or something, and nodded. The other chap went out.

"You always put me in mind of my mother, Iris, whenever I see you," Syd said. "Made from the same 24 carat gold, the pair of you." He took a postcard off his desk and handed it to Iris. "She's having a great time on her cruise. Canary Islands."

"Ooh, lovely," said Iris. "She's lucky to have a son like you to take care of her. You've always been fond of your mam, haven't you, Syd? How old is she now, she must be knocking on."

"Eighty-two," he said. "And she doesn't look a day over seventy." He took a picture of his mother in a solid silver frame down from the mantelpiece and kissed it. "She always speaks highly of you, Iris. You're her favourite bingo companion."

"That's nice, love. I've always had a soft spot for your family. And you've done well for yourself, haven't you? I mean, this house isn't exactly a two-up, two-down council property, is it?"

"We've not done bad between us. My brother Brian is a postman and our Evelyn is now a social worker with the council." He turned to me. "Do you remember our Evelyn from school, then, Doreen?"

I didn't, to be honest, but I managed a weedy smile and said: "Oh yes, your Evelyn. Smashing lass. We used to get up to all kinds of tricks. I always knew she'd get on."

The phone rang as the other chap was serving the tea, and Syd picked it up and walked over to the other side of the room and turned his back to us. Although he was whispering, I could hear quite clearly what he was saying. And his personality was completely changed. The perfectly plain, ordinary, chatty, man was suddenly replaced by this sneering, scowling, dangerous-looking person. "Don't give me that bollocks," he was snarling into the telephone under his breath. "I'm telling you now—if this isn't sorted by dinner time tomorrow, I'll make sure you get a lesson you won't forget... Oh stop your fucking whining and get on with it— and remember what I said, you miserable cunt, if you don't deliver, you'll be very sorry."

With that he slammed the phone down and turned back to us. The smile reappeared immediately. I pretended not to have heard.

"Come with me, Iris, I've got something to show you," he said, all friendly and nice. "You come as well, Doreen. You'll like this."

He led us into another room and switched on the light. Inside it had been made into a sort of shrine to his mother. There were pictures of her all over the place on various holidays. There was even one that had been made into a poster where she was meeting

87

the Queen at some function. There were daft verses in frames hanging on the walls with these right sentimental poems called things like "Mother of Mine" and "Ode to the best Mam in the world". The sort of crap you get in seaside souvenir shops.

"And what about this," he said, reaching under his collar and pulling a locket on a chain out of his shirt. "24 carat gold is that." It was heart-shaped, with the initials S and G engraved on it in tiny diamonds.

"That's posh," said Iris, as though she were talking to a five-year old. He didn't seem to mind, in fact, appeared to like it.

Syd opened the locket. It was one of those were you put a photo in each half. On one side was a picture of his mother, on the other one of him.

"What do you think of that, then?" Syd was as pleased as punch.

"Oh, it's lovely, is that. Int'it, Doreen? Right smashing," says Iris.

I nodded and gave a feeble smile.

"You'll note that the house is a pig hole without her," said Syd, putting the locket away. "She'll go mad when she comes back and sees the state of it. She's the only one who keeps me on the straight and narrow. I don't know what I'd do without her."

"You're certainly going to miss her when she's gone," I said without thinking.

The atmosphere changed instantly. It was as though somebody had gone through the room with a blast freezer. Syd was fixed to the spot, mortified. I noticed a little tear in his eye.

Iris saw what had happened and tried to rescue me. "Doreen means when she's gone on holiday again. You'll miss her when she's on her next cruise. That's what you mean, isn't it, Doreen?"

"Don't talk about it," said Syd in this low, rumbling voice. "It sends me into a state. If somebody sets me off talking about... *that*... I can be in a state for days afterwards."

He looked up at me with an expression of pure evil. If somebody had said the devil had possessed him, I'd have believed them "People don't like me when I'm in this state," he said.

"No, don't get the wrong idea, Syd," said Iris, desperately trying to rescue the situation. "Your mother's a young woman in many ways."

He defrosted a little. I could see what Iris was trying to do, so I thought I'd better do my bit to reassure him as well.

"Iris is right. She's a lot younger than she might be. Some old women are much older than your mother. She's not as old as they are by a long chalk. In fact, I'd go as far as to say that your mother isn't half as old as some people I could mention."

His lips were trembling as he tried not to imagine life after the dreaded day of his mother's final departure.

"Anyway, your locket's smashing," said Iris. "Any mother would be thrilled to bits to have a child buy her something like that."

He perked up a bit.

"Do you really think she'll like it?" he said.

"She'll be over the moon."

He turned to me, and the devil had disappeared. "You ought to buy one for Iris," he said brightly. "She deserves one, too. Every mother should have one of these."

I nodded, but I thought: the only thing I'll buy for her is a wooden stake and a mallet to hammer it into her chest.

"Try this on for size," he said, and walked over to me and put the chain over my head and round my neck. Then he started rearranging it, and his fingers were on my shoulders, and touching my throat. I couldn't keep thoughts of his poor wife out of my mind, and I began to feel a bit weak around the knees. This is exactly how she would have seen him on the day he strangled her—with his big hands stretching out.

I managed to stay upright until he took the necklace off, and then he led us out of the room and back into the office.

"Right, now then, Iris, what can I do for you? A bit of business you said." He went back to his tea and slurped it.

"Well, it's about our Doreen's chip shop," Iris said. "She's just setting up down Balaclava Street, taken over from Mr and Mrs Deans. Well, she's signed up with you—you know, for insurance purposes and that..."

"Well, don't you worry about that, Iris. Any friend of my mother's is a friend of mine. I'll instruct the lads to by-pass your place when they do their rounds next week. We don't want your money, lass. I mean, after all, if we can't do a few favours for family friends, who can we do them for?"

"Well, it isn't so much that," Iris said. "It's the damage your lads are doing to the shop. I mean, it's not that we don't keep up to date, but they're destroying the premises. It's just a bit mystifying knowing what we've done to deserve it. I was just wondering if perhaps they've got the wrong party. You know, whether they should be knocking somebody else about who isn't quite so regular with their contributions as we are."

He looked puzzled. "I know nowt about that," he said. "Balaclava Street, you say. Hold on a minute." He picked up the phone again and dialled. He walked into to his little corner and turned his back again.

"Gerald? Is it your fucking crew of bastards that are covering Balaclava Street? Well, what's this I'm hearing about them trashing the fucking chip shop?" He listened for a few moments, then said: "Don't give me that crap—find out about it. I want a full report before the end of the day. That's by tea-time. And don't twat me about."

He turned back to us, and the sunny disposition returned. "There seems to be some kind of misunderstanding, Iris. But I'll get to the bottom of it. I've got my lads on it and they'll find out what's been going on. Some of my employees can get a bit above themselves. They get big ideas. Think they can take the law into their own hands and fiddle me out of what's rightfully mine. You can rest assured that somebody's going to get it in the neck for this."

In the neck! "Oh no!" I shouted, suddenly thinking of his wife under that hedge. "I don't want nobody strang... er, punished." I had visions of people being buried in cement and made part of a motorway. "Just stopping, that's all. Perhaps with a bit of gentle chastisement."

He looked at me, and the devil was back. He said: "Do I tell you how to fry chips, Doreen?"

I shook my head, petrified, my eyes bulging. He put his hands on my shoulders again.

"Well, then, don't tell me how to do my job. OK?" He was smiling as he said it, but it was a very threatening smile.

Then he was all charm again: "Mam will be pleased to hear that you've visited, Iris." He signalled to the other bloke, who took Iris's arm and led her to the door. I followed. "If you have any more trouble, give me a call, but I think you'll find the mistake has been rectified. You'll not be bothered again."

"Thank you, Syd, love. You're a good lad." Iris said as she was forced out through the front door.

I've never been so glad to get out of a place since the last time I went to the dentists for a filling. I took a couple of breaths of fresh air, and we ran up that driveway as though we had fleas up our arses.

"I feel quite unclean, Iris," I said. "I'm getting a bath as soon as I get home. I've never met such a frightening man in my whole life. He's demonic."

"His mother's a cow as well," she said. "Only I've kept in with her because she's my ticket to the occasional free knees-up. He showers money on her. Gives her whatever she wants. You see what I mean about steering clear of the topic? His ex-wife used to slag his mother off something alarming. And look how she ended up."

"I hope never to see him again," I said, and shivered all the way home.

* * *

I was confused and didn't really know what to expect. Iris seems confident that all the trouble is over and that we can refit the shop and get it up and running without any further problems. That's going to take a good three weeks.

"Well, look on it as a bonus," she said. "With the insurance money we can do the shop up in modern fittings, and we can have a lovely new sign made. What about this."

She handed me a business card she'd had printed. It said: "Iris and Doreen's Fish and Chip Shop, 16 Balaclava Street. Props: I. Potts and D. Potts"

"Hang on a minute," I said. "How come your name's first on this? 'Iris and Doreen's Fish and Chip Shop.' Chuffing cheek!"

"It's only temporary. Besides, it's usual business practice to put names in reverse alphabetical order in such situations. Saves arguments. I hope you're not going to be petty about it."

* * *

Our Sylvia has been maundering round the house like an undertaker's assistant since I had to postpone her moving into the flat. She gives me the cold shoulder most of the time, and worst of all is trying to turn our Charmaine Bernadette against me as well. She sits there on the settee, pointing me out to the babby and saying: "See that woman? That's your grandmother. Make a note of her face and never trust her. That's the woman who doesn't keep her

91

promises. Don't take a blind bit of notice of anything she says. She's wicked."

"Don't give me a bad name with the babby," I says to her. "Not for the sake of a temporary postponement. You'll get your flat once all this trouble's blown over. I'm doing it for your own safety."

"Don't listen to her," our Sylvia whispers to the babby. "She speaks with forked tongue. She never had any intention of letting us have that flat. She's the devil's spawn."

Then she turns away from me and won't let me make a fuss of our Charmaine Bernadette. It's getting me down. I'm sure I'm not the devil's spawn (although I can't swear to it, given that I'm not quite sure what it is). It's a good job the babby isn't old enough to understand what's being said.

During our morning tea break in the front room, Iris says to me: "What's the matter with our Sylvia. She's walking about with a face that could turn custard lumpy."

I told her about the rift that had developed between us.

She said: "Can't you see what she's up to? She's manipulating you. Pushing your hot buttons. You don't want to let her get away with it."

"As you're an expert on emotional blackmail, Iris," I said, "I have to take note of your specialist knowledge. But what can I do? I hate it when there are family fall-outs. It makes me feel really down in the dumps."

"Bring her to heel. Let her know who's boss," says Iris.

"And how do I do that?"

"Have a bit of back bone for once. Call her bluff. Tell her that if she doesn't stop being so mardy, you'll rent the flat to the highest bidder. Then give her a smack across the face to show her who's in charge."

"There's quite enough violence in the world, thank you," I said. "We shan't be requiring no further examples in this house."

"If you let her twist you round your little finger like this, it'll never end. Kiddies have got to be disciplined. Tough love they call it."

"You're right," I said. "This has gone on long enough. I'm going to put a stop to it."

"So, what are you going to do? Belt her? Spank her? Shut her in the coal hole?"

"What do you think I am, a Catholic nun? No, I'm just going to tell her straight," I said. "I'm going to tell her that she can move into the flat next week."

"That's tough, I must say," says Iris, pouring herself another cup, despite her contempt for my tea.

"I mean," I said, "that Syd Warren promised there'd be no further trouble, so it should be OK, shouldn't it?"

"Oh yes, if Syd says it's OK, then it is."

"Then we might as well let her go."

I called our Sylvia downstairs to give her the glad tidings and there was an immediate sea change in her attitude. She was over the moon. Her face relaxed. She loved and kissed me. A proper little ray of sunshine she was.

"Isn't your nana lovely?" she says to our Charmaine Bernadette. "Isn't she the best nana in the whole world for giving us this flat? We're going to have our own little home, just you and me." She shoved our Charmaine Bernadette at me so I could have a little kiss and cuddle.

"Spoiled brat," says Iris. "I still think the coal hole would have been a better option."

After that, me and Iris took a walk round to the shop to see how the shopfitters were getting on. They've given us a completion date of a fortnight, so opening time shouldn't be too long now.

We've had the place completely done out in pale blue, with a lot of tiles with a fishy motif. I didn't want plain tiles because they can make the place look like a public toilet. The friers are brand, spanking new. They're shiny and sparkling and I can't give over buffing them up.

Meanwhile, Iris likes to give the impression of being very efficient. She keeps going round with what she calls her "inventory" (a bit of paper on a clipboard) and checking that everything is where it should be.

And we've had security gadgets galore installed. There's a burglar alarm and one of them metal grilles that you can roll down over the main window when the shop's shut. That'll put a stop to them casual bricks-through-the-window in the small hours.

I get a little thrill every time I look at the place. My own little empire.

After the shopfitters were finished for the day, and I was going round putting little touches here and there, Iris gave a contented sigh and just for a split second I felt glad that she was around.

That soon wore off, though.

*   *   *

It's all happening! In fact, so much has happened in the last couple of weeks, I haven't had time to write my diary. But now I've got a few minutes, I'll bring it up to date.

Well, the shopfitters and decorators finished off, and the place is an absolute picture. The insurance money has meant we've been able to more or less start completely fresh. We've got concealed lighting that makes the place glitter, even when it's dark outside. The tiles and the paintwork are works of art. The whole place looks really smashing.

Everything was going smoothly until we had that frightening set-to.

It started when our Sylvia moved into the flat. She got all her belongings together and we shifted her and the babby in. The flat has been done up lovely also. It's a proper little home from home for them. When Mr and Mrs Deans left it looked like what it was—a home of old people. Ancient furniture, dark wallpaper, doors that didn't fit properly. Our Sylvia said she'd taken advice from a friend of hers, a professional designer and decorator. Matt, I think he was called. I don't know how she'd got to know him, I think he might be the same one as did up our Gary's flat. But he advised her on colour co-ordination, told what would look nice. I understand he helped her a bit with the work, too, the painting and that.

Now she's got cream-coloured walls (with a hint of apple), a beige thick-pile carpet, lovely bright curtains and brand new Ikea furniture, including a book case—even though our Sylvia hasn't read a book since her Janet and John days.

It's very comfortable, I must say. It's got a cosy little sitting room with a settee, an armchair and a television. There's a diddy little kitchen, just big enough for someone who can't cook. And a double bedroom at the back that she's done out in pink, with frilly curtains and a pastel duvet cover. Very feminine. And finally, a panoramic view over Balaclava Street from the front window. Not

94

that there's a lot to see at the moment except that empty warehouse that's scheduled for demolition.

"Int'it lovely, Mam?" our Sylvia says, "Int'it smashing?" You'd think she'd moved into Buckingham Palace the way she was carrying on.

"I want to have a little housewarming party, to christen my new home," she said, so me and Iris and Derek and our Gary went round with a big bottle of prosecco and we toasted the flat and wished our Sylvia every happiness in her new home.

Well, our Gary sipped his bubbly and then said he had an urgent appointment and went off as soon as he could. Derek looked equally bored and made his excuses to go down the Trades Club to play darts. But me and Iris stayed until midnight, talking over our plans, and trying to get our Sylvia fired up about the venture. She was too busy putting that poster of her star sign up to be bothered.

Anyway, just as we were getting ready to leave, I heard this banging noise. I went to the window and looked out. In the street below, there was these three burly lads trying to break the shop window. Of course, since we had the grille put on, it's not so easy, but they had a snooker cue, and they were poking it through the gaps and trying to smash that plate glass window with that.

I opened the window and shouts down to them: "Stop that, you bleeding hooligans. I'll have the bobbies out to you if you don't bugger off."

The man who was battering at the window stopped and looked up at me. He was wearing a black woolly hat, the sort that's so fashionable on these hidden camera crime programmes on the telly. People who wear these hats are always robbing building societies or jumping over the counter at off-licences.

"Oh, so there you are," he says to me.

"I mean it," I said. "If you don't fling your hook, you'll end up with a prison sentence."

"Doreen, is it?" he says.

I was took aback. "How do you know my name?" I said. "And no, it isn't."

"Just the lady we're looking for. We've got a bit of bad news for you, Doreen. And we want to deliver it personally. You've been a naughty girl, haven't you, and now you've got to take your medicine."

He looked straight up at me and punched the flat of his hand with his other fist. "Know what I mean?"

I was nearly sick out of the window there and then. He looked so violent—all three of them did.

"OK lads," he said to the other two, "Let's get up them stairs and sort this out once and for all."

They left off trying to break the window and the three of them made their way round to the side door that leads upstairs to the flat.

"Quick," I says to our Sylvia. "Get the door locked."

"It is locked," she says. "I wouldn't leave it open at this time of night."

Fortunately, the reinforcements that had been installed by the Deans's were still in place, and although these men were kicking at the street door, it wasn't quite as easy to open as they'd thought. The bolts and metal bars were holding quite well. But they wouldn't last forever, they were up against a determined barrage.

"Call the police," I says to our Sylvia. She had already picked the phone up, but from the expression on her face it was obvious that it wasn't working.

"It's out of order," she says. "They must have cut the wire downstairs. How am I going to ring my friends now?"

Downstairs they were taking it in turns to kick at the door. The loud thuds made my hair stand on end. The door was beginning to give.

"Get into the bathroom, and take the babby with you," I said to our Sylvia. "Lock the door, and if they manage to get in, throw bleach in their faces."

"I haven't got any bleach," she was wailing. "Will Head 'n Shoulders do?"

I pushed her through to the bathroom and closed the door. Me and Iris waited in the sitting room. We would have to hold them off, somehow.

Iris was pulling the plug out of the back of the phone and sticking another one in.

"Don't forget Doreen, we've got two lines, one for here and one for the shop. I can connect the other line to this handset."

She dialled furiously when she had the connection.

"Have you got through to 999 yet?" I said to her. "Tell them to hurry."

Then she said. "Hello. Can I speak to Syd, please?"

"Syd?" I shouts. "We want the chuffing police, not the gangster who's trying to kill us."

I tried to get the phone off her, but she shoved me away. Then she said: "Hello, is that Syd? Hello, love, it's Iris Potts again. I'm sorry to trouble you at this time of night, Syd, but we've got a bit of a problem here at the chip shop on Balaclava Street... Well, there's these men at the door, and I don't think they're trying to deliver pizza. They're trying to kick their way in. Are they your lads, Syd? Because if they are, could you call them off, duck? They're frightening the babby."

"Frightening the babby!" I shouted. "They're scaring the cack out of me."

"OK, lovey," she was saying into the phone. "Lickety-split, if you can."

She rang off and said, "They're not his lads. He's sure of that. He's getting his own lot out here straight away. They're always on call."

"Give me that phone. Let me call the police."

"Hands off, Doreen. We've got to get these buggers off our backs once and for all. Only Syd can manage that. Calling the police will just drag it out for longer. Be patient."

There was another violent bash at the door.

"Patient? What are you talking about?" I went to the window and opened it again. I started to shout for help, but then I realised that the whole area was like a desert after ten o'clock. There wasn't a soul anywhere nearby to hear me. How does it go? In space no-one can hear you scream? Well, it's the same thing in Balaclava Street after dark.

Then the kicking stopped and the man in the woolly hat came back round to the front of the shop. He looked up and saw me at the window.

"Don't worry, Doreen," he said. "We'll soon be up there with you. You've been a naughty girl, and you've got to be punished."

"The bobbies are on their way," I shouted. "You want to make a run for it. We've got a mobile phone up here."

"Oh aye," he said, disbelievingly. "And guess what I've got here?" And with that he opened the door of his car and brought out a big iron bar. Iris came up beside me to see what was going on.

"Oh my God, it's a gemmy," she said. "They'll have the door open in no time with that."

We started to pile furniture up against the door at the top of the stairs. It had a flimsy little Yale lock on it, nothing like the downstairs one. It would take them a matter of seconds to get it open.

"Arm yourself," said Iris. She went into the tiny kitchen and came back with a carving knife. I picked up the large glass vase, one of our Sylvia's house warming presents, with the intention of smashing it over their heads as they came into the room.

Downstairs we could hear the gemmy being forced between the door and the frame, and there was a loud creaking noise as they levered the hinges out of the jamb. It took them another couple of minutes to get it wide enough open to gain access and then we heard them coming up the stairs.

I was shaking like a jelly, and my hands felt so weak I could hardly hold on to the vase. Iris was standing there with the knife raised over her head, like the mad mother in Psycho.

They got to the top of the stairs and gave a push at the door. "Now come on, Doreen," said the man on the other side. "Stop this silly messing about and open up. You know you've got to take your medicine like a brave girl. Might as well get it over with. It won't hurt—after you're unconscious."

"There's nobody here called Doreen," I said. "You've got the wrong party."

"I don't think so."

They started pushing at the door and the pathetic little lock soon gave way. Me and Iris pushed as hard as we could against the furniture on the other side, but we were no match for the three of them. The chair and settee started scraping across the floor as they forced their way in.

I charged at the first one, who was wearing one of them face masks, and tried to break the vase over his head, but it just bounced off and I dropped it. It didn't seem to have had any effect at all. Then Iris came running across the room with the knife raised. But she got her foot caught under the rug and... whoops... down she went, flat on her face, with the knife stuck into the arm of the settee.

"Alright, ladies," the man with the woolly hat said (they'd all got them pulled down over their faces now), "Time to stop playing around. You know why we're here."

"No, we don't," I managed to stammer. "We don't know what all this is about. If you're with Syd Warren, he's going to have your guts for garters."

"Syd Warren?" said the leader. "Who's he?"

With that, he picked up an ashtray and threw it at the mirror hanging over the gas fire. It smashed into smithereens. Seven years bad luck for somebody, I thought—probably me by the look of it.

"What is it that we've done?" I asked. "If we owe money, tell us. What are you persecuting us for? Tell us, please!"

"I'm paid to persecute people," the man said putting a pair of strangling gloves on. "That's my job. I don't ask questions. So, I'd better get on with it, hadn't I?"

"Right lads," he said to the other two. "I don't want any of this furniture left in one piece. I want this place looking like the reject pile at a matchstick factory before you've done. And leave these two ladies to me."

He started to move towards me. Iris ran in front of me as a sort of protection. I could hardly believe how brave she was. He grabbed her by the arm and threw her aside like a little rag doll.

But before he could have hold of me, there was a noise at the door downstairs. Then running feet, and suddenly the room was filled with all these big, hefty men. Within seconds the lot of them were fighting in a heap.

Me and Iris dodged into the kitchen, shut the door and clung on to one another. After a bit, things quietened down, and the kitchen door opened. In walked Syd Warren, calm as you like in a black cashmere overcoat.

"Iris, sweetheart!" he said. "Are you OK, darlin'?"

"Am I glad to see you, Syd," she said. "I thought they was going to murder us."

"Maybe they were," he says. "Let's find out, shall we?"

We followed him back into the sitting room, which now looked as though it had been the victim of a tornado. Five of Syd's lads—who all looked as though they were descended from the gorilla family—had overpowered the other three and were holding them still. The masks were off and we could see their faces now. A right ugly crew they were, all cauliflower ears and broken noses.

"Now then," said Syd, calm as you like. "I'm curious to know what's going on here. Who are you boys?"

"We're independent operators," said the leader, a bigly made lad with livid scars on his face.

"Are you, indeed." Syd walked round them, inspecting them from top to bottom as though sizing them up for a concrete overcoat.

Then he sat down on the settee and inspected the knife, which was still sticking out of the arm.

"Now you boys know that this is a lucrative business we're in. It's very competitive, and there are a lot of people trying to get a bite of the action. Know what I mean? It's taken me a long time to build up my little patch here. And I'm not likely to give it up easily, am I?"

He was talking to them slowly, deliberately, like three-year olds, but he sounded threatening, sinister, terrible. I'd have been scared out of my wits if he'd been talking to me like that.

He took hold of the knife handle and yanked it out of the settee. He sat there examining the blade in minute detail. "Now, I want you lads to tell me who you're working for. Who your employer is. I don't want to hurt you, you see. I've no desire to see you lads on life support. You're just doing a job for someone. I understand that. You've got a living to earn, and no doubt it pays well."

He got up and walked about the room, weighing the knife in his hand.

"I certainly pay my lads well. Don't I lads?"

Syd's lads all said, "Yes Syd," together.

"And you've no need to worry about being out of a job if your employer comes to any harm," said Syd. "I'm always looking for good workers in my firm. So come on, let's have the truth. Who sent you here, and why?"

The three of them said nothing, but I was on the verge of fainting. There was such a threat of violence in the air.

Syd got up and walked over to the leader, still holding the knife.

"I see you've got a nasty scar on your face," he said. And he had, right from his temple to the bottom of his right cheek. "Will you be wanting another to match, on the other side?"

He put the knife up to the man's face. Then he turned to me. "Don't worry about your carpets, Doreen. My lads will see to any cleaning up that needs doing."

The room was spinning in front of my eyes at the prospect of what was being threatened.

Syd put the knife back up to the man's face and said: "Last opportunity, son. Are you going to tell me who you're working for?"

The man stood firm, although I could see little gobs of sweat running down his face.

Syd's hand started to move, and the knife came closer to this chap's eye. I couldn't stand it any longer and I spewed my prosecco all over the floor. Iris put her arm round me.

"See," said Syd, to this man. "You're upsetting the ladies with your stubbornness. They don't like to see people getting hurt, don't ladies, particularly if there's a lot of blood."

Then one of the other chaps who'd been threatening us suddenly broke and said, "It's a man called Hackett—Mortimer Hackett."

"Shut your fucking mouth," said the leader.

"Mortimer who?" said Syd. "I thought I knew everybody in this business. This is a new one on me."

"He works for Addison's, the fish and chip empire. Arnold Addison, that's who he works for." said Iris. "It's that fat twerp who wanted to buy the shop."

She went over to where Syd was standing. "It all makes sense now. This Addison owns the Chips & More! chain. He wanted this shop and Doreen wouldn't let him have it."

"He must have wanted it bad," said Syd.

"He was desperate," I said. "But when I wouldn't sell he got nasty, it was about revenge and spite then, not business. But I didn't think he'd go to these lengths."

"Well, that's a load off my mind," said Syd. "I thought I was going to have a full-scale war on my hands over this turf. But maybe not. All the same," he turned to the intruders. "I'm not happy about these ladies being frightened when they've been loyal customers of mine. When I offer insurance, I don't rat on the pay-out. So, you three lads are going to go back to Mr Arnold Addison and you're going to tell him to stay the fuck off my patch. Is that clear? Because if I see any of you lot round here again, you'll be very sorry. Or at least your grieving widows will be."

He turned back to us.

"Very sorry about this unpleasantness ladies. Very regrettable, but I'm pleased to say it's nowt to do with me."

101

He turned back to the Addison men. "And don't think you cunts are going to get away with what you've done to these defenceless women. This is a grave offence you've committed."

"After all," says Iris to Syd. "There's innocent bystanders involved here. Think about it. Your mother might have been here, having a cup of tea."

Syd stopped in his tracks at the mention of his mother. You could see the scenario that Iris had suggested to him playing out in his imagination. I thought: any merciful thoughts that Syd might have been entertaining have now flown.

"You're right, Iris," he said. "She might have been."

He walked around the three men looking at them contemptuously, and then said to his own boys: "Take them to the warehouse. I want them giving a good going over before they take their message home to daddy Addison. If a few bones get broken, well, it can't be helped. But don't damage their vocal chords. I want them to be able to tell the whole tale."

With that, Syd nodded his head, and the three men were taken away by his heavies.

Before he followed them out, Syd turned back and said: "Tarra, Iris, sweetheart. You'll be OK now. If you have any more trouble with Mr Addison, just tip me the wink and I'll see you right."

He was about to leave when he turned back again and said: "Oh, and don't worry about the damage to the flat. You've got full cover from me. I'll see it's all put right. Goodnight, darling."

And then he was gone.

* * *

I didn't sleep for a week after that horrible night. I kept waking up in a cold sweat wondering what had happened to them men. On Tuesday night, about three a.m. in the morning, I got up and went to the kitchen to make myself a cup of tea. I sat there cradling it in the dark and prepared to relive the whole thing yet again in my head. Flashbacks is what they call it.

There was so many unanswered questions: Was he really going to kill me, that man, or was he just trying to frighten me into a change of underwear? And what happened to them in that warehouse? I kept imagining what the sound of bones breaking would be like. I kept thinking about their screams of agony.

I toyed with the idea of going to the police, but then I decided that it was all best left alone. The bobbies hadn't been very interested the last time I tried to report Syd Warren. And if Syd found out that I'd been talking to the police about him, he'd no doubt reek his revenge on us in some terrible way.

No, much better to heed Iris's advice and keep on the right side of him.

I sat there for about half an hour, seeing it all in my mind's eye over and over again, and then Iris came downstairs in her long dressing gown, looking like a ghost.

"What is it, Doreen?" she says. "You're not still worrying about Arnold Addison are you?"

"I don't know how you can forget about it all so easily," I said. "It was horrible. I've been dramatised by the whole experience. I'm beginning to wonder if I need counselling."

"Counselling be buggered," she said. "You'll get over it. Just be glad that Syd has sorted it all out for us, and we can rest in peace now."

"That's what I thought I would be doing. Pushing up daisies. I keep seeing that scar-faced man coming towards me." I gave a little shudder and warmed my hands on the cup of tea.

"Think positive, Doreen. Tomorrow is the grand opening of the shop. Our dream will become a reality. You should be thrilled, but you look as though you've just been sentenced to be hanged by the neck until dead."

"I'm all up and down about it, Iris," I said.

She poured herself a cup of tea, sniffed it, made a retching sound and then sat at the table with me.

"We can't be having no crisises of confidence at this late stage," she said. "We're committed to this project now. We've *got* to make it work. After all, it's not just our futures that are at stake, but those of our employees."

"What—you mean our Sylvia? We'll be lucky to get her downstairs out of that flat, let alone working for us."

"Not just her. Our future employees. The ones we'll be lifting from poverty and personal despair—that is, taking them off the dole—when we open up our chain. Think what we'll be doing for the fishing industry and the potato industry. Not to mention the savaloy and chip fat industries. A lot of people will be depending on us."

"You make it sound ever so noble," I said.

"Making a success of yourself is noble, Doreen. And don't ever forget it. Now, shape yourself and get a good night's sleep. We've got our problems sorted out, we've got our advert in the paper, we've got our leaflets delivered. Now we just have to go out there tomorrow and fry the best chips we are capable of. It's going to be a busy but rewarding day."

I must say, Iris is very good at giving pep talks. She's almost as good at making you feel good as she is at making you feel bad.

She sent me back to bed with a spring in my step and I slept much better after that.

* * *

Well, the big day dawned and we were down at the shop at the first chirp of bird call. Naturally, we've had a couple of trial runs to make sure we've got the hang of the friers, and everything is ready. The batter is made, the fish laid out ready, the potatoes are chipped and the fat is bubbling.

We've got bunting up and a special introductory offer of 20% off gherkins.

The layout of the shop is as follows. You come through the door, which has got a buzzer on it in case we're in the back when a customer comes. There are three formica tables, screwed to the floor, each with a fishy pattern on top, for those who like to eat their fish and chips in the comfort of a steam-filled room. Then it's the counter, a really fancy job, quite high, topped by a marble-type substance. It has a till and a shelf for the wrapping paper. Then there's our two fryers against the back wall and a price list over the top. There's a door to the side which leads into our little room at the back.

It's just like when you were a kid playing at shop, only better because it's real. There are the little scoops for serving the chips, and the wire stirrers for agitating in the frier. We've got an excellent supplier, fresh fish every day from Grimsby—none of your unidentified frozen muck.

Anyway, doors open at five o'clock, and we're dead excited.

Round about four-ish our Gary and Bill arrived with a bottle of champagne and some flowers. They opened the wine to wish us all the best for the future, but Iris wouldn't let me have any, due to me not being able to co-ordinate properly. She said she wasn't having me drunk in charge of boiling fat. (As soon as our Gary and Bill had gone, she chucked the flowers in the bin saying that they might be construed as unhygienic.)

We were thrilled to bits as the big moment arrived. There was me, our Sylvia, Iris and Derek standing behind the counter, counting down to five o'clock.

"Five, four, three, two, one!"

"This is it," says Iris, lifting the gate over the counter and walking through the shop to the front door. With a flourish she pulled the bolt back and turned the sign over so that it showed "Open."

Immediately the door was opened, our first customer came in—a little lad, no more than about nine. He was a mucky little tyke as well, filthy hands and a torn jacket with crusty sleeves.

"Small packet of chips, open," he said.

We'd already drawn lots to see who was going to serve the first customer, and I'd won. So, I shovelled the chips into a cone and handed them over. I took his money.

"Here," I said to him. "You want one of these little wooden forks. Your hands are filthy. You'll get germs eating your chips with them."

He took the fork and looked at it and threw it on the floor. Then he went out, happily eating the chips with his disgusting fingers.

So that was our first customer. Not what you'd call thrilling, but our first pound coin in the till.

It was dribs and drabs after that, a trickle. My friend Marje Bickerstaffe arrived, just to wish us luck. She didn't buy anything. Below her dignity to be seen buying chips.

"Best of British, Doreen and Iris," she said. "And let's hope that you're not going to go the way of so many other under-financed small businesses."

After she'd gone, my next-door neighbour Beryl Cathcart arrived, accompanied by Mary O'Boyle from the other side of Evergreen Close.

"I'm that excited for you," said Mary, "I've been to church and said a prayer for your success."

"That's lovely of you, Mary," I said. "Have a complimentary pickled onion."

They both had haddock and chips and sat and ate them at the table.

It was steady after that. Not really enough to keep us all busy. Derek soon got fed up and went off to the Trades.

"It'll take time for people to realise we're here," Iris said. "We can't expect miracles on the first day."

By nine o'clock we had fifty-two pounds in the till.

Then, about half past nine, this big car pulls up outside. It looked familiar. The buzzer rang and in walks Arnold Addison, still as fat and ugly as before, the same wobbly jowls and the same horrible coat stretched across his obscene middle. He was accompanied as usual by his spindly son, Ainsley. What a pair. They looked like an unfunny version of Laurel and Hardy.

Arnold walks up the counter, bold as you like, smiling like a baboon. Iris looked him straight in the eye and said: "You've got a chuffing nerve, showing your face in here after all you've done."

"Now, now, Iris. I've not come to cause bother. I'm simply here as a fellow in the trade, to wish you the best of luck with your enterprise. I saw your advertisement in the paper, and I said to Ainsley— didn't I Ainsley?—I said we must go down there and wish them well." He looked around the shop with a professional eye, taking it all in, but there was no expression on his face to show what he thought of it.

"Not bad for amateurs," he said. "But you've a lot to learn. A great deal." he said. "Don't be tempted to try novelties, ladies. That's my advice. Give the public what they want. Folk don't want new, they want what they know. When it comes to food, they like the familiar. Comfort eating is what fish and chips is all about. You'll come to realise that our business thrives on stress and unhappiness. Trade were at an all-time high on the day of Princess Diana's funeral. A few more dead royals and I'll be retiring to the Bahamas."

He took a look behind the counter at our equipment.

"And don't underestimate the part that excessive alcohol plays in fish and chip consumption. Beer is our best friend as far as turnover goes. Always try to open your shop near a pub. That's a tip I'm giving you free, Doreen. All my shops have got pubs nearby, and I stay open till well after closing time. There might be a bit of violence, but the profits are excellent, and the staff are easy enough to replace if they occasionally get beaten up by drunken louts. See,

I'm giving you all this advice free, gratis and for nothing, just to show there's no hard feelings."

"Well, it's not mutual," Iris retorted. "We've got plenty of hard feelings about you, and the bruises to prove it."

"I'm not cognisant of what you're on about. You're talking in riddles."

"Them bully boys of yours..."

He looked shifty and said: "Them bully boys, Mrs Potts Senior? What are you saying? I don't have no bully boys, I'm a legitimate businessman. I know nowt about no bully boys."

"No, I expect you cover your tracks well," she said. "Get others to do your dirty work for you. Mortimer Hackett for instance."

He turned to me and said: "You want to get your mother-in-law under control. She's got a mouth on her like a runaway train. I could take court action with the insinuations she's making."

Then he turned to his son, "Have you heard this, Ainsley. It's slander and libel is this. They're making me out to be a criminal."

Ainsley looked at the floor, but mostly he was looking at our Sylvia, making goo-goo eyes at her as though he'd never seen a lass with a big bosoms before. Well, not one that was so anxious to show them off to him, anyroad.

"You're worse than a criminal," Iris said. "At least criminals are honest about it. They don't send third parties out to beat up two old women."

"Er, *one* old woman and one middle-aged one," I corrected.

His smile disappeared. "Well, that's the thanks I get, is it, for going out of my way to wish you well and offer invaluable advice. I don't know why I bother."

"We don't want your lousy advice," says Iris. "You can stick it up your..."

"Now then, now then," he said. "I've tried the friendly approach, but I see that's not going to work. So, I'll have to tell you this, Mrs and Mrs Potts. All's fair in love and war. Yes, that's what I'm saying. All's fair in love and war."

"And what's that supposed to mean?" I said. "Another threat, is it? Because we've got powerful friends, we have, haven't we, Iris? You can't just push us around like you can other people."

"There's more than one way to skin a cat, Doreen," he said. "You'll see who'll come out on top. You've made some very silly decisions about this place."

"Have I?" I said. "If I've been so silly, how come we're up and running despite your efforts to stop us? Can't have been that silly."

He looked furious. So did I. "If I didn't want to keep the place immaculate, I'd chuck a piece of wet fish at you. Now scoot, you and your runt of a son. Get out of our shop."

"And remember," Iris shouted after him, "Don't get any ideas of starting your tricks again, because we know where you live—and so does Syd Warren."

He stormed through the door, dragging Ainsley with him. The poor lad managed to turn round and mouth "Sorry" before his father overpowered him.

I was trembling again.

"Bleeding cheek," Iris was muttering.

"Who was that lad?" our Sylvia says.

"What, Ainsley?" I said. "I think he's a product of Arnold Addison's illicit affair with a squirrel."

Iris chuckled, but I was still worried.

"What do you think he's up to?" I said.

"I don't know. But something."

* * *

After the fuss and the congratulations, the routine quickly settled in, but I didn't mind. I was waking up first thing in the morning full of excitement. I couldn't wait to get cracking on the day. It's a long time since I've felt like that—ready to get up and get working. Every so often this little thrill of excitement would go through my internal organs as I thought about the business—my business, my very own little empire! I'm over the moon about it all, and I'm so glad I persevered, despite all the trouble.

People seem to be generally pleased that we've opened. Trade is building up slowly but surely as the locals get to know about us.

"I think this is going to work," Iris said to me after the first week. And I was that pleased I gave her a little kiss—just on the cheek, kind of thing—so you can tell how happy I was.

It was this lunchtime that the bombshell burst. Mrs Chakrabarti from the newsagents next door came in to say goodbye.

"We've sold it at last," she said with a great big grin on her face. "We've got it off our backs."

"Oh, I am sorry to hear that," I said.

"Well, we've been trying to get out of this place for long enough. Just when I thought we'd never get rid of the shop, out of the blue comes this offer."

"Who's taking over, then?" I said.

"Well, we sold it to the Arnold Addison company. They made us an offer we couldn't refuse. Very generous."

My heart dropped into my boots. "Arnold Addison?" I said. "I didn't know he was into newsagents' shops."

"Neither did I," said Mrs Chakrabarti. "But we just had to go with it. We're desperate, you see, Doreen. Desperate."

I called Iris from the back. When she heard about it, she hit the roof.

"What the hell is he up to now?" she said.

"It's obvious, isn't it. He's going to open a Chips & More! right next door to us."

She stormed into the back room and I followed her. She was on the phone in a shot to the Arnold Addison head office. "Put me through to Mr Addison," she says, but obviously the switchboard girl wasn't too keen. "It doesn't matter who's calling, just put me through. It's personal... I don't care if he is a busy man, I want to talk to him urgently."

She waited, drumming her fingers on the table. Then she mouthed to me: "She's enquiring."

"Ah, is that fatso Addison? It's Iris Potts here, former victim of your intimidation... I don't care if you do sue me, it's true. Now listen, wobble-gob, we've just had Mrs Chakrabarti from next door in saying you've bought her shop. Is that right? ... Well, we want to know what you're up to. Are you planning to set up in competition with us, because if you are we shan't take it lying down... Well, you can't do that. You can't just change the usage of the shop. You need permission... You may think you're above the law, but we know what's what. We'll lodge a complaint with the council. We'll raise objections. We might even get a petition up."

She listened for a bit and then slammed the phone down.

"What did he say?" I asked.

"He says there's nothing we can do about it. He's got the best legal brains in Rotherham on to the matter. He says it's personal now. And he's going to ruin us, profit or no profit."

She sat thinking for a moment, then said, "I'm going to see Bob Kennedy about this. He'll be able to tell me what to do."

"Who's Bob Kennedy when he's at home?" I said.

"He's our local councillor. We're going to have to get him on our side."

* * *

We made an appointment to see this Councillor Kennedy at his house in Treeton. Nice enough lad, he were. A bit young, I thought, lacking authority, but he seemed to know what he was talking about.

"I've looked into your problem, Mrs Potts," he said. "And I fear that Mr Addison may be right. You really can't dictate what people sell in their shops, so long as it isn't against the law. His shop falls within the same class as yours as far as planning permission is concerned. If he wants to change what the shop sells, I'm afraid he can. It would be against everyone's interests if you could just object to competitors because you thought they would damage your business. If that were the case, we'd only have one newsagent's chain and one electrical retailer and one supermarket company. Do you see what I mean? Our society is all about competition. We all get advantage from that."

I felt a heavy feeling, like a lump of lead, descend on my stomach.

"Now, where you might be able to raise an objection would be if Mr Addison were to propose any major alterations which would require planning permission. But I think he's probably thought about this very carefully, and he'll make sure that he doesn't do anything that the council would take exception to."

"But he can't just come here and drive us out of business. It's not fair."

"There again," said councillor Kennedy, "It wouldn't really be fair to him if the council prevented him opening a shop, would it? He has rights, too."

"But we were there first. We're established."

"Makes no difference," he said. "You see, Mrs Potts, I'm in a bit of a cleft stick here. As the local representative, I'm very anxious that the area around Balaclava Street should undergo some kind of revival. We need to take the whole place upmarket a bit, and that would help so many of the problems that beset the place. We've made a start with the housing estate, and now if we could revive that parade of shops, things could definitely change for the better. I don't want to discourage anyone from doing anything that is going to help in that process. Some call it gentrification and the Chips & More! chain does carry a certain prestige from that point of view."

"But..." Iris began.

I grabbed her arm and stopped her. "It's hopeless, Iris, they've got us well and truly stitched up. I expect Addison's got the council in his pocket as well."

"Please don't think of it like that, Mrs Potts," Kennedy said. "This might be to your benefit, too. The whole community would be winners if Balaclava Street could be brought back into the respectable world."

"Don't talk so chuffing barmy," I said. "Arnold Addison is out to shut us down, at any price. How can we come out winners in that?"

"Don't give up hope, Mrs Potts," he said, getting up and indicating that the interview was terminated. "Take on the challenge and go into battle with Addison's. You never know, you might triumph."

I gave him a look that could have stripped paint, and me and Iris left the place feeling despondent.

* * *

I was mooching about the house all Sunday while Iris sat in her room conniving. I kept sighing and putting the kettle on. Our Sylvia rang from her flat and asked if me and Derek would like to go round for our Sunday dinner. I declined on grounds of melancholia and then put a right sad record on—Herb Alpert and the Tijuana Brass playing Moon River.

"For God's sake, Doreen, what the hell's the matter with you?" Derek said. "I'm the one in this family who's supposed to be subject to depression. What about putting that leg of lamb in the oven and roasting a few potatoes?"

"You've no sympathy, have you, Derek? You've just seen my dream come crashing round my ears and all you can think about is having something to eat. Well, I've got no appetite. I just want to sit and feel sorry for myself."

He shrugged and retired behind the Sunday People.

I went into the garden, looked at the state of it—covered in weeds and the grass knee high. I've been neglecting it since we started the shop. In fact, I've done nothing but think about the shop from getting up till going to bed since I bought it. Now my ambitions are doomed.

I decided to have a little walk down to Balaclava Street to see how things were shaping. To my surprise, the workmen were busy at the new Chips & More!

"I didn't know you worked on Sunday," I said to this lad in a vest who was mixing cement.

"An urgent job, this. Spare no expense type of thing. I'm not complaining. I'll take double time anywhere I can get it."

I looked from my modest little establishment, which I held in the fondest regard, and over to next door, where a new shop front was taking shape. There were architects with plans and an important looking man with a clip board. I went over to him.

"When do you expect this to be finished?" I asked.

"No more than a week to ten days," he said. "It's coming along at a cracking pace, and Mr Addison has got us pulling all the stops out."

"Mr Addison," I said with another sigh.

"Aye, Mr Addison," this loud and uncouth voice behind me says. I turned round and there he was, the man himself.

"Come to admire my new branch, have you, Doreen?" he says, with a nasty smile. "I knew I'd get one on Balaclava Street one day. I was determined—by hook or by crook."

"Mostly by crook," I said. The man with the clipboard sniggered.

"Well, I'll give you a run for your money. Look at that" he pointed to our shop. "Amateurs thinking they can just elbow their way into the trade and make a quick buck."

"I'm not an amateur," I said. "And our shop is a service to the community, not just a money-making exercise aimed at giving as little as possible for as much as you can get."

"Service to the community!" Addison sneered. "You want locking up. The Arnold Addison community is the only community I'm interested in." Then he turned to the man with the clipboard and said, "Harold, have you seen that lad of mine?"

The man with the clipboard shook his head.

"Fat lot he's going to learn about the trade while he's skiving off. If you see him, tell him I'm looking for him." He turned back to me. "I'm making Ainsley manager of my new prestige branch here. Let him get to know the business from the bottom to the top. Now, you and that disgusting old faggot of a mother-in-law of yours are

112

laughing on the other side of your faces, aren't you? That'll teach you to get above yourselves. As soon as my emporium is open, you might as well shut yours down, because it'll be no contest."

My frustration must have been showing because he burst out laughing and then walked off.

I was that mad I could have picked up a brick and bashed his brains out there and then, but instead I just shouted after him: "Oh shut your gob, you fat berk."

I felt even worse as I walked home, and when I got in the house I found a note from Derek saying: "Given you can't be bothered to cook any dinner, I've took mother to the Trades. We'll get pie and chips there. Come and join us if you feel like it."

But all the energy had just drained out of me. I was beaten.

* * *

Serving in the chip shop is now a bit like serving at the Last Supper. You just feel it's all a waste of time. Iris carries on as though nothing has happened. "We're not beaten yet," she keeps saying, but we are. Now I'm just going through the motions. Fry the chips, batter the fish, wrap them up, take the cash, go home, go to bed, get up and the same thing again.

The Joy de Veev has gone out of it and there's this sense of gloom hanging over the place. There are what seems like hundreds of workmen next door. I expect they'll be trading within a fortnight. They're even putting a neon sign that flashes on and off over the top of it. "Chips & More!—the nations favourite fast food!" it says.

"Try smiling, Doreen," Iris says to me as I walked about with a face as long as Blackpool pier. "We'll never keep our customers loyal if you keep scowling like that. They want friendliness. Come on, pull yourself together. Take the bull between your teeth. We're not beaten yet."

"If you say that once more, I'll clout you," I said.

Then, to make things worse, the local free paper was shoved through the door. Arnold Addison had taken the whole of the front page for an advertisement advertising the opening of his new branch.

"Civilisation reaches Balaclava Street" it said. "A personal message from the chip-master himself, Arnold Addison."

Then underneath, in the form of a letter which he is supposed to have written himself, it said: "It's been a long time coming, but at last there's to be a decent fish and chip shop for the residents of the Balaclava Street area. You all know Chips & More!—the nation's favourite fast food outlet—well, now it will be there on your own doorstep, available for you whenever you get that familiar pang of hunger. Why make do with inferior imitations when the real thing is on offer? That unmistakable crunch of the Chips & More! chip, with the accompaniment of our mouth-watering selection of breaded and battered fish dishes. It's traditional, but it's modern. Most of all, though, it's satisfying and delicious. Remember, the big opening day of the brand new Balaclava Street Chips & More! is this Thursday. Make sure you and your family are there for FREE balloons, t-shirts and other prizes. There'll also be the chance to meet the one and only Chips Chipperson, who'll be choosing one of our customers to take a dream holiday in Paris for two. Don't miss out! Get into the Chips & More! habit today!"

Iris read it with goggle eyes. "Who the hell is Chips Chipperson?" she said.

"It's a soft toy," I said. "They have a man dressed up as a big yellow chip with a face on it. It's their mascot. It's the Ronald McDonald of the fish frying industry. Haven't you seen them adverts on the telly where he's always running down the street with hordes of hungry kids running after him, threatening to eat him?"

"I haven't, but we shan't be able to top that," said Iris. "I think we might have to prepare ourselves for a poor trading day on Thursday."

"And Friday, and Saturday," I said, "and forever more until he closes us down."

Our Sylvia came down the stairs at that point, carrying the baby with her. "I've just heard Chips & More! advertising their new shop on the wireless," she says. "They're giving away a weekend in Paris. All you've got to do is buy a chip supper and your name could be drawn out. I can't wait."

* * *

The awful day dawned and Chips & More! opened. You should have seen the performance. They had a brass band leading a lorry, on the back of which was Chips Chipperson, the cuddly french fry, and his also-cuddly friend, Fishy Fry. The Chips & More! banner was blowing in the wind. All these little kids were running behind the lorry, skipping and waving balloons, and wearing paper hats that had been given out by girls in short skirts walking along the road. People were picking up the vouchers for a free fish and chip supper (while stocks last).

Not to mention the chance to win a weekend for two in Paris.

I turned back into our shop, deeply depressed. "It looks as if the circus has come to town instead of a chip shop opening. All they're short of is an elephant."

"Speaking of which, isn't that Arnold Addison bringing up the rear, with his trained flea of a son," said Iris. Then one of these lasses with all the make-up pushed a leaflet through the letterbox. Iris picked it up. It was an entry form for the competition.

"I wouldn't go to Paris if they paid me," she said. "It's a filthy hole. A frog-eating, snail-eating, slug-eating hole."

"Don't exaggerate, Iris," I said. "They do not eat slugs in France." But I didn't have the heart to argue with her. What's the point when Argameddon is rolling towards us on the back of a lorry.

When the parade reached the outside of the Chips & More!, Arnold Addison marched to the front, waving and smiling—and wobbling. There was quite a crowd gathered at this point, watching the proceedings. None of them had come into our shop.

Arnold was helped, with some difficulty, up on to this a rostrum they'd had erected. There was a bit of suspense as he mounted the platform because the sheer weight of him looked as though it was testing the timber to the utmost. The ribbon was waiting to be cut, and the new branch officially opened.

Our Sylvia came downstairs all dolled up in her dreadful clothes.

"And where are you off to?" I asked.

"I'm going round to find out what it's like next door," she said.

"Oh, but you're not," said Iris, standing in front of the door and barring their way. "None of our family is going to be seen patronising that place."

"You can't stop me," said our Sylvia. "Besides, there's nothing to do here. Nobody's going to buy chips from us when there's a Chips & More! next door."

"Doreen—tell her," Iris ordered. "Forbid her to go."

"What's the use?" I said, all hopeless. "You can't turn back the tide, even King Midas couldn't do that."

115

So, Iris reluctantly stepped aside, and our Sylvia went. It seemed like the final slap in the face.

"And besides which," I said, "she's right. We're finished."

Over the loudspeaker, I could hear Arnold bragging off about the superior quality of his products. "And now," he says, "I want to introduce you to someone you're all going to get to know—the new manager of this shop. Here he is, none other than my own flesh and blood, Ainsley Addison. Come and say hello to your new customers and soon-to-be friends, Ainsley."

I couldn't resist a little peak out of the window to see Ainsley being manhandled on to the platform by his loud-mouthed dad. He looked mortified at being made a show of and even more mortified when his father handed him the microphone. Ainsley looked as though he'd been handed a red-hot poker. He couldn't say a word.

"Come on, lad, introduce yourself. All these folk are friendly, aren't you?" No-one responded.

There was a silence as Ainsley struggled mightily to make words—any words—come out of his mouth. Arnold elbowed him in the ribs. "Say summat, lad, say hello."

Ainsley's mouth moved, but all that came out of it was a squeak you could hardly hear. Then there was a pathetic "Hello" followed by an hysterical coughing fit.

Somebody in the crowd laughed, and then somebody else. Ainsley's worst nightmare was coming true: he was being humiliated because of his shyness.

Arnold wasn't best pleased and rapidly shoved the lad off the stage.

"He'll find his feet as time goes on," he said over the microphone. "You'll find you've got a friendly hands-on manager at your local Chips & More! when he settles down."

I turned back into the shop feeling very sorry for anybody who had that barrel of lard for a father. "He's horrible to that poor lad," I said to Iris. "I hope the fat pig comes a real cropper one day."

No sooner were the words out of my mouth than a big cheer went up from outside.

"I expect he's cut the ribbon," I said.

"No," says Iris, who was standing by the door watching the proceedings. "The platform's given way. Arnold's flat on his back with his legs in the air and a pile of splinters all around him."

It was gratifying to see Mr Big in such an undignified pose, but even that didn't make me smile.

* * *

Trade had been so bad since Chips & More! opened its doors that it hardly seems worthwhile firing up the friers. We just stand around or sit in the back watching the portable television. The only person to stick their head through the door yesterday was my old 'friend' from the Housewives Register, Marje Bickerstaffe, and she'd only come round to crow.

"I just thought I'd pop in and see how things are doing," she said, looking round at the empty shop with some satisfaction. "I hear you've got a bit of competition next door."

"You could say that," I said in an unfriendly tone. "How can I help you, Marje?"

"I've just come to try and raise morale. I know it must be flagging a bit. You should see the queue next door, it's right round the corner. They must be taking a fortune. I don't see what people see in all this fast food. I don't believe in it myself. I much prefer to make stuff fresh at home, and you can get such lovely things from Marks and Spencers these days, can't you? For the price of one of these fishy nuggets they're selling next door you can get a Chicken Tikka Marsala for two, which is much nicer and more nourishing."

I didn't respond. I just wanted her to go.

"I don't understand young people, they're all fast food mad, aren't they?" she persisted. "As long as it's in fancy boxes and looks as though it's being served by Americans, they'll eat any old junk, won't they? And they're scattering them containers all over the road. It looks a right mess out there. I'm just glad I don't live round here."

She went on like this for a good half hour, carrying out her threat to "cheer us up". By the time she'd finished, she'd cheered me up to the point that I was considering sticking me head in the electric chipper and switching it on. She's always been a spiteful madam has Marje. She thinks she's a cut above, but I know all about them little shoplifting jaunts she goes on. Although why she feels the need to stick tins of marrowfat peas up her jumper, I don't know. You'd think she'd go for something a bit more expensive than that, a tin of salmon or something. She's banned from Tescos and Morrisons—that's probably why she has to go to Marks's.

After Marje had gone (and I'd checked that the salt and vinegar dispensers were still on the counter and not in her coat pocket), that little lad who'd been our first customer came in. He looked as if he hadn't had a wash since the last time he was here.

"A small bag of chips, open," he said.

I filled the cone and handed it over. He gave me the pound.

"Just a minute," I said, as he walked to the door. "How come you're not next door with all your mates? Do you prefer our chips?"

"No," he said. "Only the queue's too long next door and I'm hungry."

* * *

A week into the great depression and the only trade we are getting is the back- wash from Chips & More!—them on the end of the queue who haven't got the patience to wait. We've had to cut back the fish order, and the potato turn-over is very modest, pathetic, in fact. Some of the sacks we've got in the shed at the back will have to be chucked—the taters are going green and sprouting. And to top it all, the business-rate demand has just plopped on to the doorstep. It seems like an awful lot of money, given what we're taking over the counter. We've already had the electric and gas bills, and they aren't paid yet, either.

On Sunday, I was out in the garden at Evergreen Close, trying to revive my flower beds and rescue them from the weeds, when my next-door neighbour Beryl Cathcart put her head over the fence.

"Feeling any better about things?" she asked.

"Not really, Beryl," I said. "There's no change. It's hopeless. That Addison swine is laughing up his sleeve as he sees us slowly sinking in the East. All this worry is making me poorly."

"I do feel sorry for you, Doreen. You've put so much into it. Is there anything I could do?"

I shrugged my shoulders. "Not unless you feel like murdering Chips Chipperson or assassinating Fishy Fry."

She laughed, then said: "Have you thought about a re-launch?"

I shook my head and yanked out a weed with great satisfaction. "What's the point of re-launching the Titanic? It'll only sink again."

At that moment, Iris came shooting out of the house and into the garden.

"Re-launch?" she said to Beryl.

"Do I ever have any privacy from you?" I said to her. "I don't think there's a single word I utter that you don't hear."

Iris disregarded me and said to Beryl: "What do you mean, re-launch?"

"Well," says Beryl, "it's something I read in a magazine last week. All these famous firms that didn't manage to get off the ground first time, but managed to re-launch themselves with a new image, and then went on to great success."

"Such as?"

"Well, there was that breakfast cereal company. Brought out a new kind of breakfast biscuit, Hello Crispies. It was a total failure. They were on the point of going out of business, when somebody suggested they call it something else—Grain-o-Pure—and pack it nicely in a greenish box and suggest it had health benefits, even though it was forty per cent sugar. Appeal to a different audience, you see. It was originally for children, but they started marketing it as a healthy breakfast for adults, full of fibre and vitamins, and it suddenly took off, and now it's the third best-selling breakfast cereal in the country."

"What's this got to do with us?" I said.

"Well, nothing directly. I just thought you might be able to re-launch your chip shop in some way. Change its image."

"And how are we going to do that, might I ask? We haven't got any money left in the kitty. You can't do that kind of thing on the cheap."

Beryl nodded. "Yes, I suppose you're right. Sorry I mentioned it. Pop round and have a drink later, if you want."

"Beryl." Iris said. "Can I have a look at that magazine of yours?"

I could almost see the cogs in her brain whirring away.

"Before you start, Iris, don't be getting no fancy ideas about relaunches. It can't be done. To start with, we're almost broke. How do you plan to get over that?"

"We'll burn that bridge when we come to it," she said, "have you never heard of small business loans?"

* * *

I didn't have to wait long before Iris called a full board meeting (which consisted of me and her at the Formica-topped table in the shop with a couple of folders and biros).

"Now let's think this through," she said. "Let's have a barnstorming session. What exactly is it that they've got next door that we haven't got?"

"Customers," I couldn't resist saying.

"They're selling basically the same product what we are, so it must be the marketing what's making them prefer Chips & More! to us."

"So, what's new?"

"So, we've got to copy them," she said. "I mean, they've got a brand image. They've got lasses behind the counter in baseball caps and striped pinnies, they've got them Styrofoam boxes that clog the gutter up, and they've got Fishy Fry and Chips Chipperson. And when they've served you, they hope you have a nice day. 'Have a nice day' they'll say. It's called customer relations is that. So that's what we shall have to do. We shall have to start saying 'Thanks for buying your chips at Doreen and Iris's, have a nice day."

"Y'what?" I said. "If you think I'm standing behind that counter telling people to have a nice day all day, you've got another think coming. I'd rather cut me tongue off than wish Marje Bickerstaffe to have a nice day. Besides, it's too American. We don't go in for having nice days in Rotherham, it's unnatural."

"That's what folk seem to want. If it isn't American, they don't want it."

"You can be pleasant without having to talk that kind of gibberish, Iris. There are other ways of having relations with the customers without talking like a parrot."

"Like what?" Iris said.

"Like, for instance, 'thanks love, how's your hubby keeping these days?' That's the traditional way of talking to people in a chip shop, as if you're interested in them. Chip shops are local enterprises, not international conglomerates that take their lead from New York. Besides, nobody takes any notice of this 'have a nice day' shite. It goes in one ear and out the other."

"You might be right there," she said. "They take notice if you're interested in them personally. Customer care. It might not be modern, but it's got to be took into account. We could keep a little notebook and put down any titbits of information that they tell us and next time they come in we can refer to it. Personally tailored fish and chips served up with local gossip and enquiries regarding their private life."

She sat and thought for a minute and then started writing.

"We can have some of them daft caps printed with our logo cheap enough. But we're going to have recyclable cardboard trays, not Styrofoam, and then crack on its environmentally friendly. That's all the rage. Taking care of the rainforest and dolphins and that. If that's what they want, that's what they shall have."

"This here logo that you're talking about. What exactly is it?"

"It doesn't have to be anything special, Doreen. Look at McDonald's—all they've got is them golden arches. Anybody can come up with something like that."

"Oh, can they?" I said. "Go on then."

She doodled for a minute and then turned the pad round to show me.

It was a square with a diagonal line in it.

"Is that it?" I said. "Is that what's going to get us instantly recognised around the world?"

"It is," she said. "It'll be vermillion with a yellow line through it. They'll be our corporate colours. Now, we want a mascot. We'll go for something they haven't got. What can we make into a funny character, something suitable to be made into a cuddly toy and irresistible to all children, everywhere? Something we could make into a costume so that we could have somebody running round the streets promoting our fish and chips? Derek could do it. They've got Fishy Fry—so what could we have?"

I was fed up with this, so I just said: "What about Elvis the Savaloy or Cliff the Gherkin?" thinking she'd realise what a mad idea this was and pack it up.

Instead, she said: "That's not bad. I think we'll go with Elvis the Gherkin. Our Gary used to be good at art when he was at school. I'll ask him to draw me something that looks like Elvis the Gherkin and then I'll make it up into a stuffed toy."

I lost my temper at this point. "Don't talk so chuffing barmy, Iris. Elvis the chuffing Gherkin—it's crackers."

"You'd have said the same thing about Fishy Fry when the advertising agency came up with it," she said. "Now half these kids think lousy Fishy Fry is a real person."

"Well, if that's it, if that's the big idea," I said, "I'm not convinced. It'll all look amateurish compared with what Addison can do."

"I've not finished yet," said Iris. "All that is obvious enough, but I've got a peace of resistance up my sleeve. Listen to this..." She straightened her pinny and announced: "Low fat chips."

"Low fat chips?" I said, mystified.

"Low fat chips," she repeated.

"There's no such animal," I said.

"Oh, but there is, Doreen. Haven't you seen them in the supermarket—low fat, oven chips. 95% fat free."

"Oven chips? Have you tried them? They're like cotton buds."

She looked at me as though I were an idiot. "It's a marketing ploy, Doreen. Haven't you heard of marketing ploys? You make your disadvantages into advantages. Look at Polo Mints and Aero Bars — they sell us fresh air and make out they're doing us a favour. So, if oven chips taste like burnt firewood, we have to say something like: taste the delicious, crunchy, just-smoked flavour—you'll love it."

"What a lot of cock you talk, Iris."

"That's what they said about Joan of Arc, but she went ahead and built it anyway, didn't she? Look, I'll explain it to you in words of one monosyllable. Think about all them women over on that new estate, they're all desperate not to become fat old hags, right?"

I nodded.

"They've all got this obsession with calories and low-fat diets, right?"

I nodded again.

"They wouldn't come anywhere near a fish and chip shop, would they? But what if we sold low fat chips, cooked in the oven? As well as regular, high-fat chips, of course—we mustn't forget our core clients, slobby men with beer guts and kids playing hooky from school. These slimming fanatics, though, they wouldn't have to feel guilty about eating chips if we could put '95% fat free' in big letters in the window, would they? They'd feel as though they were doing themselves a favour by having their fish and chips cooked in the oven."

"But we haven't got an oven. We've only got these friers."

"Then we'll get an oven. We could fit a small one in that alcove at the back there. It won't cost much in the great scheme of things."

122

I thought about it for a minute. "It doesn't sound right to me. Nobody else is doing it. Surely Chips & More! and all that lot would have thought about it if it was going to work."

Iris snorted. "Sometimes it's so obvious these clever dicks don't see it. I think it could be the making of us, Doreen. The first chip shop in the land to sell low-fat chips. Think about it. An absolute original. Them lasses on the estate would be queuing round the block."

"You make it sound reasonable," I said. "But it sounds like you're grasping at the straw that broke the camel's neck. There must be a catch in it somewhere. Let me think about it for a few days."

"But keep it to yourself, Doreen. Don't go blabbing about it. Walls have ears and we don't want nobody stealing our thunder."

That night I rang up our Gary and asked him to come round. He sounded glad to be getting out of the flat for the evening.

I thought him and Bill had been rowing, but he wouldn't say.

When I explained what we were doing he sat down with a piece of paper and proceeded to draw his idea of Elvis the Gherkin. When he was finished, he held up the bit of paper for us to see.

"Elvis the Gherkin?" Iris said with contempt. "That's more like Willy the Banana. You've got phallic symbols on the brain, you have. Have another try. Straighten it up a bit and give it a few more bumps. Gherkins are lumpy and green."

He looked frustrated. "How am I supposed to make a slimy pickled vegetable look cuddly?" he wanted to know. "What child is going to want to cuddle up to a gherkin when it goes to bed?"

"He's right, Iris," I said. "I think we might have picked the wrong vegetable to home in on. Gherkins might be tasty, but they're not going to replace teddy bears, are they?"

Iris tutted with impatience. "You just don't get it, do you?" she said. "Kids don't want teddy bears any more. They want weirdness. They want their cuddly toys to be irrational. Look at them Teletubbies, look at Furbies, look at Thomas the Tank Engine for heaven's sake! They don't make sense. They're that— what do you call it?—off the wall. And that's what Elvis the Gherkin is going to be, totally barmy, but that's what kiddies want. If we can get Elvis established as a character, the fact that he's a gherkin will count in his favour. Believe me."

Our Sylvia was sitting there with our Charmaine Bernadette, watching all this. Iris said to her: "I wish that babby could talk, then she could be our focus group and tell us whether her friends would like an Elvis the Gherkin."

"She hasn't got no friends," our Sylvia says, "only little Jean-Claude and he's allergic to soft toys."

Our Gary shrugged his shoulders and set to work again and came up with another version of Elvis. This time the gherkin had a big smile and long eyelashes and tiny little arms and legs sticking out.

"That's better," Iris said. "But there's still something missing. He's got to have a gimmick. Like something that's unique to him, that other gherkins don't have."

She thought for a moment, and then she said: "A crown. Put him a crown on."

"It's bloody crackers is this," I said. "A gherkin with a crown on? What's it supposed to mean?"

"It doesn't necessarily mean nothing," she said. "That's the whole point. He's a character. But if you think about it, Elvis was the king, wasn't he?"

I shook my head in disbelief at her thought patterns. They defeated me, but she was so confident about it I didn't have the wherewithal to argue with her.

"Right, now we've got to make a prototype," she said. "We'll get some felt and stuffing from the hobby shop tomorrow, and you can knock up the first Elvis on the sewing machine, Doreen."

"I can't make soft toys," I said. "I'm hopeless at arts and crafts. I was excused from the class when I was at school because of an accident with a pair of scissors and a bodkin. When she came back from the hospital, the teacher said I wasn't safe to be given sharp tools. No. You'll have to do it, Iris."

"I can't sew to save my life. What about you, Gary?"

Our Gary was getting his coat on at this stage, having served his purpose as artistic director. "I've got enough problems of my own, Mam, without taking on any more. But I hope it works out for you."

Iris went over and gave him a little kiss. "Thanks, Gary, love. You've made a lovely job of it. And I'll tell you what—if Elvis the Gherkin ever takes off in a big way, we'll make sure we remember who the father was, and you'll be rewarded in cash money."

He smiled indulgently at his Gran and went.

Iris went over to our Charmaine Bernadette and tickled her under the chin. "You're a bonny lass, aren't you?" she said. "Would you like your granny Iris to make you a nice Elvis the Gherkin dolly? Would you?"

She smiled. She likes it when Iris talks silly to her.

"We'll have to get somebody who can do this kind of thing to make the first one for us," Iris was saying. "Can you think of anyone, Doreen?"

"As it happens, yes I can. You know that accident I was telling you about that I had at school? Well, it involved the girl who shared the work bench with me. I stuck that bodkin through her hand because she was always better at sewing and knitting than me— accidentally, of course. Always showing me up. And her name was Beryl Slack née Cathcart. Yes, her next door! She used to be a dab hand at needlework and making things. Even before she got the feeling back in her hand, she could still make gorgeous embroideries and knitted jumpers. I'll ring her up and ask her if she can help."

So, I got on the phone and she came round.

Iris was her usual cautious self. She more or less made Beryl swear on the Official Secrets Act that she wouldn't say a word to nobody about our relaunch plans. Beryl was goggle-eyed at the intrigue of it all.

"You can trust me, Iris. I'm no spy. I wouldn't sell you down the river," she said.

So, Iris told her what we were planning. Now when Iris gets an idea in her head, she could convince Imelda Marcos that she doesn't need any more shoes. And as she explained her plans to Beryl, you could see Beryl getting more and more enthusiastic about it.

"Int'it exciting, Doreen?" she kept saying, as Iris unfolded her masterplan and made it sound like the relaunch of ICI rather than a backstreet chip shop.

After she'd given her the low down, Iris said, "So what do you think, Beryl?"

"It's brilliant. You're a genius, Iris. A bloody genius."

"Aye," I said. "She's definitely missed her vacation. She should have been managing director of some big corporation by rights, then the world would have known about it."

"You don't know how lucky you are, Doreen, having such excitement in your life," says Beryl. "I'd give anything to be having something like this happening to me."

"What? You think having a failing chip shop on your hands, and a mad granny about to run us into thousands of pounds worth of debt with a crackpot scheme revolving round a gherkin is exciting?"

"She's got no vision," Iris said contemptuously.

"Don't think negatively, Doreen," Beryl said. "Give it your best shot. If you convince yourself from the outset that you're going to fail, you will, as sure as eggs is eggs."

Iris smiled a broad smile and patted Beryl on the back. "Thank you for that, Beryl. I'm glad to see there's somebody with a bit of go in them. It's a shame you're not my partner instead of her. With your attitude and my conniving brain, we could rule the world."

"I'll tell you something," Beryl said. "I'd buy Doreen's share like a shot if she'd sell it. I think it's dead exciting. It beats sitting in the house all day watching that daytime television. If I see another cookery programme, I swear I'll turn bulimic."

"Well, you can do your bit by putting your handicraft skills to good use," says Iris. "Would you be able to come up with a prototype Elvis the Gherkin, based on our Gary's drawing?"

"I'll have a bloody good go," said Beryl, who revealed she'd made soft toys before for her grandkids. "Leave it with me for a day or two. I'll see what I can do."

And off she went, clutching that stupid Elvis the Gherkin picture as though it were a bone china tea service.

Iris rubbed her hands with satisfaction. "Well, everything's coming up roses," she says. "I've got a good feeling about this."

I grimaced at her and said: "Do you think she was serious about buying me out?"

* * *

I was awoken this morning about seven a.m. by this demented knocking on the front door. I went down in my dressing gown and found Beryl standing there, looking like an excited kid, with a Tesco bag in her hand.

"I've done it," she said. "I've been up all night at that sewing machine. I've had a few false starts, but I think I've got it right now."

She held up the bag. "In here, Doreen, is Elvis the Gherkin version one."

126

"Come in, Beryl before we both catch our deaths of cold," I said, pulling my dressing gown tight.

"I'm that excited I couldn't wait another minute to get round here and show you," she said, coming into the lounge.

Iris was standing there in her house coat.

"Morning Iris," Beryl said. "Elvis is ready for unveiling."

"Put the kettle on, Doreen," Iris ordered. "Make us some coffee."

"Oh, bugger off," I said to her. "You make the chuffing coffee. I want to see what Beryl's come up with."

"Look," said Iris. "We want us wits about us dealing with this. Get the kettle going, will you?"

I realised that resistance was futile, so I went into the kitchen. Thankfully, Beryl insisted on waiting till I got there before she revealed what she'd come up with.

While I was making the coffee, our Sylvia pitched up with the babby. She'd come to collect the baby food she'd left behind in the kitchen cupboard.

We gathered around Beryl who then, with a flourish, opened the bag and pulled out Elvis version 1. He was about eight inches tall, made out of green felt, with little beads on to give the effect of them lumps that gherkins have. He had diddy little arms and legs that flopped about and was topped off by a bonny little face—cheeky grin made of red felt, wild eyes made from white, and on top a little gold crown she'd taken off the Christmas tree fairy.

Iris gave it a serious inspection, turning it over in her hands, examining it from all angles. Beryl was watching her face expectantly, like a Labrador waiting for its master to chuck a stick.

Iris looked at me and said: "What do you think, Doreen?"

"I think he's lovely. He's a right character."

Iris didn't look convinced.

"He's cute enough," she said. "But what's going to make him recognisably different from any other stuffed toy gherkin? How will a child know if it's got a genuine Elvis?"

"I don't think there's much competition to be honest, Iris," I said. "Kiddies aren't really into toy gherkins, are they?"

"You'd be surprised," she said. "Kiddies are fickle. And that's going to be Elvis's appeal. His unique rarity value."

She took Elvis and handed to our Charmaine Bernadette who looked at it, then smiled.

"She loves it, Mam," our Sylvia says. "There aren't any loose parts are there that could choke her, like there were on that Chinese Barbie doll that I got her off the market."

"Elvis will be tested to destruction by the health and safety authorities. There's nothing dangerous about this soft toy. Is there, Beryl?"

"Oh no—there's nothing loose or sharp involved. No choking hazards, as such. Although you don't want to put it too near a naked flame—I've stuffed it temporarily with something that might cause you to get fatally gassed if it goes up in smoke. That's all I had in the house. But we can correct that in the final version, can't we?"

Iris looked thoughtful.

"Do you like it, then?" Beryl was gagging for some kind of verdict.

"You've done a grand job," Iris said to her. "But it isn't finished. What I want you to do, Beryl, is make him a little sash to go round his middle, and on it I want you to embroider 'Elvis the Gherkin' and our logo. Can you do that?"

"That'll be easy enough," Beryl said. "I've got some silver ribbon in my work box. I'll use that."

"Well get on with it, girl. I think we've cracked it."

Beryl was all smiles as she ran from the house to get started on the sash. She didn't even wait for the coffee. So, me and Iris sat there in our night clothes, sipping our first cup of the day, with our Sylvia shovelling baby food into our Charmaine's mouth at a rate of knots. The babby, in the meantime, was clinging to Elvis the First. At least it's a hit with her.

After a while of silence, in which Iris was deep in thought, I said: "What are we supposed to do when she's done it? I mean, what use is one soft toy?"

She looked into the distance and said: "It's merely the beginning, Doreen." And all the while her mind was ticking over like a Formula One racing car.

* * *

You'd think I'd have learned by now never to underestimate my finagling mother-in-law. A week after she had made the prototype Elvis, Iris had persuaded me to allow Beryl to invest in the business.

128

"We shall need some capital to fight this Addison creep," Iris said. "And Beryl's got it. She's got a nest egg sitting doing nowt in the building society. She wants to put it to use."

"Yes, but is it a good investment? Are we leading her astray with her life savings?"

"You put *your* money into it, didn't you?"

"Yes," I said. "But that was pre-Addison. I'm not sure that I'd do it now."

"Look, what she's putting in will pay for the production of a couple of hundred Elvis's and it'll allow us to have some bespoke packaging printed—fancy stuff that looks professional. And I've had a uniform made up for us. Only a couple of pinnies with the logo on it and these like trilby hats to wear. We've got to look the part."

"So, now we've got all this stuff, how are we going to let people know about it? I mean, we can't afford full-page adverts in the paper and commercials on the telly like Addison can."

"Leave it to me," Iris said. "I've got a bit of an idea."

I smiled and said, "When haven't you?"

* * *

Just after the dinner time rush (three small cods, a fishcake and five portions of chips sold), I thought I'd pay a visit to our Sylvia in her flat and see what she was making of it. When I got up the stairs and opened the door I was confronted by Ulrika, our Sylvia's friend from the single mother's support group. She was cutting her toenails.

Her own kiddy, a little toddler by the name of Jean-Claude was sitting on the settee with our Charmaine Bernadette. They were scribbling in a painting book with crayons.

"Where's our Sylvia?" I said. "Is she shopping?"

Ulrika looked at me as though I was speaking Chinese.

After a bit she gathered her thoughts and said: "She's gone for a date with her boyfriend. I'm looking after the kids."

"Boyfriend?" I said. "What boyfriend is this?"

"I don't know, she hasn't said."

"Well, I think I'd better take our Charmaine Bernadette home with me until our Sylvia decides to show her face," I said. I wasn't smitten with the idea of Ulrika as a babysitter. "Tell her, will you, that the baby is safe at our house. And remind her that she's on duty tonight in the shop."

"OK," she said.

"That'll mean you can go home as well now, Ulrika. Take the little lad with you and I'll lock the place up."

"I am home," she said. "I live here."

"You what?" I was taken aback. "You live here? Since when?"

"Sylvia says we can live here with her and Charmaine. I'm fed up with that B&B, it's mucky."

What could I say? Either our Sylvia has given the pair of them a home out of the goodness of her heart or she's after a share of the benefits that Ulrika is on. Mind you, I wouldn't wish that bed and breakfast on anybody—they aren't even allowed to cook their own grub in there, consequently they live on chips and other even less nourishing rubbish.

I gathered up our Charmaine Bernadette and left Ulrika to continue clipping away at her toenails with a tiny pair of nail scissors. Still, it'll be company for our Sylvia and a little friend for our Charmaine Bernadette to play with.

As I was walking back down Balaclava Street, I noticed a big poster in the window of Chips & More! It took a while to register but when I got a bit closer it said:

"ERIC THE GHERKIN IS COMING! Launching next week–our fabulous new cuddly toy that every child will love! You've got Chips Chipperson and Fishy Fry—now there's a new friend to add to the gang —Eric the Gherkin (registered trademark). Come and collect your Eric the Gherkin toy from next Monday (terms and conditions apply)."

The drawing of Eric the Gherkin on the poster was almost identical to our Elvis.

I was fuming. I could hardly believe it. I was going to go in and play hell, but the shop was closed until 5pm.

When I got home, I spluttered the whole story out to Iris. I was that angry my face was throbbing. "They've pinched our idea, stole it hook, line and sinker," I said.

"How could they have?" Iris says. "Nobody knows about it except you, me and Beryl Cathcart. I'm sure she wouldn't have blabbed."

"Well, somebody has. It's a bit too close to home to be a coincidence."

"Industrial espionage," Iris says. "That's what it is. There's a spy in the camp. Else they've got us under surveillance."

"Bugged?"

"How else could they have known?" She started looking round the ceiling, trying to locate a hidden camera. But there was nothing, except a spider lurking in the corner.

"They've got us well and truly stitched up. He must have acted fast to get it all done in just a few days."

"Well," says Iris. "When you've got a big staff team and a PR agency to outsource to, he probably designated it a rush job. They won't have had it made in China like we was going to. It must have cost a fortune. That Addison must really hate us."

"Is there still time to cancel the order from that Chinese factory? Otherwise, we're going to end up with hundreds of the lousy Elvises and nothing to do with them."

A mood of deep misery has fallen on Evergreen Close. Me and Iris are that disappointed that we've been played for fools. But what can we do about it? Even Iris was stumped.

I'd invited our Gary and our Sylvia round for their teas, just to take my mind off things. Our Gary said he was busy, but our Sylvia came round—she's never behind the door when there's a free meal to be had. I was glad to be able to feed our Charmaine Bernadette something other than chips.

We sat at the table in silence. Derek soon caught the mood and started to look dead gloomy. He's prone to depression, at the best of times, and I could almost see the black cloud forming over his head. I thought to myself, if he's not careful he'll be on tablets again.

When we'd had our meat and tater pie and I was serving up the Ambrosia Creamed Rice, our Sylvia said: "Mam, can you look after our Charmaine Bernadette for me next weekend?"

"Why, where're you going?" I said. "You know you're on the rota for Friday and Saturday. And I can't watch the baby. I shall be rushed off me feet."

"But you won't be, Mam. Hardly anybody comes to the shop. Even on Saturday. You don't need three of us in there."

"Well, where are you going that's so special?" I said.

"I'm going to Paris," she says.

"Eh?" I was too stunned to say anything sensible.

Iris says: "Paris? You mean in France? How're you managing that on benefits?"

"I won that Chips & More! draw. I got the first prize."

"Well, at least somebody's got summat to celebrate," says Derek, perking up a bit.

"And who are you going with?" I said.

"Me and Ulrika are going. We'll be alright. She took French O-level so she can ask where the toilet is. She's palming little Jean-Claude off on her mother for a couple of days."

"Well, I hope Ulrika can speak French better than she can speak English," I said.

"And you'd better take some sandwiches with you," Iris advised, "because they eat some right muck in Paris. Snails, slugs, the lot. You take some English food with you."

"Take no notice of your gran," I said. "She's living in the past. Besides, she's never been further than Cleethorpes for her holidays. They have lovely food in France. You want to take the chance to try something new. Pancakes and that. Widen your culinary horizons."

"We will, Mam. Ulrika says they've got McDonalds in Paris now, so we'll be having French Big Macs. That'll be exciting."

Well, I couldn't begrudge the lass a chance of a little break, particularly as it would be at the expense of Chips & More! so I allocated her shift to another member of staff (Iris) and I'd look after our Charmaine Bernadette.

But, of course, I couldn't resist going down to Balaclava Street to see how business was doing at Chips & More! There was a queue round the block as usual for them, and a deadly silence at our place. The people coming out of Chips & More! were clutching their Styrofoam supper and the new soft toy—Eric the Gherkin. It stabbed at my heart. But even worse was a new notice in the window.

"COMING SOON TO YOUR LOCAL CHIPS & MORE! – 95% fat free chips! Yes, for those watching their weight, we have a new product that will help you on your way without the need to deprive yourself of your favourite Chips & More! supper. Slimming has never been so easy."

I gasped at the sheer cheek of it. The unfairness of it. The nastiness of it.

I charged straight in to challenge that lad of Addison's who's supposed to be running this rip-off joint.

I stormed up to the counter, fuming. A lad shouts out: "Hey up, Mrs—there's a queue here. Wait your turn." Others behind him started to object as well.

"I've not come to buy any of the muck they sell here," I said. "I've come for a confrontation with the manager. Where is he?"

The lass behind the counter, wearing one of them sunshade type things, says: "Ainsley's not here, can I take a message?"

"Yes, you can. You can tell him from me that he's a rat and a thief, just like his father. And you can tell him when he gets back that I shall be round here to have his guts for garters."

"Come on, Mrs, shove off," says this lad at the front of the queue, "we want our supper."

"Oh, shut your cakehole," I said, ready to direct my anger at anybody who got in my way.

I stomped out of the shop, ignoring the "We've been here half an hour" comment from the queue.

As I got outside, I noticed through the corner of my eye that there was a light on in our Sylvia's flat. "Typical," I thought, "leave all the lights on and Mam will pick up the bill."

I got the spare key out of my bag and let myself in. I could hear the television from the bottom of the stairs. So, I hurried up into the flat and there was Ulrika and Jean-Claude, large as life on the settee.

"What're you doing here?" I said to her.

"I live here," she said.

"No, but I thought you'd gone to Paris with our Sylvia."

"No," she said vacantly.

"Has our Sylvia gone to Paris?"

"Yes, I think so."

"Well, who's she gone with?"

"I think she's gone with her boyfriend. She's took her boyfriend with her. I think that's who she's took, her boyfriend."

"And do you know who this boyfriend is?" I said to her.

"I think it's him next door. You know, that lad next door. Him at the chip shop we go to."

"What, Ainsley? Do you mean that Ainsley lad?"

"I don't know what he's called. It might be Ainsley. Something like that."

I nearly fell down the stairs I was in that big a rush to tell Iris. I went into our shop and she was sitting in the back, watching the telly. I could hardly get me breath I was that angry.

"What the hell's the matter with you?" she said. "You look as though you've run a marathon."

Eventually I got my breathing under control and managed to tell her what had happened—about Chips & More! pinching our low-fat chips idea and about or Sylvia consorting with the enemy.

"Well," Iris said. "We know who the spy is now, don't we?"

"I can hardly believe it—after all I've done for her, letting her have that flat, giving her a job, paying her bills, and this is how she repays me. Wait till she gets back! I'm going to screw her neck round."

"He's seduced her," Iris says, "he's using sex to get her to do his bidding."

"What, that weedy little squirt? Are we talking about the same person? He's about as sexy as a tube of haemorrhoid cream. I thought our Sylvia had a better taste in men. She wouldn't entertain him, would she?"

"From what I've heard she'd entertain…"

I stopped her. "I know what you're going to say, Iris, and there's no need to go into all that again. The magistrate accepted our Sylvia's explanation that she was not actually employed at the Happy Endings Massage Parlour but merely on a zero hours contract for when they were short-handed. She took an intensive three-hour massage course to get that."

"It looks as if Addison has robbed us of our final throw of the dice, Doreen. We're all out of ammunition. This could be the straw that broke the camel's neck."

When Iris admits defeat, you can be sure that defeat is final.

* * *

I was sitting in our Sylvia's flat on Monday morning, waiting for her to pitch up. Her friend Ulrika was there, looking very uncomfortable as I drummed my fingers on the arm of the settee. "Just wait till she shows her face," I was muttering.

Poor old Ulrika could sense I was browned off and that there was an explosion approaching. She was anxious, bordering on frightened. She kept glancing at me out of the corner of her eye every few seconds to see whether I was going to vent my fury on her. She was in that flight or fright mode.

Eventually she could stand the tension no longer. She got little Jean-Claude ready and said: "I'm just popping round to me mother's to see if she's got any knock-off cigs from Poland this week."

I was on the point of asking her if she could get me a few packets, but I didn't want to spoil the mood of violent foreboding, so I kept on drumming.

It was about half past eleven when our Sylvia comes waltzing in, dragging her suitcase behind her, knocking lumps off the stairs, and looking as though butter wouldn't melt.

She was surprised to see me. "Oh, hello Mam, what are you doing here?" she said.

"Did you have a nice time in Paris?" I said, in a tone of voice so sharp it could cut through stainless steel.

"Yes, it was lovely, thank you." She picked up straight away that I was on to her.

"And did Ulrika enjoy it?"

"Ah well, I meant to mention that. She couldn't go in the end because her mother's got fibroids."

"So, you went on your own, did you?"

"Well, no—I took a friend." She reached into her pocket and pulled out a paper bag. "Look, I've brought you a present. French cinder toffee from Paris."

She handed me the bag, which contained a quarter of cinder toffee, which I happen to know was off Mrs Craven's sweet stall in the market—the name was printed on the bag—and had never seen Paris.

Ignoring her blandishments and her attempt to distract me, I said: "And was this friend of yours male or female?"

"Why? What do you want to know that for?"

"And did this friend of yours just happen to be a mortal enemy of our family, by any chance?"

"Oh, alright, it was Ainsley from next door."

"Now we're getting there. What are you doing consorting with a backstabbing, rotten little bleeder like him? And why have you been giving him our state secrets? You're nothing but a Martha Hari. A traitor to the cause."

"I don't know what you're talking about, Mam. I'm in love with Ainsley. He's the man of my dreams."

"Who? Him? That little runt," I said.

"We went to Paris to celebrate our seven-and-a-half-month anniversary, all expenses paid, up to the value of £75. He fixed that competition so that I would win and so that we could cement our relationship in the capital of love. He was talking about marriage at one bit. It was while we were eating our anniversary dinner at Burger King."

"Marriage. Is that what convinced you to tell him all our plans, so that him and his dad could pinch them off us?"

"I didn't spill no secrets, Mam. I didn't know we had any secrets. You never said nothing to me that they were secret. It was just something to chat about. He got me talking, you see, and I just talked about the lovely things you were doing with Elvis the Gherkin and them oven chips. I'm that proud of you and me gran that I wanted to brag off about you. I wanted to show him that I've got a clever family. He was ever so interested, with him being in the trade and that."

"I'll bet he was. Getting you all worked up into a frenzy of lust and then wheedling the information out of you. He's a crafty sod, just like his father. You've been took advantage of, girl. Exploited."

"Oh no, Mam, he really loves me. He says he's going to buy me a ring this week."

"I'm going to see about this," I said. "I'm going to have it out with him and that great blob of a father of his. Let's see what your granny Iris has got to say about it. She won't be so forgiving. She might insist that I invict you from this flat and chuck you out on the street."

"Don't spoil it for me, Mam. This might be the chance I've been waiting for."

I rang Iris and asked her to come round so we could plan strategy. She was equally suspicious of our Sylvia as what I was. She was going to take some convincing that our Sylvia wasn't a little liar who has sold her own family down the river for a potage of gold.

After she'd grilled her for half an hour, Iris said: "If you want us to believe what you're saying, you'll have to prove it."

"What can I do to prove it? Tell me what I can do and I'll do it," our Sylvia was saying.

"I want you to get that lad to tell us what plans the Addison empire has got for the future. See if you can find out what they're going to do next to try to drive us out of business, what other dirty tricks they're plotting."

"A double agent!" I said. "What a brilliant idea."

"I can't do that," our Sylvia wailed. "It might get him into bother with his dad. He's a bit scared of his dad."

"Oh, I see, it's alright to get *us* into bother, is it, but not him. Well, you've got a choice to make now, lady. You can either spy on Addison and company or you're out of this flat and into that bed and breakfast where you found Ulrika and her sprog. And not only that, but I shall have our Charmaine Bernadette took off you by the authorities. So now then."

"You couldn't do that, Mam. You can't make me homeless and childless."

"Oh, can't I? You didn't hesitate to risk making *us* homeless and bankrupt, just to satisfy your passions and indulge the spite of Arnold Addison."

"Listen to your mother," Iris said to her. (It's something I never thought I'd hear her recommend.)

"Well, what have I got to do?" our Sylvia says. "I don't want to break his heart. It'd break my heart to break his heart."

"You'll have to crack on that you still love him," Iris said.

"But I do," our Sylvia said.

"You've seen the sort of character he is. He's used you something merciless. Now it's your turn to turn the tables. You've got to be crafty."

Our Sylvia burst into tears. "You rotten old cows, the pair of you. You're going to make me lose him."

"You'll see that we've done you a favour in the end. There's nothing but heartbreak and misery to be had from this doomed affair," Iris said.

"Why don't you invite him round to Evergreen Close for his tea," I said. "Make out that you're anxious for him to meet us. We'll be as nice as pie, make him think we approve of this romance. Then you can start work on winkling out the information that we need."

"It's not nice. It isn't honest," our Sylvia sobbed.

"That's never worried you before. Especially as regards the benefits system," Iris said. (I thought to myself, she's some need to talk. Iris is a world champion at diddling the welfare.)

"What if I won't do it?" Sylvia said defiantly.

I went to the sideboard and picked up the key to the flat and waved it in her face. "This is hanging in the balance. If we can't trust you to keep your trap shut, you can sleep on a park bench tonight."

"Alright. Well, I'll prove to you that Ainsley is not the nasty piece of work that you think he is. I'm sure his father made him do it. I'll invite him round for his tea tonight and you can see for yourself how nice he is and that he means what he says about marrying me."

Well, she kept her word, and we closed the shop for the evening, not that anybody would miss it. She turns up at Evergreen Close with this Ainsley lad. A poorer specimen would be hard to imagine. Pale, thin, squeaky voice, everything that a romantic idle is not.

"Nice to meet you, Ainsley," I said, all smiles but taking note of his scrawny neck for purposes of future throttling, "being as how we're fellow tradespeople in a similar line of business."

"What, you mean we're both running fish and chip shops?"

I looked at Iris who was sighing with frustration. "Our Sylvia says you had a lovely time in Paris. Did you go up the Eiffel Tower? I believe that's in Paris, isn't it?"

"No, we never," he says. "We couldn't find it, could we Sylvia. We looked all over. Then it started raining so we stopped in the hotel most of the time, having drinks in the bar. There was a Burger King next door, so we didn't starve, did we Sylvia? We didn't go out much in case somebody spoke to us in French, and we couldn't understand them."

I tried not to roll my eyes, but I couldn't help thinking that perhaps he might make a good match for our Sylvia, being an ignoramus, just like her.

"How's your dad keeping, Ainsley?" Iris says.

"Well, y'know, he's alright."

"We admire his business skills, don't we Doreen? We wish we could run a successful business like that, all fair and square and honest."

"I haven't seen him for a while," Ainsley says. "Which suits me fine. He's horrible, I hate him." He suddenly stopped and bit his lip. "Sorry, I shouldn't have said that. Its nasty is that. Take no notice, Mrs Potts."

"I quite understand your feelings, Ainsley," I said. "I share them to a great extent. I expect it's hard to get close to a full-blown captain of industry like that, even if it is your dad. Mind you, with his stomach sticking out so far I don't suppose you can get that close to him in any sense."

I thought I might have overstepped the mark, but Ainsley suddenly burst out laughing.

"He is a bit of a fat sod, isn't he?" he said. "He's got this idea that I'm going to take over his empire when he's gone. He makes me go to these board meetings to plan new initiatives. I haven't got no initiatives. I'm not even sure what they are. He knows I don't like talking in front of posh people, but he insists that I say something at these meetings, so I just tell him what's going off locally with my branch."

"Oh, so that's how he came to know about Elvis the Gherkin and our plans for low fat chips, is it?"

"Yes. Your Sylvia told me about it, and I thought how clever it was. I just mentioned it for something to say at one of these board meetings. I'm surprised you never carried out your plans, Mrs Potts. I thought they was great ideas. Me dad thought they was, an'all. He decided to make his own versions. They're doing quite well."

"You know they were trade secrets, don't you?" Iris said. "We spent a fortune on R&D."

"Nobody said nothing to me about secrets. If your Sylvia had said they was secret I wouldn't have said a word. I love your Sylvia and I wouldn't do nothing to hurt her. Nor you, Mrs Potts." He looked at Iris, "Nor you Mrs Potts."

"And nobody said nothing to me about no secrets, neither," our Sylvia pipes up, "so you can't blame us."

"Well, it's a relief to know that betraying us and bringing us to the brink of ruin wasn't done with malice aforethought."

"So, Ainsley," Iris said, serving up the corned beef hash. "How did you and our Sylvia meet?"

"Well, if you remember, Mrs… er… If you remember, I came to your house once with me dad, when he was trying to buy your business off you. Do you remember? I saw your Sylvia then and me heart skipped a beat. It was love at first sight. I was smitten with her. When I went home, I couldn't stop thinking about her and so I made a point of seeking her out and we started knocking about together, didn't we Sylvia? I'm also took up with little Charmaine Bernadette. She's cute, in't she?"

"We think so," I said, warming to Ainsley, which was most unexpected given that I'd been ready to murder him ten minutes earlier.

Iris said: "What are your intentions as regards our Sylvia, Ainsley? She seems to be under the impression that there's matrimony in the offing."

"I don't know about that, but I was going to propose to her later in the week, when I've been to H. Samuels to get a ring. Me dad'll go mad when I tell him, but I don't care. I'm fed up of always doing what he wants."

"Quite right, lad," Iris says. "A young man should strike out on his own. But you want to choose your moment. Make sure you're OK for the future. Don't burn your bridges before you come to them."

We had a slice of Vienneta ice cream for pudding and a cup of tea. Then our Sylvia says: "Shall we go for a canal walk by the canal, Ainsley? I feel dead romantic."

The lad didn't need no persuading and off they went, a right pair of mismatched souls, him tall and gangly, her small and dumpy, both of them three sheets to the wind.

After they'd gone, and we were washing the pots, I said to Iris: "What do you think? Do you think he's genuine? He could be cracking on that he's as thick as a plank just to mislead us up the garden path. He could be using our Sylvia as an ongoing resource."

"I think he's probably doing that already, Doreen, although nothing to do with industrial espionage. Our Sylvia has always been free with her favours. But I think Ainsley's too naïve to be a spy. He's as daft as a brush. He wouldn't have the low cunning to deceive us."

"Just think—if all this is above board and Bristol fashion, our Sylvia could be marrying into a fortune. Imagine, when Arnold Addison drops dead from a heart attack— which he will if he doesn't start eating his own low-fat chips—Ainsley will be his heir. The whole Addison empire will be within our grasp."

Iris suddenly stopped wielding the dish cloth and looked thoughtful. "You're right, Doreen. This could be a turning point. If we plan carefully, Ainsley could be our lord and saviour. We've got to think this one through."

* * *

140

Iris was taking her time looking at all the options for exploiting Ainsley to the detriment of his father.

"What we've got to do is make sure Ainsley doesn't take no rash action that would get his father to disinherit him. We don't want changes to the will at this stage, or any family break ups. The most important thing is to keep the news of our Sylvia's infatuation away from Arnold. He'll go berserk if he hears about that and any plans for marriage."

"But our Sylvia won't be able to keep it to herself. You know she wears her heart up her sleeve," I said.

"Well, she's going to have to be told. This could benefit us all if we can keep Arnold in the dark."

So, we got Rotherham's very own low-rent Romeo and Juliet round to our house for top-level discussions.

"We've been thinking about your futures, haven't we Iris?"

Our Sylvia was straight on her high horse. "You can't do nothing. I'm over twenty-one, I can do what I like. You'll not stop me marrying him. We'll run off to Gretna Green, won't we Ainsley?"

Ainsley hutched up a bit closer to her on the settee to show solidarity and looked equally defiant. "We're going to get wed, Mrs Potts," he said and again turned to Iris, "and also Mrs Potts. We are both grown up adults. We can live our lives as we see fit."

"Look, Ainsley, love, I'm not trying to interfere with your life...well, only to a certain extent," I said. "I mean, what will your dad have to say about it all? You know he can't stick this family. Did you know he tried to harm us? Put a contract out on us, type of thing? Our lives were threatened, weren't they Sylvia?"

"Yes, but that had nowt to do with Ainsley, did it? He wasn't responsible for the fact that they was going to rough us up and chuck us down the stairs."

Ainsley was shocked. "This is the first I've heard about it, Sylvia. Me dad doesn't tell me nothing about what he's doing and that suits me fine, because I'm not interested."

"Oh yes, he put our Sylvia and Charmaine Bernadette at the mercy of a gang of yobbos. We had a narrow escape from a severe case of assault and battering. It was touch and go as to whether our Sylvia's pretty face was going to be rearranged."

"And you're saying me dad did it?"

"Well, not personally, of course, but he was responsible, I'm afraid Ainsley. He put them big lads up to it. We've got proof."

Ainsley looked shocked. "I know he can be a bugger in business, but I didn't think he'd do this to innocent people like Sylvia."

"So, you see, Ainsley," Iris said. "We're worried about our Sylvia's future."

"He'll not touch a hair on her head," Ainsley said, with a determination I hadn't seen from him before.

"I don't mean her physical safety," she says. "I mean her financial future. When you're a husband with a family to look after, you can't afford to put yourself in the poorhouse. If you upset your dad to the point that he renounces you and disinherits you out of his will, you'll not be in no position to look after Sylvia and any further children you might have. You want to keep in his good books for all your sakes."

"I know, but…"

"It'd be a tragedy to put yourself and our Sylvia—and bonny little Charmaine Bernadette—at risk of penury, wouldn't it?"

"I don't know," he said. "I don't really know what penury is."

"No, and I hope you never find out," Iris said.

Our Sylvia started to look shifty. She wriggled a bit in her seat and bit her bottom lip.

"The trouble is, mam, you see, the thing about it is…" She was struggling to get the words out, so I braced myself for more bad news. "Me and Ainsley are having a baby. And Ainsley's father, Mr Addison, will be the grandfather."

Iris audibly gasped. I felt a lead weight falling into my stomach.

After a bit I gathered myself and said: "Well, that's put a spanner in the bag. Have you told your father yet, Ainsley?"

"No," he said. "I'm waiting for the right moment."

Iris snorted: "There will never be a right moment for this news. He'll go off like Mount Venusian when you tell him. It'll make the destruction of Pompeii look like a kiddies fireworks display."

A look of fear came over Ainsley's face as he projected his mind into that dreaded confrontation.

"I shall have to tell him," he said. "After all, your Sylvia is going to present him with his first grandchild. He's got a right to know."

"I can't argue with you, lad," I said. "But don't fret, if worse comes to shove, there's always a place for you here. And if you want some backup, we can speak to him on your behalf and give our Sylvia a character reference."

"Hold on a second…" Iris said. "A character reference? Our Sylvia?"

Ainsley said: "I'd better tell him straight away before I lose me nerve. Will you come with me, Sylvia? He might not get violent if there's a pregnant woman who's having a baby involved."

"That's the way," Iris said. "You've got to take the bull between your teeth before your courage fails. And remember what Doreen says—you can always come here if it all goes bottoms up."

The two of them went out of the house looking as if they were off to a funeral. Mind you, knowing the lengths Arnold is prepared to go to, that might be the case.

* * *

Derek was not best pleased at the prospect of becoming a granddad for the second time. He was even less best pleased when I told him who the daddy was. "I wouldn't have thought he had it in him," was his only comment before he set off for work, glad to be out of it I suspect.

Iris and me knew that there was going to be consequences. Arnold must know by now and there had been silence from his direction. But it couldn't last and, of course, before long Arnold pitches up in his big motor car, walking up to the front door with a face like thunder. "Hey up, he's here," I says to Iris.

I let him in. He took his coat off and handed it to Iris as if she were the cloakroom attendant. "Pop that on a hook, grandma," he said without looking at her.

She chucked it directly on the floor.

"Now, what's going off here," he said. "My lad says your lass has got him into trouble."

"Eh?" I said. "It's her that's in trouble, carrying your Ainsley's kiddy—your grandkiddy."

He snorted. "Aye, well, I've only got your word for that. I understand your daughter has got form as regards having babbies out of wedlock. Don't worry, I've told him straight out that he's not marrying her—what's her name—Sally is it?"

"You know very well what her name is. And you also know very well that there are such things as DNA tests these days. I've seen it on Coronation Street—and Emmerdale. You'll not be able to deny who the father is when the child pops out and we send off for a kit."

"He's been entrapped, that's what he's been. Led astray by that strumpet of yours. Don't think I don't know what your game is. Setting him up so you can get your hands on my brass."

"Believe me, Arnold, I have no desire to see our Sylvia chained to your family in holy wedlock. She's better than that."

"I don't think so. I've had a few enquiries instituted about her. She leaves a lot to be desired as regards her former reputation. Oh no, she's not snaring our Ainsley. It'd break his mother's heart to see her only child married to a hussy like her. She'd never be able to face the vicar again."

"Might I remind you…" says Iris.

"You keep out of it, granny. It's not something old folk need concern themselves with. Go and have a cup of Sanatogen."

"Might I remind you," Iris continued, regardless, "that both these children are adults. They are both over twenty-one and if they decide that their future is together as man and wife, there's nowt you nor nobody else can do about it."

"Is that right?" he said. "Well, we'll see about that. There's more ways than one way to skin a moggie. Don't forget I've still got control of my own money and I can insure you that none of it is coming your way. Not a brass farthing. Oh no, you won't win against me—any more than you did with your shop." He gave a nasty little snigger. "How is the shop going by the way? Still tottering along is it?"

As he picked his coat up, Iris stuck her face right up against his, jutting out her chin in a threatening manner. "We know you were responsible for that attack on Balaclava Street. Don't deny it. Them men you hired didn't fare so well, did they? They was seen off by a friend of mine—you might have heard of him, Syd Warren."

The smirk on Arnold's face was replaced by a shifty frown. "I don't know to what you are alluding to," he said, pulling his coat over his vast girth. "That were nowt to do with me and there's no way you can connect me with it."

"All I'm saying," says Iris with a voice full of threats and menaces, "is that Syd has vowed to take care of this family. Doreen will back me up on this, she was there when he said it. The last thing he said to us after your thugs had frightened us to death was, 'let me know if you have any more bother from that Addison bloke and I'll make sure he won't be in any position to do it again.' Yes, he mentioned you by name."

144

"I can confirm everything that Iris says," I said. "He's a scary chap is that Syd Warren. You wouldn't want to get on the wrong side of him."

"You're not frightening me with your silly tales," he said. "It'll take more than that old witch and her overactive gob to scare me."

"Well, if you think it's silly tales, I suggest you have a word with them heavies you employed. I think the broken faces might tell a different story. A horror story."

"I've had enough of this," Arnold says, making for the door. "She's off her rocker that mother-in-law of yours, Doreen. But make no mistake, I shall continue with my plans to expand the Chips & More! empire on Balaclava Street. But it will all be legitimate and above board. I shan't have to lift a finger."

He put his gloves on and the smirk returned. "As I understand it, your pathetic little shop will be on the scrapheap of history before the month's out. Tell me I'm wrong, Doreen. You can't, can you? That'll give me the opportunity to get the shop at a bargain price and double the capacity of Chips & More! I might even set up a sit-down restaurant in the extra space. Oh yes, it's just a matter of waiting and watching and enjoying the sight of the last bits of your cash dribbling through your fingers."

He opened the door. "And you can get the sound of wedding bells out of your ears. There's to be no nuptials—not for our Ainsley and that lass of yours, anyroad."

He slammed the door hard enough to cause splinters.

"Well," says Iris, "he's blind-sided us this time. I don't think we'll be able to manipulate him with the use of the grandkid. He's not going to put up with our Sylvia being a member of his family, child or no child. And that means no inheritance and that means goodbye Mr Chips to our chip shop. I thought the ball was in our court, but he's put the boot right on the other hand now."

* * *

Iris and me were sitting in the front room, trying to ponder what we could salvage from the wreck of the shop, when the door opens and Beryl Cathcart from next door comes in.

"Hello, Beryl," I said, hardly daring to look at her as she saw her life savings going down the swanee with our hopes and dreams. "Come and have a cup of tea."

145

"I've got some news for you both," she said. "It's regarding the chip shop. I've come up with an idea."

"It'd better be a good one," said Iris, despondently. "Because we're looking at total annihilation by Arnold Addison."

Beryl took this letter out of her pocket. "I saw an advert in the *Advertiser*. It was from this TV company, looking for a suitable location for their new series. *Celebrity Shopkeeper* it's called. Apparently, they want to film a different celebrity each week trying to run a local business. They want to show how difficult it is for independent traders to make a living when they're up against these multi—nationals. They think it will be hilarious, but also make an important point."

Iris perked up a bit.

"Well," says Beryl, "I wrote off to them for further particulars, mentioning that I was an investor in just the right place for them. A woman rings me up from this TV company, and she says they are interested. They think a local chip shop will be an ideal location for one of their programmes. They're thinking of a comedian to run it for a week, see how they get on."

"That's well-spotted Beryl. This is interesting," Iris said, stroking her chin.

"But what's in it for us?" I said.

"Well," Beryl says, "they're offering what she called a location fee, and they'll repair any damage that is done by this comedian showing off and breaking things."

"And not only that, but think of the publicity," Iris said. "This could put us on the national map. Oh yes, this could be a game changer."

"But Iris," I said, "we're on the brink of a complete financial collapse. We've used up all the credit that the bank will allow. My cards are maxed out, there are unpaid bills piled up in the waste bin. I've juggled and lied to buy us time, but there's only so long you can rob Peter to pay the piper. We simply can't keep going long enough to wait for this TV programme to happen—if it ever does. It could be months away."

"Listen," said Beryl. "I'm so excited about this idea that if they decide to go ahead with it, I'll put up another few thousands. I've not touched me Premium Bonds. But they could keep us going just long enough."

"Oh no," I said. "You've done enough, Beryl, I can't let you…"

146

Iris grabbed my arm to stop me. "You mind your business, Doreen. Beryl's got a mind of her own, let her do what she feels is right."

All the same, I don't think Iris is motivated entirely by concern for Beryl's financial welfare.

* * *

So, we arranged with this woman at the TV Company, Snark Productions, to come round for 'negotiations' as Iris calls it. Fiona was her name. Nice lass, about 30, beautifully dressed in designer jacket and slacks, very charming although somewhat poshly-spoken.

"I think you've got a vague idea of what we're planning," she said to Iris and Beryl and me, as we sat in the front room with her. "It's basically entertainment but with a serious social purpose. We know that small businesses are having a bad time at the moment, and we wanted to show what this means in reality for the proprietors. Each of our celebrities will take on a struggling business for a week and see if they can turn it round. We've got Jim Loxley MP taking on the butcher's shop and Annie Soper from Gogglebox doing the mini-mart."

"And who's going to be doing the chip shop?" I asked.

"Well, our initial thought was Charlie Wilkinson from the quarter final of Swimming with the Stars," she said "but then we thought maybe Clara Ellis who came fifth in Masterchef in 1993. We haven't settled on it yet."

I said, "I don't want to seem rude, Fiona, love, but I thought we was talking about celebrities here? Charlie Wilkinson? Clara Ellis? I've never heard of them."

Iris snorted with contempt. "Oh, don't worry, Doreen," he says, "they've bandied the word celebrity about so much on the television that it's become meaningless. Celebrity these days just means they've had their photo in the *Daily Mail* with their doo-dahs on show."

Fiona looked narked. "You've got to understand that our programme is not a prime-time show. If it was on, say, BBC1 at 9 o'clock, that would be different. As it is, we have budget restraints. It would be lovely to have big stars, but we just can't afford it."

"So, what are you expecting from us?" I asked.

"Well, beyond the use of the chip shop for filming, there would probably be interviews and an assessment of how the celebrity is doing. There'll be three episodes for each shop, Monday to Wednesday, and you'd be required to score him at the end. We hope it's going to be great fun—lots of opportunities for disaster."

"Oh dear," said Iris, "it's going to be one of them celebrity shows where they cock everything up for the sake of the cameras. You know the sort of thing—they get on a baking show and end up dropping their cake on the floor. It's all so fake and staged. It gets on my chest that kind of thing." She turned to Fiona. "If you want slapstick with your fish and chips, send for Laurel and Hardy—at least they'd be funny."

"Don't worry, Iris, as well as the celebrities, we've got a retail expert on hand, Maxwell Horton he's called. He's going to analyse the businesses and find the weak spots and then try to come up with a rescue plan."

"We need more than an expert to solve our problems with Chips & More! we need a genius," I said. "The man who owns Chips & More! is trying to run us aground."

"Oh really? Oh, that's perfect," Fiona says, "this is going to add an excellent bit of drama, a bit of conflict. Before the end of the week, we'll have the viewers rooting for you. A David and Goliath battle. Fantastic. And the good thing is that we can edit the show to give the impression you're coming out on top. It's all good human interest stuff. We'll end on a cliff-hanger each episode to make sure the viewers come back for more."

She looked round at us, trying to work out what we were thinking from our expressions.

Well, ladies, what do you think?

Beryl was all for it. "What is there to lose?" she said.

"Our dignity," Iris said. "They can make you look right fools if it suits their purpose."

"Oh no, Iris, we wouldn't do that. The whole purpose of the show is to explore your dilemma in a positive light. There are hundreds of small shops around the country in your situation. You'll be the heroes. Can I tell my producer that we're on?"

"I'm on," Beryl said again, full of excitement.

"Oh, go on then," Iris said.

And finally, I gave it my blessing and Fiona seemed well satisfied. She promised to have all the papers drawn up, the legal wavers (no idea what that is).

"And the cheque for our troubles?" Iris said, "will that be drawn up, too?"

"Of course," said Fiona. "I'll be in touch with details in a couple of days."

* * *

Our Sylvia is walking about in a dream. She keeps singing "I'm in Love with a Wonderful Guy" as she dispenses the haddock and chips (with and without mushy peas). I've never seen her so happy. I'm pleased for her because she's wanted a decent boyfriend for some considerable time. Her and Ainsley have been together now for eight months, which is twice as long as any of her previous boyfriends.

Oh yes, Ainsley's a good lad—if you leave aside the fact that he's as dim as a nine bob note. I'm coming to really like him. He seems to properly care about our Sylvia and little Charmaine Bernadette. He's always showering her with presents and little treats.

He lives in the flat over the Chips & More! so him and our Sylvia are next door neighbours. After close of business, they take turns at popping round to each other's flats and cuddling up on the settee to watch *Celebrity HGV Drivers* on the television. Our Sylvia's condition is starting to show now, the little babby inside her is kicking and Ainsley keeps popping round from his shop to ours to check that she's alright and having a feel of her belly. In the end, I gave her extended leave of absence, given that there isn't really enough work in the shop for the three of us.

Ansley's dad is still fizzing furious about the romance. I think he's banking on it all falling apart due to our Sylvia's flighty reputation. But this one's different. In the past she's given off the wrong signals with her short skirts and tight jumpers. Well, of course, if you carry on like that, you're bound to attract lads who are just after one thing, and when they've had it, you won't see them for dust. She was in perpetual mourning about the end of one hopeless relationship after another.

But now, Ainsley's showing a more general interest in her. He's not just after a quick fling and then goodbye dolly grey. He's got domestic ambitions. He's talking in terms of them moving in together and starting to create a cosy little home for our Charmaine Bernadette and whoever else is on the way. I can't wait to see the new addition. I love babbies.

One evening, Iris and me were in the shop, waiting for the customer that never comes, and in strides Fatso Addison.

"What're you after?" Iris said sharply, by way of welcome.

"Never you mind, grandma. I want to speak to the organ grinder, not the monkey," Arnold says.

"As it happens, I'm forty per cent organ grinder in this business," she said. "Now, what is it you're after?"

He turned to me. "You've never gone into business with that old bat, have you Doreen? If you have, you're dafter than you look, and that takes some doing. That mother-in-law of yours is doolally. Sooner you put her away the better."

Iris was so furious she couldn't say anything, so she pulled her tongue out at him.

"Look," he said, "We've got to get this business of our Ainsley and that lass of yours sorted. If it's money she's after, we can open negotiations."

"They seem very happy together," I said. "There is no need to break them up and I don't think any amount of money is going to force them apart. He reveres her. They're deeply in love."

"Deeply in love? Sentimental claptrap. Deeply in love me aunt Fanny! Everybody's got their price, Doreen, now put in your first bid."

"You're a heartless great lump," Iris said. "Is money all you ever think about?"

Arnold turned to her and said: "If I'm not wrong, that is precisely what you are thinking about. Am I right? Of course I am. Conniving to get your hands on my hard-earned brass."

He took a breath and calmed down a bit. He'd been getting a bit red in the face. "Now look, we could see your Sandra—or whatever she's called—very comfortable. And she's no need to be saddled with another babby. I could arrange that for her. I've got medical contacts who could relieve her of the burden. It could all be over by this time tomorrow."

150

"You're a monster," Iris says. "You'll never get our Sylvia to harm that bairn. She's looking forward to having another mouth to feed, even if she can't afford it. And so is your Ainsley. He'd be devastated if he thought he wasn't going to be a father."

"His life will be ruined if he ends up with her hanging round his neck," Arnold shouted, going red again. "And the thought of having her genetic jeans being mixed up with mine makes me heave. But I'll tell you this, if he doesn't change his mind, he'll be no son of mine. I shall disown him—and that'll spike his guns. And yours an'all."

"Well, who'd benefit from that?" I said. "You'd be cutting off your face to spite your nose. Ainsley's your only chance of keeping your bloodline going."

Arnold harrumphed and looked round the shop. "What I don't understand is how you're still in business. I happen to know that your funds have run dry."

"We have a new investor, thank you," Iris announced, with great pride.

"Who's that, then? Somebody even dafter than you, you old crow. They must have more money than sense, whoever it is. Chucking good money after bad. Who is it?"

"Maybe you should send your spies round to find out," I said. "You'll have to get a new one, though, because your Ainsley has sworn allegiance to his perspective new family. You'll not be able to use him against us again. He were right upset when he found out you'd used him to get at us. Well, you want to watch out, Mr Chips & More! you've got a big surprise coming."

"Oh aye, what's that, then? Another of your crack-brained schemes?"

I smiled at him in a way that suggested we had something up our sleeve that he wouldn't like.

His eyes narrowed. "Whatever it is you're up to," he said, "it had better not be nothing to my detriment or I shall kick off again."

"Oh, but you won't," Iris says, with a smile of triumph, "not unless you want your face knocking straight off the front of your head, compliments of a dear friend of mine called Syd Warren."

He gave her a murderous look and stomped out.

* * *

The next big surprise came when our Sylvia revealed that her and Ainsley was engaged to be married. She came waltzing into the house with a great big grin on her face to tell us.

"He got down on his knees and everything and proposed, just like you're supposed to."

I thought about Derek's proposal to me, all them years since. "Do yer fancy getting married?" he said to me one day out of the blue in the pub. "Oh yes," I said, "I didn't know you were even thinking about it." Then he went to the bar and got me a brandy and Babycham and no more was mentioned until me mother arranged the church and sorted out a reception in our front room. And that were it. About as romantic as a bout of measles.

"Int'it smashing, Mam? And, he's bought me a gorgeous ring," our Sylvia says, flashing this diamond solitaire as though it was part of the crown jewels. "Int'it lovely mam, though, int'it smashing, int'it gorgeous?"

"Oh, it's lovely, is that, Sylvia," says Iris, taking hold of her hand so she could examine it more closely. "It looks expensive, an'all. You want to look after that because in a hundred years' time they'll have it on the Antiques Roadshow and they'll all be going mad over it."

Our Sylvia gave a little sigh of pleasure. I've never seen her so happy.

* * *

On the Monday morning Fiona and her producer/presenter Stephanie arrived to put final preparations in place for the TV filming. Stephanie was another posh lass, but a bit older, carrying a big briefcase stuffed with papers.

They poked around the shop and then Stephanie says to me: "Now Doreen, we're going to install some hidden cameras around the place so that we can film all the antics without people feeling self-conscious about it. Is that OK? We'll be monitoring it all from a room upstairs. The young lady who lives there has rented it to us for the week. We'll make sure everything's left as we found it."

Iris stepped forward. "Antics?" she said. "What do you mean by antics?"

"Well," said Stephanie, "you'll have Des McIntyre with you for the week, and he's bound to want to inject a bit of fun."

"Who?" says Iris.

"Des McIntyre," says Stephanie. "Host of *Use It or Lose It*, the latest hit quiz show on Channel 5."

"Never heard of it," said Iris, "although it sounds mucky to me. The doctor used to say to my husband 'use it or lose it' when he was having trouble with the functioning of his downstairs department."

"Oh no, it's a family show," said Stephanie. "You'll like Des, he's a real laugh."

Iris didn't crack so much as a polite smile. "I hope he isn't going to get on my nerves," she said. "I don't like people laughing indoors and I'm not keen on people with big faces, neither. Has he got a big face?"

"Don't be unreasonable, Iris," I said. "He's a comedian. It's his job to show off and amuse folk. And the size of his face is not germane to nothing."

"Well," said Stephanie, suddenly not quite sure she'd made the right decision about us, "our engineers will be in later today to install the cameras and mikes, and we'll start filming in the morning if that's OK. I just want you to carry on with your usual routine and when Des arrives, just treat him as you would any new employee. Give him a brief induction course and then, when that's done, let him work a shift in the shop. Then we'll ask you to assess his performance and give him a score out of five. Would he or wouldn't he make a good Mein Host of your business? Take into account everything, including how he gets on with the customers as well as his technical skill with the frier and with his knowledge of fish species."

"That all sounds straightforward," I said to Stephanie, but Iris was still pulling a face like an angry pug. Stephanie thought about shaking her hand on the way out, but she was met with that speciality scowl that is unique to Iris. It intimidated Stephanie to the point that she just said: "Well, goodbye ladies," and left.

"That was a bit rude, Iris," I said.

But like everything that Iris does, it was premedicated. There was a method in her madness.

"If they want a show, we'll give them a show," she said. And then she noticed that Stephanie had left a file of papers behind on the table.

* * *

153

Apparently, this programme is now going to be called *Service with a Smile* although they're going to have to work hard to get a smile out of Iris. We were in the shop bright and early, making sure everything was sparkling.

Then Stephanie turns up with her crew, to let us know that Des McIntyre was due in at ten. All the cameras and microphones they'd installed at various points in the shop had been tested and were working. From upstairs they could watch us and record us from all angles. It was a bit creepy to think we was under surveillance at all times, but they insured me that they had not installed a camera in the lav, so we couldn't be caught occasionally forgetting to wash us hands, and we were all set to go.

Well, ten o'clock came and no sign of Des McIntyre. Half past ten and still he hadn't turned up. Iris looked up at one of the cameras and said: "Excuse me, but how long are we supposed to be standing here like spare parts?"

"He should be here soon enough," Stephanie said, talking to us through a microphone she'd also had installed upstairs. "We're trying to contact him now."

Eleven o'clock came and went and Iris kept glaring angrily into one camera or another.

At a quarter to one a taxi pulls up outside and out he gets, this Des McIntyre.

He was tall and slim, mid-thirties I would think, wearing a fabulously tailored navy-blue suit, very flattering to his figure. There's no getting away from it, he's a good-looking lad—hair beautifully coiffed, clean-shaven and a spotless complexion.

Iris was not impressed. As he paid the driver she said: "Look at the size of his face. I can't be doing with people with big faces."

"So you've made clear," I said. "Try to be pleasant to him."

Des comes into the shop, all hail-fellow-well-met sort of thing. Obviously thinking his very presence was a treat for us.

"Hello, ladies, lovely to meet you. I'm Des McIntyre," he says, all fake smiles. I thought: he knows he's being filmed. These so-called celebrities can sniff a camera out at a hundred paces. "I think we're going to have a fun few days together don't you think? It should make a cracking show. I'll just have a coffee and then we can think about starting."

Iris walked straight up to him. "Where do you think you've been?" she barked in her I'm-not-amused voice. "We've been waiting here like fools."

"Sorry…" he started to say, but Iris cut him off with angry gesture. He was about six foot two and she's five foot nothing, so it made quite a comical sight with her chuntering at him at chest level. I thought to myself, they're both going to have cricks in their necks before the end of the day, with him looking down and her looking up all the time.

"I'll tell you something, my lad," she said, "If you really was starting work at this shop and you pitched up at this time, you'd be out on your ear straight off. Where do you think you've been anyroad?"

He tried to smile thinking Iris was just joking, but when he realised she wasn't, and that his usual I'm-in-charge approach wasn't going to work, he said: "Where's Stephanie? I think I need to have a little word."

"Never mind where Stephanie is," Iris said. "And never mind having little words. You're supposed to be working for us now. Haven't they explained the rules of this programme? Now, why are you so late?"

Des was a bit discombobulated by Iris who was in her scary Yorkshire terrier mode. On his quiz show he was always the one in authority, asking folk personal questions, showing them up when they were nervous and pulling them about so that they were standing in the right place. He wasn't going to come that with Iris.

She stood there looking at him with her hands on her hips, as if to say "Well?"

"I had to see my agent, there was an urgent matter I had to discuss. It went on a bit longer than I'd thought, but nothing for you to concern yourself about."

"I'm not in the least concerned," Iris said, "But what your behaviour tells me is that you put your agent's needs well ahead of ours. Do you know we've been sitting here twiddling our thumbs for nearly two hours while you go gallivanting off to meetings and not telling us about it? It's clear you don't think our time is worth anything, is that what you're saying?"

Looking increasingly like a little lad caught pinching sweets from the comer shop, Des said: "Well, I'm sorry. It wasn't my intention

155

to inconvenience you. I'll try harder tomorrow. Where is Stephanie, by the way?"

Iris pointed at one of the cameras. "She's up there, and I hope when you meet with her, she's going to give you a similar rollicking to the one I'm giving you. And dock your wages. It's most disrespectful treating us like that."

Des looked up at the camera. "Are you there, Steph? If you are, can we have a bit of a pow-wow, please?"

"No, you can't," Iris shouted. She looked up at the camera: "He's not available for no pow-wows, Stephanie, given that he's wasted enough of our time this morning already having pow-wows with his agent." She turned back to Des. "You're supposed to be working here and we're supposed to be training you. So, get your coat off and roll up your sleeves and we'll get started. You might regret wearing that expensive shirt as well before the day's out."

Des was looking up at the camera with a pleading expression in his eyes. There was no response from upstairs.

"Well?" Iris barked. "Coat. Sleeves. Chop-chop."

He was reluctant, but Des realised that nobody was coming to his rescue and so he had to follow Iris's instructions.

She started off apprising him with what she called "the ground rules".

"To start with," she told him, "there'll be no acting about in this shop. This is a proper job, not an excuse for a lot of show biz showing off."

"But…" he said.

"And if I find you're spoiling food in the process of trying to get a laugh, I shall have something to say about it. Is that clear? If you start dropping fish on the floor or knocking over jars of pickled eggs to entertain your viewers, you'll have me to answer to."

Des was completely flummoxed.

"And I don't want you wasting time telling jokes to the customers. They come in here for their supper not to hear about the Englishman, Irishman and Scotchman. So, get the grub served and move on. Is that clear?"

"Look, Iris," Des said. "You're not being fair. This is supposed to be an entertainment programme, not The World at War. They've brought me in to lighten things up, not be berated by an Eva Braun wannabe. I'm here to get ratings. I'm a big draw on reality television. I think you ought to have some respect for me as well as the other way round."

"Respect has to be earned," she said. "And you haven't got off to a very good start. I thought this was supposed to be about rescuing our shop from ruin and that isn't funny. Why they've fetched a comic in, I can't fathom."

"I think there's a bit of confusion about all this," Des said, but before he could expand his point, Iris handed him a white coat and a cap. He looked pleadingly at the camera again, but once more there was no response. I just looked on open-mouthed as the rottweiler continued to worry its prey.

"Right, let's crack on," she said. "We've got to catch up for lost time."

* * *

I don't know what's got into Iris, she's a right tartar as regards that poor Des. I think he's wishing he'd never got involved. She gave him a run-through of the health and safety regulations and warned him that if he did anything that resulted in a visit from the authorities, there'd be hell to pay. She then tested whether he'd been paying attention by quizzing him on the topic as if it was the specialist subject on Mastermind. All it lacked was the drumbeats and the black chair.

She explained the process of firing up the friers and getting the oil to the right temperature, and then chipping the potatoes. She then let him try it himself. She had a beady eye on him at all times, looking for any signs of playing to the gallery. He was ever so tense as he fed the taters into the chipper, worried that he might accidentally drop one and bring down the wrath of Iris.

On his own show, he had these games involving balls and balloons and balancing things on top of one another while blindfolded. Some of those games were quite hard and if the contestants were cack-handed and mucked it up, he would humiliate them merciless. Now the boot was on the other hand.

After he'd done the chips without mishap, we came to the enrobing of the fish fillets with batter. "Doreen will explain the process. She is fully conversant with it. In fact, if they issued certificates in fish battering, she'd have a gold medal, so take notice and learn from an expert."

I explained the formula to him—take the fillet, hold it by one end then dip it in the batter. One drag to the left, one drag to the right, one more to the left, then let it drip for a moment, then straight into the oil.

Des picked up the fish and held it over the batter pan. "Ooh, this is messy," he said with a childish grin, "I'm going to enjoy this,".

Iris was straight on him. "You're not thinking of abusing that batter are you? You're not being tempted to pretend you can't manage it and then splash it all over? This is not *What's My Line*— or whatever that dam quiz show of yours is called. This is about feeding the nation, not causing uproar. Supper is a serious business round here and laughing in a chip shop is not appreciated."

"No, I've gathered that," Des said, despondently.

After we'd been through the process and timing of frying the fish and the chips in separate friers, Iris explained the process of shovelling the chips into the boxes and placing the fish on top. He was being far too mingy with the chips in her opinion and she had to reprimand him again. "Folk round here like plenty of chips, a mountain of them. Give it to them or they won't come back."

Then she had to tell him about the many other aspects of a fish supper, how to tell cod from haddock, the difference between wrapped and open, the various pickles and meat pies, the correct way to ladle mushy peas and when it was appropriate to include fish scraps.

Des was picking it up reasonably well and, by teatime, we deemed him ready to assist with service the following day.

At this point Stephanie came into the shop with a cameraman, toting a big camera on his shoulder. She was all smiles.

"That was fabulous," she said. "Well done ladies. This is going to be great."

"What about me?" Des said. "That was one of the hardest day's work I've done for ages. And I have to object to the way I'm being treated by these ladies. There's not much scope for comedy here."

"Oh, put your big boy pants on," Iris scolded.

"Now, the last thing on the agenda for today is the scoring," said Stephanie. "This is where we rate how Des has done on his first day." She signalled to the cameraman to start filming.

"What did you think of Des's performance today, Mesdames Potts?"

"He's going to have to pull his socks up," said Iris.

"I've done everything you asked, and I've done a good job of it, too," complained Des. "It's like being in Wormwood Scrubs with Cruella de Ville in charge."

"You was over an hour late this morning, which is going to cost you points on the scoreboard."

"And what about you, Doreen? How would you rate Des?" said Stephanie.

"Well," I said, not wanting to be quite as brutal as Iris. "He did OK. He battered the cod lovely, but then he unfortunately left it in the oil too long. When he took it out, the batter was dark brown, bordering on black, not the lovely golden that it's supposed to be. But I'm sure he'll get it right with practice. We all have to learn."

"So, now to the score," Stephanie said. "Iris, please rate Des out of five."

She didn't hesitate: "One," she said. "That late arrival got right on my chest. I'm still fizzing about it. I can't be doing with tardiness, so he'd better look sharp in future and get here on the dot."

"Just a minute," said Des, all miffed. "I don't think you're being entirely fair here..."

"Excuse me," says Iris, all bossy, "I think it's us what's scoring you, not the other way round."

Stephanie and the cameraman were trying hard not to laugh.

"And you, Doreen?"

I tried to moderate what I said so as not to completely destroy Des. "Well, he did his best and he hasn't made too many mistakes. And he's got very lovely teeth, just like they are on telly, so I'll give him four. I'm afraid I agree with Iris, though, that the late-coming was really aggravating, otherwise it would have been five, or even six due to his teeth."

Stephanie turned to the camera and said, "Well, there we are, the first day of Des McIntyre's assignment at the Balaclava Street fish and chip shop here in sunny Rotherham. Hardly a resounding success for Des, but he's still got two days to redeem himself. Join us tomorrow, when Des will be let loose on the hungry customers."

Des let out a great sigh. "God, I'll be glad to get back to the hotel and have a drink after the day I've had with these two."

"Well, you'll be able to do that when you've finished cleaning up," says Iris.

"Cleaning up?" says Des.

"Yes," said Iris. "You know from the extensive training I've given you in health and safety that the place has to be left immaculate at close of business each day. We're not going to flout the rules. You'll find the cleaning materials, including mop and bucket, in that cupboard in the back. Just leave everything sparkling and then your time'll be your own."

Des turned to Stephanie: "This is ridiculous, Steph. I never signed on to be an under-house parlour maid."

"Everybody knows that when you're apprenticed to a new job you have to do the skivvying," Iris reminded him. "It's traditional that the junior employee has to clear up. And make sure you do it right. I shall be back in an hour to inspect and if you've left so much as a speck of muck, you'll be kept behind until its fettled to my satisfaction."

"I don't think so," said Des, defiantly.

"Well, if you don't, this whole charade will be over. And if this programme doesn't get finished because of something you've done, I understand there's a penalty clause in your contract. No programme, no cash. Isn't that right, Stephanie?

Stephanie nodded, a bit embarrassed, "Well, yes, that's true—but how did you know that, Iris?"

She produced the file Stephanie had left behind. "You forgot this when you was here last. I didn't mean to read it but I'm afraid I'm compulsively nosey. It's a diagnosed condition I've got. I couldn't help it. But, there again, me and Doreen have no such obligations to remain, have we Doreen? We haven't signed no binding contract."

"No," I said. "We're as free as birds, we can walk out any time, no problem."

"Charming," said Des to Stephanie, "what kind of confidentiality does your firm provide, when any Tom, Dick or Iris seems to know my private business?"

He was furious and was obviously contemplating storming out, but after a moment's thought about the consequences, he went into the back and we could hear the angry rattling of mops, brushes and buckets.

Stephanie signalled to the cameraman to stop filming and the two of them let out the laughter they had been holding in. They were tittering as they left.

* * *

When we got home, I said to Iris: "That was a bit cruel. You showed that lad up something dreadful. He almost looked as though he was going to burst out crying."

"Well, they said they wanted a show and we're giving them one. It won't be like any of the other episodes they're making, where everybody bows down to the so-called celebrity and tries their best to be polite and charming. Our episode is going to stick out like a sore thumb."

"Does that mean that Des is in for another mauling? He's such a handsome lad, I could fancy him meself?" I said.

"His face it too big for my liking. It's out of proportion," she said.

"It looks alright to me. Although I've a suspicion he's got cosmetics on to make his skin look that smooth."

"And he smells like a mucky woman's boudoir. He's wearing more scent than they've got on that knock-off stall in the market."

"You shouldn't hold that against him, Iris. I wish my Derek would use a bit of after shave from time to time. It sometimes smells as though I'm in bed with a wet dog."

"Mr McIntyre has got to be shown his place," she said.

"I don't know how you can do it, Iris, being so nasty to such a nice lad."

But a moment's thought told me that I know exactly how she can do it, having been on the receiving end myself often enough.

* * *

Day two of the filming and Iris was giving Des (who was there on the dot of ten o'clock, now dressed in more suitable clothing) instructions on the correct way to wrap orders for taking out. He mucked up the first few efforts and she berated him until he got it right. I can see that this would have been an excellent opportunity for a bit of the usual clumsiness that gets these reality stars a cheap laugh. But Iris wasn't going along with any of that.

Then we had a run-through of a serving. I had to pretend to be a customer while Iris stood beside Des, issuing detailed instructions.

I walked up to the counter and he said to me: "What can I get you?"

Iris stopped him. "No, no, no. You have to make it personal. Say something like: 'Is your Maureen out of the hospital yet? She's having a hard time, isn't she, what with one thing and another'. We're trying to make the customers feel as though they're amongst personal friends."

Des replied: "But I don't know any of the people coming in the shop. How am I supposed to ask about their family if I've never seen them before?"

"You'll soon get to know the regulars," Iris said. "See that little book under the counter? If anybody comes up with a titbit that you can refer to at a later date, make a note of it."

Des looked confused. Iris then reminded him that he was not here as a TV personality for the duration of this exercise, but as a simple fast-food retailer. "Don't take no notice if they start asking for autographs or wanting to ask questions about your private life. We don't want none of that. Now try again. Remember: personal. It's about them, not you."

So, he turns back to me and says: "Hello, Doreen, how's that cow of a mother-in-law of yours, doing? Still using her face to strip paint, is she?"

I couldn't help but laugh. Iris realised he'd got one up on her, so she ignored it and said to him: "Come on, ask what she wants. We're here to shift fish and chips, not pass the time of day."

"I'll have a rock salmon, two portions of chips, a fishcake, two pickled gherkins, one meat and potato pie and a saveloy," I said to him. "You'd better include a can of Tizer with that. How much do I owe you?"

Again, he was tongue-tied, looking round for help.

"Come on lad," chivvied Iris. "You've got to reckon up faster than that. Did they not teach you mental arithmetic at school? When they come down from the factory with the lunchtime order, they'll want a lot of different things, including cans of pop and the occasional Cornetto, and they don't want their lunch break wasted while you try to compute simple adding up. It's not exactly rocket surgery, is it?"

Des was stymied, so Iris got one of the menus off the plastic table with all the prices on it.

"Take that back to your hotel tonight and memorise it. There'll be a test tomorrow, so don't think about skipping it. Now..." she said, "Having taken your order, you need to pack it and take the money. So, let's see you pack everything appropriately."

Des looked at her, then at me. "What was it you wanted?" he asked.

Iris sighed loudly. "You can't be asking everybody twice what it was they wanted. You'll have to listen properly and commit it to memory. Doreen can remember a fifteen-item order first time of asking, and she's not exactly Alfred Einstein, is she?"

And so it went on, everything that Des did, Iris found fault with. His confidence was sinking slowly through the floor. His TV persona—'everybody look at me' type of thing—was nowhere to be found.

Eventually we stopped for a tea break and Stephanie came down to join us.

"This is great stuff," she said. "I'm really enjoying it."

"You're enjoying seeing me being made a fool of," said Des. "Iris is getting away with murder. I expect I look like a right berk. I want you to put that right in the editing, Steph. I want you to take out her jibes and insults and give me the chance to shine a bit. I can hardly get a word in edgeways with her."

"Well, that's up to the editor," she said. "I'm sure it will be balanced in the final cut. When we've had tea, I think we'll stop for today. We'll just do the scoring and then you'll be free to go…"

Iris quickly reminded Des "*You'll* be free to go when the place has been cleaned up to my satisfaction…".

Des was furious but he knew he had to buckle down. Iris put her coat on and went home with a satisfied smile on her face. But I decided to stop behind and help Des out. I felt that sorry for him.

We soon whipped through the chores and he was grateful.

"I was thinking of having a little meeting this evening to discuss how things are going – you know, with Steph. We're going out to dinner and I was wondering if you'd like to join us? After all, you're an important cog in the wheel, being the owner of this place."

"Only partial owner. You know that Iris also has a stake."

"Yes, but as I understand it, you're the majority shareholder, right? The chairman of the board sort of thing."

"Well, yes."

"Then you're the one who should be present at the planning meetings. Besides, it would be nice to get to know you a bit better, socially I mean."

He smiled and them glorious teeth was revealed again. And I couldn't help noticing how green his eyes were. If only I was ten

163

years younger (well, maybe fifteen) I would have jumped on him there and then. I was getting a bit swoony and thinking "Am I in with a chance here?"

"Oh, that would be lovely," I said. "What time shall you pick us up?"

"Just you, Doreen, the little ferret is not included. I always think these business meetings work better with just the principals involved. The more people you have, the more acrimonious it gets."

I thought, yes, what you really mean is if Iris comes along it'll be World War Three. And that isn't good for the digestion.

* * *

At home I told Derek about how awful his mother was being to Des McIntyre.

"It can't be that bad," he said. "Me mother wouldn't hurt a fly. Perhaps he's misunderstanding her."

I said to Iris: "You know, the worm is going to turn before long. No man is in Ireland. He won't stand that level of showing up before he cracks."

"All the better," says Iris. "We're going to be TV stars, Doreen, and the shop is going to be famous. Just you watch what happens."

* * *

When I came downstairs, all dolled up in my best TK Maxx evening gown, lipstick applied, perfume daubed on, Derek didn't even notice, but Iris was on it in a flash. "Where are you going with your best frock on?" she said.

"I'm going to a business meeting with Des and Stephanie," I said. I'd been dreading telling her because I knew she'd hit the roof.

"Why didn't you tell me earlier—now I'm going to have to rush to get ready," she said.

"Sorry, Iris, you aren't on the guest list," I said. "Only the principals in this matter are included."

Her face turned thunderous, but I thought: hold your ground, Doreen, don't let her get the upper hand. She was about to let rip when the doorbell rang. "I'll be back later," I said to Derek. "Don't wait up for me."

"I won't," he said, not looking up from his *Racing Post*.

164

I went through the front door as quick as I could and swiftly shut it behind me, hoping to prevent Iris from shouting abuse after me. Des was dressed in a fabulous jacket and trouser ensemble with matching tie. It was definitely not off the peg and showed of him off lovely. I thought, it's a good job our Gary isn't here, he'd be unconscious with excitement by now.

Des had his fancy car parked ready. He opened the door for me and I felt like a princess as I installed myself.

"Are we picking up Stephanie at her hotel?" I said.

"Actually, Steph can't make it. So, I'm afraid it's just the two of us," he said. "I'm sure we can have a good time between us."

My stomach did a little bit of an acrobatic turn. Was it—could it be—that I was out on a date with a gorgeous young man who could charm the birds off the trees and was relatively famous with it?

As we drove over to Sheffield in the car, Des said to me: "You know, Doreen, you're one of the few people I've ever met who is exactly what she appears to be. No side. No sarcasm. In my business you meet a lot of phonies and jerks. Everybody's on the make, but you're different. Do you know the term wysiwyg?"

"Well, I've heard our Gary using it in connection with his computer. Is that it?"

"In a way, yes. It stands for what-you-see-is-what-you-get. And that's precisely how I see you. It's all spelled out upfront and no complications. I know you're not being devious like so many of the people I have to work with—always after something. I feel safe with you."

I wasn't quite sure whether it was a compliment or an insult. Did he mean I was shallow and also had no depth? Was he saying I was without any real substance? I decided to give him the benefit of the doubt for the time being, as arguing with him at this point in the evening might have been a bit embarrassing.

"You know," he said, "I think Iris imagines I'm a jumped up, no-talent chancer who just walked in to his own TV show with no effort. But the truth is, I've had to serve a long apprenticeship, Doreen. I was no overnight success. I spent years when I was younger trying to establish myself as a stand-up. It was the same for a lot of others, we toured all around the country doing one-night stands at these comedy clubs, every night a different Travelodge and eating junk food at eleven o'clock after the show. I became very familiar with fish and chip shops and pizza parlours and Indian takeaways and motorway services. My diet was terrible. I was piling weight on. But I put up with it because I was learning the trade, you see, finding out how to hold an audience, testing out my limit, dealing with unruly drunks and hecklers. It was hard work and very lonely. But I'm not complaining. It gave me the grounding I needed to get into television. But can you see why I get so annoyed with Iris belittling me all the time. I don't think I deserve it."

He suddenly seemed like a young lad in need of reassurance rather than this over-confident TV personality, shouting the odds and being in charge.

We went to this new restaurant from South America where they serve all kinds of meats, one after another, especially steak. They bring them and slice them at the table, and you can have as much as you like. There are also salads, but who's going to have a salad when there's all this chicken, lamb and beef to choose from? (I noticed that Des had a salad and some green veg. He's learned his lesson and found you don't keep a figure like his by neglecting your broccoli).

Des looked glorious sitting at the table, very confident and at ease with himself. There was a kind of glow about him. A few people were staring at him, especially girls. I didn't blame them—I could hardly take my eyes off him myself.

Eventually this young lass came over and said: "Are you Des McIntyre? If you're not you're the dead spit of him."

"I am," he said.

"Can I have an autograph, please, Des? Only I collect autographs, see. I've got Larry Grayson, Jimmy Tarbuck and Ann Widdecombe so far."

Des asked the waiter for a piece of paper and pen, and he wrote his name on it with a personal dedication to this girl, Debbie I think she was called.

"Thanks ever so much," she said. "I hope you and your mam have a lovely evening."

That brought me down to earth with a bump. It was clear I wasn't going to be mistaken for a mystery girlfriend.

"Well, this is all very nice, Des, but what was it you were going to discuss? Some kind of business?"

"Not really business," Des said, topping up my glass of wine (third one, not that I was counting, he wasn't having any, due to driving). "I just wanted to know how you thought it was all going. This could be an important development for your business."

"Well, I've never been on the television before, so I've nothing to compare it with. How do *you* think it's going? You're the expert."

"Well, it's all grist to the mill for me. I've done dozens of these cheapo reality shows, they all blend into one after a while. But this one is different. Mainly because of Iris."

"Yes, she can be a bit of a tyrant, can't she?"

"Tyrant? She's like Pol Pot, Idi Amin and Vladimir Putin all rolled into one. But really, that's what I wanted to discuss with you. I mean, you're the owner of the business, right?"

"Well, majority part owner. You'd never guess it, though, when Iris gets going."

"That's it, you see, Doreen, I think she's lording it over you and stealing your thunder. You should be the star of this show, not her. You're far more interesting than she is, and I'm sure the viewers would take to you much more easily. You're far more likeable. I mean, if it's publicity for the shop you're after, you need people to feel that they're secure and safe to come in and buy their fish and chips from you, don't you? But with Iris, you're going to need a Beware of the Granny notice outside."

I had to laugh. "But what can I do?" I said. "She's been very useful in keeping the shop open during some very difficult times."

"You'll just have to step forward and make your mark. Don't let her dominate everything. Maybe you could ask her to stay away for the rest of the week."

"Oh, no chance of that," I said. "She'd kick the door down rather than be excluded. But I'll try to side-line her a bit. Make her a bit less prominent."

"I'd quite appreciate that, too, Doreen, because, as you know, she's given me a very hard time and it's difficult to retaliate against an elderly lady without coming over as a bully."

"Oh yes—she's well aware of that and she'll play on it something ruthless."

He topped up my wine again and gazed into my eyes with those crystal-clear green peepers. I was almost melting. "So, anything you can do to get Iris off my back would be appreciated."

Yes, I would put an end to Iris's brutality. He was too lovely to be subjected to any more of her attempts at showing him up.

167

On day three of the filming, I came in with a bit of a hangover, Iris had been at me at home since I got up to tell her what had gone on with Des the night before. But I was adamant that I would not be drawn. She was furious. She didn't like not being in complete control and stamped about in the shop waiting for Des to arrive.

It was quarter past eleven when he walked in, looking much more confident than he had on other days. I've a feeling his lateness was meant as a deliberate provocation. Iris was about to go for him in a big way, when I stood between them and said: "Morning Des. Would you like a cup of tea? Iris will make it."

"Y'what?" Iris roared. "I'm not making no tea for him."

"Oh, but you are," I said, with renewed determination. "You can make a cup for all of us."

"It's his job to…"

"Iris!" I commanded. "Tea, please, and quick about it."

"I will not!" she said, equally determined.

"Then I shall have to ask you to vacate the premises," I said. "There can only be one chief amongst the Indians and, in this instance, I am Geronimo. So, do as you're told or go home and do some hoovering."

"How dare you…" she started

"Can I remind you, Mrs Potts senior," I said, with all the majesty of a superior position I could muster, "I am the founder and senior partner of this emporium and you are a minority shareholder and employee who came late to the party. So, get the kettle on, else I'll take steps."

She moved forward with the intention of defiance, but I put up my hand to stop her.

"Kettle please, Iris, and quick about it."

I looked at Des and he was beaming widely putting his full dental magnificence on display.

"You'll regret this, Doreen Potts," Iris said, but all the same she went into the back to mash the tea.

Des gave me a thumbs up and said, quietly, "That's the way, Doreen. Keep it up."

After she'd made the tea—and there was that much door-slamming and banging of mugs and spoons coming from the back room it could have been a localised earthquake—she pulled me to

168

one side and said: "I see what this is about. I now know what went off last night. You're a sucker for a pretty face, you always have been."

"Is that so?" I said. "Then how come I got lumbered with your Derek?"

"Look," Iris said (and when she says 'look' in that way, it generally means 'listen'). "You don't want to side up with him. He's trying to drive a wedge between us. Can't you see that all this arguing and nastiness and tormenting of him is just to make sure they have a good programme to put on? If they get that, it'll benefit all of us."

"I'm perfectly well aware of your game, Iris, and I don't like it. It's cruel."

"I'm only viciously tormenting him on a temporary basis, just till we finish this programme."

I turned away from her and said, "Well, we'd better start getting ready for the lunchtime rush. Fire up the friers, Des, and get them chips ready. I'll go and make the batter. Iris, start warming up the mushy peas and defrost a few pies. I hope the fish delivery's been."

I went to get started on the batter while Iris gave Des an evil stare. He gave her a little smile of triumph in return.

"You heard her ladyship—get them chips seen to," she ordered.

I knew the big test would come when the customers arrived. Des had done well in the training, but the fish and chip trade is a lot more complicated than most people realise. It takes a while for even the most cleverest people to master it.

I think Stephanie's idea had been to chuck Des in at the deep end and watch him flounder. Of course, I think on the quiet, Des was hoping it would all go belly up as well. Plenty of opportunity for the type of clowning that Iris so detested.

What Stephanie hadn't told us—and what I should have realised she'd do—was that she had invited a lot of locals to come in and have a fish and chip lunch all expenses paid. And when I say a lot, I mean thirty or forty, who all turned up at once demanding to be fed.

Iris looked at me as if to say, "Now then, miss big chief Sitting Bull, you can deal with this without my experience to help you."

I said to Des, "I'll fry while you and Iris serve. Keep your wits about you."

The first three or four customers were fine. They were simple orders of fish and chips that were dispensed satisfactorily in a reasonable time. But then came the people who wanted to make the most of their freebie, ordering multiple kinds of fish and some sausages as well as our new line of chicken curry and battered black pudding, which we've only just added to the menu, so each one has to be fried individually.

As instructed, Des was piling on the chips, which was emptying the pan really fast. I was chipping like mad trying to keep up and then tipping them into the frier at a rate of knots. People at the back were singing "why are we waiting?" The rush was so hard that I began to make mistakes.

I put one bucket of chips into the frier without letting them dry a bit and so when the water hit the fat there was a bit of a hot oil explosion that went all over our overalls and sprinkled on to our hands and faces.

"Watch what you're doing, Doreen, you nearly burned my eye out then," Iris said. She was doing her best to keep up, but panic and impatience was setting in and then, to cap it all, Carol Cartwright came in with her three kids—one in a right big pushchair—and wanted to stand and have a chat about her Ken's psoriasis. Iris got annoyed with her and told her to bugger off.

Des says to her, "What happened to the personal touch, Iris? Shall I write in the book that her Ken's got a skin complaint, y'know, just for future reference?"

"Get on with your work," she snapped, wiping her brow.

Just as we thought we were getting through the first mob, another one of equal size arrived.

"You'll have to wait a while," I shouted. "The chips aren't ready yet and we've run out of cod."

"This is Stephanie's doing," Iris was saying. "She's set us up to fail."

Then suddenly the friers turned off. They just conked out. I fiddled with them for a bit in the hope that they would obey instructions and start working again if I spoke to them harshly enough. But it was no good. I'm no engineer and this was a job for the professionals.

"I'm sorry," I shouted over the noise of the impatient crowd. "The equipment's failed. There'll be no more fish and chips today."

There was a menacing rumble of disappointed from the people in front of us. The shop was crammed to the doors, everyone furious that they weren't going to get their free lunch.

"I've come all the way from Rawmarsh for this," one woman was saying. "I think it's a bloody cheek dragging us all this way for nowt. I had to take two buses to get here."

"I'm sorry," I said. "I shall have to have the experts in. I can't repair specialist equipment."

Still the crowd didn't disperse, and the anger seemed to be growing. I was getting quite nervous and started going through in my mind whether we could make an escape through the back door if worst came to shove.

Iris suddenly climbed up on the counter, so that everyone could see her, and she shouted. "Attention please. Please give attention ladies and gentlemen," the crowd went quiet and turned to hear what she had to say. "You heard what Doreen here said, we can't serve you, so please leave the shop immediately in an orderly fashion. Thank you."

Nobody budged, but there was an element of rumbling anger.

"Go on, sling your hooks," Iris was yelling. "You're only here because you thought there was summat for nowt. Well, there isn't, so do one, the lot of you."

From within the crowd somebody threw a wooden fork at her, this was followed in short order by one of the menu stands that clipped her ear.

"I can see who's chucking stuff—like you Harold Harper, you chucked that," she was saying.

"Come down, Iris," I said. "You're a plastic duck sitting up there. It'll be the salt and vinegar dispensers next, and it won't be funny if one of them clocks you in the face."

Some big lads were pulling at the two tables that were screwed to the floor. "Stop that, you bleeding hooligans," Iris was shouting at them. "I'll come down there and smack your arses if you don't give over."

As predicted, a vinegar shaker winged through the air and just missed her head. Somebody at the front got hold of her overall and started pulling at it. "Gerroff," Iris shouted. "Let go or I'll kick you in the chuffing face."

This amused some of the rough lads that had joined the mob. Someone grabbed her ankle and gave it a real tug. She flew through the air head first into the crowd, which was packed so tight that they were able to catch her and pass her around, like they do at pop concerts—I think they call it crowd-surfing. When I heard the

171

language she was shouting at them, I thought "If this is on film, they'll have to put their bleeper to good use."

As the crowd heaved her about the room, she eventually ended up back at the front and they installed her back on the counter. A cheer went up.

"Get down from there, and stop inciting them, you're only making it worse," I said.

Des helped her down and then he climbed up on to the counter himself. He took off his hat and somebody in the crowd said: "That's Des McIntyre. Him off the telly!"

A little shriek of delight was heard and suddenly the crowd turned from hostile to delighted.

"In't he gorgeous," this girl said to her friend. "I wouldn't mind having a go with him."

"Listen," Des said. "I know you're disappointed, and we're very sorry, we don't want you to go hungry, so please, go next door to the Chips & More! and I'll personally stand everyone to lunch—whatever you fancy."

A cheer went up and there was a mad exodus from the shop, with folk falling over one another to get to the front of the queue at the Chips & More! As soon as the last one was out, I rushed to the door and locked it, rapidly turning the sign to "Closed".

I was so worked up I was on the verge of collapse and had to fan myself as a reviver. Eventually I turned to Des and said, "Thanks Des, that was starting to get really frightening. You've saved us from a riot by being so generous."

"Don't worry," he said. "Stephanie knows this will be going on my expenses."

At that point he went next door to make the arrangements with Ainsley to take on our overflow.

"Are you alright?" I said to Iris.

"I'm fine," the 'little ferret' said, "that were quite exhilarating."

* * *

Stephanie expressed her delight in the way things were going. She said they had some cracking stuff, and the programme was going to be sensational.

I said nowt about her putting our lives at risk by encouraging a rampaging mob to invade the shop. People round here take their

172

fried foods very seriously and they also take promises of something for nothing very seriously, an'all. I remember that opening day promotion they had at Tescos that time—free sandwiches and bags of crisps while stocks last. Well, they didn't last long and that resulted in extensive damage to the fruit and veg section and the manager being rushed to A&E.

Des was satisfied that he'd come over as the hero of the day and that his actions in the face of the disaster would make up for his earlier belittlements.

On the final day of filming, Des had brought in a bottle of champagne to be cracked open when it was all done.

But before we got there, the time seemed to be taken up with him and Iris exchanging insults. She said he ought to get a real job instead of prancing around on the television like a big, daft jessie. He replied by asking if she needed a licence to be so evil. She couldn't leave his face alone, of course, and she said that a survey had shown that people with big faces were lacking in intelligence.

I mean, honestly, I can't see anything wrong with his face, size-wise.

Fortunately, with the friers being on the blink, we didn't have any customers, so we passed the time buffing up the brassware, re-stocking the cruets and cleaning the tables a few more times.

Then Stephanie came down, accompanied by this so-called Retail Guru, Maxwell Horton, who was going to give his opinion of the business and make suggestions for improvement. So, we was all sat in a row and he commenced to give his assessment.

"I don't think there is anything fundamentally wrong with this business," he said. "It has a great deal of potential, given the area it's in. I think the obvious reason it's not doing well financially is because of the presence of the Chips & More! right next door."

"How much are they paying him to do this?" Iris whispered to me, "we want him to tell us something we don't already know, not stating the bleeding obvious."

"But the biggest advantage that this shop has is its adherence to tradition. People like tradition, they like the familiar, and they like a good quality product. And these ladies – and Des, of course – are providing the kind of dependable, freshly made food that people like. Chips & More! is all well and good, but the products they offer are not prepared on the premises, as they are here. They're all delivered par—cooked from a central production unit in

Hackenthorpe, and they are the same—exactly identical—whichever branch of Chips & More! you buy them from. There's nothing wrong with that, of course, nothing at all, it's standard practice for many food outlets these days. But you can't deny that freshly cooked has a different flavour and texture."

"They may sell crap," Iris said, "but it doesn't stop them cornering the market, does it? However good we are, all the punters are still going next door for their stuff."

"I wouldn't go so far as to dismiss our competitor's product out of hand. It has quality ingredients. It could well be that what Chips & More! is offering is simply cheaper," said Mr Horton. "That is an important consideration for many people—especially round here in an area of deprivation. They would love to come and have your superior fish and chips, Mrs Potts, but if there are cheaper alternatives, I'm afraid they'll take them ."

"Well," I said, "We're doing our best to hold the prices down, but have you seen the cost of fish at the moment? It's gone through the roof."

"Overfishing," said Maxwell. "Some fish species are becoming unsustainable, as I'm sure you know. The answer might be to introduce less familiar types of fish, the sort that are not under threat and might be a little less expensive. Pollack, coley, hake or whiting are possibilities. Most of them are indistinguishable from cod to the not-very discerning consumer. And, of course, other products. I notice that you've introduced your fried black pudding and haggis and the selection of pies is expanding. That is all good news. As fish becomes out of the reach of many people, an imaginative alternative is good. But you have to keep ahead of the competition, keep people interested with more and more alternatives to fish."

"He'll be telling us to have fried Mars Bars next," said Iris.

"We're not having that," I said firmly. "I draw the line at fried Mars Bars. They're far too sweet. We could try frying Kitkats, though, that might be nice if the biscuits didn't go soggy. But Mars Bars, no."

"So, what you're saying, Mr Maxwell," said Iris, "is that we're doomed because of the presence of a cheaper alternative next door, namely, Chips & More!? Right? We might as well shut up shop now and go home."

"Well, it's a big problem and there isn't an obvious solution except, as I say, to keep on trying with new temptations for your customers."

After Mr Horton had said his piece, Stephanie put Des on the spot to ask how he had found his week at the shop.

"Strangely, despite a bit of hostility, I've enjoyed it. It brought back a lot of happy memories of my childhood and the weekly visit to the chip shop with my mates. We'd sit outside the local shop on the bench they provided and really enjoy a great big bag of chips and fish bits. And it's the same kind of memories that people will get if they come to Doreen's chip shop on Balaclava Street— comfort and joy and a warm welcome. And I can testify from having tried the fish and chip supper here in this shop, that it's one of the best you'll get anywhere in the country. And I've had plenty to compare it with from my time on the road. All made with love and attention to detail."

"And nobody is going to tell you to have a nice day," chimes in Iris.

Finally, we had to score him for the last time.

"Well, Doreen, how would you rate Des as an employee and as a worker?"

"Oh, he's been lovely, Stephanie, a right pleasure to work with. He's a nice lad and I'll give him five out of five, with a few bumps in the road that have been ironed out."

"And what about you, Iris. I think you may have been the cause of a few of those bumps, haven't you?"

"Well, you can't handle apprentices with kid gloves, can you? They'd learn nowt that road. No, you've got to test their mettle, make sure they're tough enough to see it through."

"And has Des passed the test?"

"He's alright," she conceded. "I can't give him the full five due to a personal dislike of the dimensions of his face. I know he can't help it, but it's four out of five from me. Oh, and by the way, Stephanie, I'm not being funny, and I know it's a personal quirk of mine, but I thought I ought to draw your attention to the size of your own face."

"Take no notice of her," I said to Stephanie. "She's mentally ill as regards the bigness of people's faces."

"Well, that's a wrap," Stephanie announced, "now it's back to HQ to edit all this footage. We've got hours of it and there are some

175

real plums to pick out. Thank you so much, ladies, and I hope that when the programme goes out it will bring you a lot of new business and keep the shop afloat."

She and the camera crew went on their way, and then it was Des's turn to open the champagne. Anyroad, he was just about to pop the cork when this this middle aged woman woman came in through the door. I say middle-aged, but she looked older. She was nicely dressed, though, but a bit vacant-looking.

"Sorry, love," I said. "Due to technical difficulties beyond our control, we aren't serving today."

"Oh, I'm not here for chips," she said. "I'm looking for Mrs Potts."

She talked in a very slow, laboured way.

"I'm Mrs Potts," me and Iris said in unison.

"I'm looking for the Mrs Potts who is the mother of Sylvia Potts."

I stepped forward, suddenly alarmed.

"Has something happened to her?" I asked, terrified. "Has there been a tragic accident involving a bus?"

"Oh no, nothing like that, love. If it was something like that I'd have been a bobby. It's the bobbies what brings you news like that, int'it? No, it's about her getting pregnant by my son," she said.

"You must be Ainsley's mother, then," I said, dead relieved.

"I've just popped round," she said, "to have a little word about what's happening."

My defences went up at that point. Iris came and stood beside me.

"Oh, don't worry Mrs Potts, I'm not here for argy-bargy," she said. "I just thought we ought to meet and get to know one another, what with us maybe about to become family."

I was a bit wary. I thought she might be setting a trap for us, sent round by her husband with some nefarious plan.

We sat down at the table.

"You see, Mrs Potts…"

"Oh, for goodness sake, call me Doreen," I said.

"You see, Doreen… I'm Irene by the way… You see, I know my husband has been on at you. He can be very forceful can Arnold."

"A big-headed bleeder, you mean," said Iris.

I nudged her as if to say, please be quiet, at least until we know what's going off.

"I know he's not everybody's cup of tea—not even mine sometimes—but we've been discussing the situation vis-à-vis our Ainsley and your Sylvia. They seem hell bent on getting married, don't they, the pair of them?"

"They do," I said.

She suddenly spotted Des standing in the corner, who was listening to all this with great interest. "Is that him off the telly? Him off *Use it or Lose It*?"

"It is," I said.

"Oh," said Irene, losing interest in Des and turning back to the business in hand as though it was quite usual for her to spot a celebrity in a local chippy every day.

"Well, you see, Doreen…" she looked at Iris. "Who is this, by the way? Is she an interested party or just a curious bystander?"

"I'm Sylvia's granny, Iris," says Iris.

"Oh, very pleased to meet you, Iris. I'm Irene."

Iris looked at her. There was a pause.

"Irene Addison, that is. Wife of Arnold," said Irene very slowly.

"Yes," I said, still not sure whether Irene Addison was a friend or foe. "And how can we help you, Irene?"

"Well, Arnold hasn't been very happy over the last few weeks. He believes our Ainsley is throwing his life away by getting hooked up with your Sylvia."

"Yes, he's made that perfectly clear."

"He's talking in terms of kicking our Ainsley into touch as regards him being our son."

"Yes, he said, and what do you think about that, Irene?"

"Well, I'm not for it, of course. What mother would be? Besides, you can't just sever the umbilical cord and pretend it hasn't happened. He'll be our son whether Arnold has refuted him or not."

"That's all very true," I said. "So, what do you want to do about it?"

"Well, I've told Arnold—I told him straight out—I said, our Ainsley is remaining a sheep in the fold. You are not going to expel him into outer darkness. The lass can't be that bad."

Iris coughed one of her cynical coughs.

"Then Arnold showed me the dossier he had compiled. Looking into your Sylvia's past, type of thing."

Iris coughed again, this time a bit more violently.

"Well, I said to him, I said, we've all got pasts, Arnold. We're none of us pure as the driven snow. We've all got skellingtons in the closet. I mean, you'd never believe it, but I was once a showgirl in a previous life."

"Eh?" I said, quite taken aback.

"Oh yes, I was a Pan's Person. You might have seen me on the Kenny Everett Show. I was third on the left."

"Bloody hell, that's some time since," said Iris, "Even I can hardly remember it and I'm ancient."

"I was very young at the time. I lied about me age you see. I was that desperate to be a dancing girl, I wanted the sequins and glitter. I wanted the lights and the makeup and the costumes. I was no more than fifteen, but I was well developed for me age, you see. I was the high-kicking equivalent of Helen Shapiro. Do you remember her? She had a right deep voice, but she was only fifteen." She starts singing, "Walking Back to Happiness, wump-a oh yeah yeah."

Then she said, "Well, I had these right muscular legs and a big bust for that age. I never thought I'd end up married to a fish and chip shop tycoon. But never mind, I danced on the television once and there's not many can say that, is there? I managed two shows before they got wind of me true age and turfed me out."

"That's all very interesting," I said, "but what's it got to do with our Sylvia?"

"Well, what I'm saying is that whatever happened in the past doesn't have to dictate the rest of your life, does it? Not unless you've murdered somebody and they've hung you. But even the most depraved person, who has cavorted in skimpy clothes in front of millions of televiewers, can repent. You see, when I finished being a Pan's Person I saw the light and brought Jesus into my life. Is Jesus in your life, Doreen?"

"Er…" I said.

"Is he in your life, Iris? Has he revealed himself to you in all his glory?"

"Nobody's revealed themselves to me in all their glory since my honeymoon night when my husband revealed himself in all *his* glory. Except for his vest, that is. That was enough of a revelation for me. I always bought him longer vests after that."

Irene continued: "No, what I wanted to say was that Arnold has had time to think things over. He's dead depressed about the prospect of losing our Ainsley. It's making him badly. I said to him,

178

I said, well you don't have to lose him, do you? It's entirely of your own making, all this misery. Our Ainsley doesn't want to break up with us—you just have to say a little prayer, asking for forgiveness and it'll all be put right in the eyes of our Saviour. He's very understanding is God the Father."

"And is he going to say that prayer?" Iris said.

"He says he's got to cogitate on the matter," Irene said. "It can be hard for men to back down, can't it? But I said to him: ask yourself what would Jesus do? But it wouldn't make no difference to me whatever Jesus would have done. I told Arnold straight, I said, choose what you say, I'm going to have that grandchild as part of my life. It's something I've always wanted, you see, a grandchild. I never thought our Ainsley had it in him. He's shown no previous aptitude in that department, thank the Lord."

"Well, you're going to have to use all your feminine wiles on your Arnold," Iris said. "Persuade him, coax him, reward him with bedtime treats—if that isn't taking your life in your hands. Failing that, threaten to divorce him and take him for all he's got."

"What I'd like to do is meet your Sylvia and get to know her. I'm sure she's a lovely lass," said Irene. "I'd like to support her during her confinement. I've fetched a box of dates and a religious tract for her."

Iris was about to do another one of her coughs but this time I kicked her.

"She's with your Ainsley in his flat over the shop next door today."

"I'll pop round now, then," said Irene. "I think our Ainsley will be OK with me. I'm not his father, you see."

So, off she went to pay a call on our Sylvia.

"Well, it's clear now where Ainsley gets his charm and intelligence from," Iris said. "But I'd like to be a fly on the wall for that little meeting."

* * *

Our Sylvia and Ainsley came round for their tea the following night. We had sausage pasta with Jersey Royals and chips, finishing off with Ambrosia rice pudding, with a splodge of damson jam. We then had cups of tea with two ginger biscuits each.

Our Sylvia is well on the way now, she's enormous round the middle. Ainsley's bought her some lovely maternity wear.

"How did you get on with Ainsley's mam yesterday?" I asked.

"Oh, she's right nice, in't she Ainsley—your mam, in't she nice?"

"Oh aye, she's OK, me mam."

"She fetched me a box of dates," our Sylvia said. "I said to her 'thanks very much, Mrs Addison—what exactly are dates?' I always thought they was something you went on with lads. I didn't say nothing to her, but I'm not eating them. They look horrible, like dog muck all squashed into a box."

"Did you come to any conclusions, the pair of you, as regards the future?" I enquired.

Ainsley looked at me gone out. "How do you mean, Mrs Potts?"

"Well, is there a reconciliation imminent between you and your dad?"

He was still confused, so Iris said very slowly, and with exaggerated lip movements, "Have. You. Made. Up. With. Your. Father? Are you on good terms with him again? Has he forgiven our Sylvia for being... well... our Sylvia?"

"Me mam says she's working on him and thinks it'll all work out one way or another."

"Well, that sounds hopeful," I said, handing round the tin of Roses chocolates that was left over from Christmas. Ainsley rooted in the tin, picking out every last one of the Hazelnut Whirls. They just happen to be my favourite, but I said nothing.

"Well, let's keep our fingers crossed," I said, shutting the lid of the chocolates before he got started on the Country Fudge, which is my second favourite.

"Are you doing alright, pregnancy-wise?" Iris asked our Sylvia. "No complications nor nothing? What are they saying at the ante-natal clinic?"

"They say everything's hunky dory, gran. Only another couple of weeks to go. Ainsley comes with me to the relaxation classes, don't you Ainsley? Then we have a cup of coffee afterwards. It's all go when you're expecting, in't it Ainsley?"

"Oh aye," says Ainsley, stuffing two Hazelnut Whirls in his mouth at once. I thought with his mouth so full he wouldn't be able to talk, but then again, I don't think anybody would notice.

I said to Iris on the quiet, I said, "How on earth does he manage that Chips & More!? How does he keep it running when he's away with the fairies most of the time?"

"Oh, Arnold brought Annie Kennedy in to run it. She used to have the sub-post office on Eckersley Street until they shut it down. Ainsley's the manager of Chips & More! in name only. He wouldn't know where to start, but his dad likes to imagine that he's got a thrusting and ambitious son. I think Ainsley's allowed to take down delivery orders over the phone, though I've even heard complaints about that."

* * *

The shop is clinging on by its fingernails. Our turnover is hardly existent, but our bills are very much existent and seem to be breeding like rabbits. Every morning we come in and find another pile of them on the mat. One morning there was a different sort of letter lying there, not in a window envelope looking like another demand for payment within fourteen days or else. No, this one was from the TV company. I ripped it open like a terrier with a rat.

"It's from Stephanie," I says. Iris hadn't brought her reading glasses, so I read it out to her. "Dear Mesdames Potts, I hope you are keeping well and the shop is thriving. I am pleased to tell you that the series "Service With a Smile" has been scheduled for broadcast each Monday to Wednesday from the 17 April at 9.30pm. Your episode will be leading the series off because we consider it the strongest. I can tell you it has been edited down to a real cracker. The viewers are going to love it. Please enjoy it and let us know what you think. And if there are developments of any kind as a result of the show, drop us a line and tell us about it. There might be scope for a follow up. It was a pleasure being with you during that week, with all kind wishes, Stephanie Bartholomew."

Enclosed was a cheque for £1,208.49 being our fee, as agreed.

"Oh, that's champion," said Iris, gripping my arm. "That's brought us back from the brink, at least for a week or two." Then she turned right serious. "But even that amount won't really scratch the tip of the surface as regards our finances. You realise, don't you, Doreen, that this telly programme is the last roll of the dice for us? It'll either make us, else break us. One of the two."

It were a Saturday afternoon, just after we'd finished the dinner time service, that I decided to pop upstairs to the flat and see how our Sylvia was doing. When I got there, Ulrika was sitting on the settee, painting her nails. Little Jean-Claude and our Charmaine Bernadette were sitting beside her, inhaling the fumes.

"Where's our Sylvia?" I said.

"She's gone to the hospikal," she said.

"What's she gone to the hospital for? Is the baby coming?" I said.

"I don't know," the dozy mare said. And not only didn't she know, she obviously didn't care. She had more important things to do, like paint her nails.

Any road, I thought I'd better get to the hospital to find out what was going off. I left Iris in charge of the shop and promised to let her know as soon as I could how things were.

When I got to the hospital reception, this girl looked on a list, but she couldn't find our Sylvia's name. "Nobody of that name has been admitted," she said. "What is the nature of her problem?"

"Well, pregnancy, if that counts as a problem."

Just then, I sees our Sylvia, kicking hell out of the refreshment dispenser over by the wall.

I went over to her and said: "What's to do? What's going off? Why are you here?"

"I put a pound in this and nothing came out," she says, giving the machine another battering. "Bloody rob-dogs."

"Are you poorly or summat, why are you here?"

"Oh, it's Ainsley's dad. He's been took badly. He's up on the ward. I just came to fetch Ainsley a drink and now this has happened."

"Is it serious?" I said.

"Well, I'm not going to put another pound in till I've got the first one out," she says.

"I'm talking about, Ainsley's dad, not the bleeding coffee machine," I said.

"I don't think it's serious. The nurse said he was on the critical list, whatever that means."

"What ward is he on?" I said. "Ainsley will need some support if he's to be imminently bereaved. You should be doing that, it's your job as his wife, to be on hand to offer comfort among the tears."

We went up to Ward 13A. ITU. Ainsley was sitting in the corridor outside the door with his mother beside him. Both of them looked like they were utterly confused and hardly aware of what was going on around them.

"Hello, Irene, love," I said. "I'm sorry to hear your shocking news in relation to Arnold's health. How is he?"

"Hello, Doreen." She said and then turned to her son. "How is he, Ainsley? You know, don't you? You've spoke to the doctor."

"Well, he's had a coronary heart attack," said Ainsley. "He just sort of collapsed in the front room, didn't he mam? He suddenly fell on to side table and it broke, with him being so heavy."

"It were me best side table an'll—genuine mahogany," Irene said. "It was quite expensive when I first bought it. I've nowhere to put the phone now."

I tried to put on a sympathetic voice and said, "Have they said what his chances are, Irene?"

"Who?" she says. "Oh, you mean Arnold? They never said, did they Ainsley. Did they say anything about what his chances are?"

"Who?" said Ainsley, paying no attention to anything.

"Your dad," Irene said. "What are his chances. Mrs Potts wants to know."

"They never said nothink about that. I don't think they did, anyroad."

What a pair of dimwits, I thought. "Well," I said. "You'll have to keep a vigil all night until the matter is resolved. Get ready for a long wait unless he should happen to go earlier."

"I'm not stopping here all night," says Irene, "Gail on Coronation Street is on life support and that serial killer is looking to switch her machine off. I'm not missing that. I'll offer up a prayer for Arnold when I go to church on Sunday."

Then our Sylvia digs me in the ribs with her elbow. "Mam," she says, clutching her stomach. "I think it's coming. The babby. It's starting."

"Oh God, your timing's perfect, as usual," I said, grabbing her hand. "But at least we're in the right place."

Sylvia let out a little yelp and doubled over. Ainsley looked alarmed. "What's up with her?" he said. "Has she got stomach—ache? Has she got diarrhoea?"

"No, you great pudding, the baby's coming. *Your* baby."

Panic spread over his face. "What have I to do? Shall I do something? I've never had a baby before."

"Best thing to do is find a wheelchair and we'll get her down to the maternity unit. It's on the floor below this, so we'll need the lift as well."

He got up and started running one way and then the other.

"What did you say I've got to do?" he says to me. "Get something was it?"

"A wheelchair! Calm down Ainsley, everything's going to be fine, just find that wheelchair."

Our Sylvia is not one for enduring pain bravely, but she does like a spot of drama—so long as she's at the centre of it — so she lets out this deafening scream. "Ainsley!" she shouts. "I want Ainsley!" (I thought: she's recreating a recent scene off Emmerdale, the one where Marion went into labour while driving a tractor. There was a lot of screaming in that.)

Poor old Ainsley comes hurtling back, still running round like a headless chicken. He hadn't located a wheelchair, but our Sylvia's amateur dramatics had brought a nurse out from the ITU.

"What's going off out here?" she said. "Don't you know there are dangerously ill people on this ward what don't want disturbing with this racket?"

I explained the situation and she went back into the ward and re—emerged with a wheelchair. "And make sure it's returned back here." she said sharply.

Well, we got our Sylvia down to the maternity ward and they took her in.

I said to Ainsley, "Aren't you going in with her to be present at the birth? Don't you want to see your little child coming into the world for the first time?"

"I might faint," he said. "I don't like blood and guts. I saw a warthog being born on the telly when I was twelve and I had to be given brandy by me mother and kept off school for three weeks. I've avoided anything to do with that sort of thing since then. David Attenborough it was."

"Well, it's up to you," I said, "but our Sylvia won't be best pleased. She'll be screaming the place down in a few minutes. But I suppose you've got the excuse of it being touch and go with your father. Why don't you pop back to ITU and sit by his deathbed? You'll feel better for it."

184

I went to find the payphone to let Iris and Derek know what was happening. Derek said he'd love to come and support his daughter at this important turning point in her life, but there was a darts semi—final at the Trades and Labour Club and he'd promised faithful he'd be there.

Iris said she'd close the shop and come round to help with various matters of births, marriages and deaths.

I was exhausted already, and we hadn't even started yet.

* * *

Our Sylvia gave birth to a bonny, bouncing baby boy at 3.26am in the morning. It was noticeable for the beautiful head of blond hair it had. Most babbies are bald, but this one was an exception.

"It's going to be a right bobby dazzler when it grows up," I said, as I sat by her bed on the maternity ward while she cradled the newborn infant.

Ainsley sat beside me staring at the bairn as though he was mesmerised by it.

"Is that really my son?" he said. "I can't believe I've got a kiddy of my own. I can't wait to take him to see Rotherham United on a Saturday afternoon. I've always wanted someone to go with. It's not much fun on your own, you feel funny about shouting. And the meat and tater pies they sell are far too big for one person."

"Do you want to hold it, Ainsley?" our Sylvia said. "Just make sure you support its head. That's right, int'it, mam? You have to support its head?"

"That's right, love."

"I won't have hold it, if you don't mind, Mrs Potts. I'm a bit scared of dropping it and it ending up funny. I'd never forgive meself."

I said nothing, tempting as it was.

Then Iris arrived. She had a bit of a coo over the child, held its little hand and said how bonny it was.

"Look at that hair," she said. "You must have some gorgeous blonds in your family, Ainsley, because we haven't got any in ours. And another thing, you'll have to stop calling it 'it'," she says, "It's a boy, int'it? You ought to give it a name – I mean give *him* a name. Have you thought of one?"

"I thought about Roderick," our Sylvia says. "Then we can call him Rod for short."

Iris wasn't smitten. She rolled it round her mouth for size. "Rod Addison?" she said. "Does that sound right to you, Ainsley? Rod?"

"Yea, it sounds alright to me," he said. "It sounds grand, in fact. I knew Sylvia would come up with a great name."

"I don't like it," our Sylvia says, all of a sudden. "I've gone off it. What about Jaroslav?"

"That's foreign, int'it?" I said. "You can't lumber a child with a foreign name if he isn't foreign."

"It's only Yugoslavian," she says.

"Do you like Jaroslav, Ainsley? Does that suit you?" said Iris.

"Yeah, it's great is that. Perfect. What was it?"

"The vicar's going to have something to say if you pitch up with a little Yorkshire lad and you want to christen him Jaroslav," I said. "He's a devil for refusing to do fancy names that will come back to haunt the little 'un at a later date. He wouldn't christen one little lad whose mother wanted to call him Rock, after Rock Hudson. Turned her down flat."

"He's the same with headstones in the cemetery," Iris said. "He won't let you put 'Mam', so, you want to bear that in mind when you have your father's headstone engraved, Ainsley. He won't let you put 'Dad' on it neither, won't that vicar. He's ever so particular. He says Mam and Dad are vulgar."

"Speaking of vulgar, how's your dad doing, Ainsley?" says Iris, "Still clinging on is he? It's a shame. Do you think you ought to pop upstairs to the ITU and comfort your mother in her time of grief? She'll be up there all alone dealing with the prospect of widowhood. She'll need her only family round her," Iris said.

"Me mam's popped out to the sales," Ainsley said. "She needs a new side table for the telephone. She's seen something she likes in Hayes's furniture store."

"Well, come on then, I'll come up to the ITU with you," I said. "Your dad could go at any time and he'll find it a comfort to know that you were heartbroken by his bedside at the time of his passing."

Ainsley wasn't thrilled with the idea. He said he was frightened of dead bodies.

I said to him "Well, your dad's not dead yet, so there won't be no corpses as such."

So, we went up to the ITU and when we got there the nurse said that Mr Addison had been transferred to men's surgical. He was down to have a heart bypass the following day.

So, we trailed down to men's surgical and there he was, sitting up in bed, large as life with the hospital pyjamas stretched to breaking point across his belly, and eating his dinner. There were various wires attached to various machines and then to Arnold, all beeping away.

"Ainsley, lad," he said, as he spotted his son. "Come here, let me embrace you."

He gave Ainsley a hug and a peck on the cheek.

Then he spotted me, "What's she doing here?" he said.

"I've come to give your Ainsley moral support," I said. "He's had a lot of stress today, what with one thing and another."

"I'll bet he hasn't had as much stress as me. I died for ten minutes, me – or so I'm told. I had to be revived by being electrocuted on the chest with one of them doingses. They had to shock me four times before I returned to the land of the living."

He pointed to the plate on the bed table in front of him. "The food here is atrocious, absolute muck. I shall put a complaint in when I'm feeling better. The custard's a disgrace."

"You should be grateful they saved your life," I said.

"Aye, but look how little the portions are. It wouldn't feed a bird, wouldn't that."

"Your Ainsley's been worried sick about you, haven't you Ainsley?"

"Have I?" he said, vacantly. "Oh yes, I have - I've been dead worried about you, dad."

"Well, I'm glad somebody has because that wife of mine is nowhere to be found." He pushed the empty plate aside and signalled to the nurse that he'd like a second helping. "You've got to be joking," she said, marvelling at the girth of him.

"It's torture is this. An abuse of human rights," Arnold said. "I'm that hungry I could eat a scabby dog."

The nurse walked away, shaking her head.

"So, what have you been up to, Ainsley? What have you been doing?" Arnold said, after he'd come to terms with no more food being on offer.

"Oh, y'know…" the lad said.

"Go on, tell him Ainsley," I urged.

"Tell me what?" said Arnold. "Is summat going off that I don't know about?"

"Your son has become a father today," I said proudly.

Arnold's eyes widened. "Not by that lass of yours is it?"

"Well, who else would it be?" I said. "She's been delivered of a lovely little lad, perfect in every way. Jaroslav they're calling him. Or at last reckoning they were—it might have changed by now."

Arnold's breathing got louder and his face started to redden. I could see that machine beginning to bleep even faster. Then he started to gasp.

"Are you alright, love?" I said.

Ainsley started to panic. "Is he going to die again? I think I'm going to run off."

I picked up the panic alarm and pressed it. The nurse came and saw that the machines were all going mad. She then pressed another alarm button, meant to summon the cardiac team.

"Can you leave, please?" she said, pulling the curtains round the bed. "They'll need all the space they can get to attend to him."

Arnold was now looking very distressed. His mouth was opening and closing like a fish out of water, his face was blue and he was struggling to breathe.

I grabbed Ainsley by the arm and pulled him away. As we left the ward, the doctors and nurses came running in with their trolley marked Resus. Team and there was a lot of shouting. I turned to speak to Ainsley, but he had gone. He was probably halfway to Manchester by that time.

* * *

Our Sylvia came home the following day, with her precious cargo (current proposed name: Umberto). I made her stay with us at Evergreen Close for a few days until she felt right. We fetched our Charmaine Bernadette back as well, safe from the "care" of Ulrika at the flat.

Ainsley wanted to stay close to his wife-to-be and off-spring, which is right and proper, so I said he could bunk on the settee. His father had been rushed for emergency surgery after his second coronary heart attack. They'd done all sorts to him, but he seems to have survived it and is now convalescing.

I said to Ainsley: "He was very lucky to be in the right place at the right time, wasn't he?"

"Who?" he said, vacant as a tailor's dummy.

"Your dad, you great lummox," I said, "Aren't you concerned for him?"

"He's alright, in't he?"

I gave up at that point and went into work at the shop.

I'll give our Sylvia her due, she is a very loving mother. She attends to that kiddy's every need. She never lets him out of her sight. Ainsley on the other hand is neither use nor ornament. When he saw our Sylvia breastfeeding, he started gypping a though he was going to be sick.

I said to our Sylvia, I said: "You want to sideline Ainsley until our little Umberto is at least fourteen, and then he might be able to cope with him."

"He's not called Umberto now," she said. "I've decided on Trystan instead. Trystan's a lovely name, int'it, mam? I considered Reinhold for a bit, but I ended up plumping for Trystan."

"Well, I hope you make your mind up before the lad understands what's going on. He'll have an identity crisis with all these names floating about. The sooner we get him registered the better, then we'll all know where we stand."

Ainsley's dad is making good progress apparently, convalescing in a nursing home (not one of his own, of course—he knows better than that). I said to Ainsley, "Do you want to pop round and visit him? I'm sure he'd appreciate it."

He was reluctant in case his father had died in the meantime and he might have to view the body, but after a bit of pressure, he agreed to go, but only if I'd go with him. I said I would if only to make sure he didn't run off again if his father had another breathing do.

It's a very nice convalescent home that Arnold has checked himself into, in lovely grounds and beautifully fitted out. It must be costing the earth.

We was shown into his room, where he was sitting in a specially reinforced chair, stuffing grapes into his mouth.

"Ainsley, lad!" he said. "I thought you'd forgot about me. I've been sitting here on me own for weeks, wondering where you was. I can't wait to get back into the swing of business."

"Hello, dad," Ainsley said.

"Oh," Arnold said, looking at me with utter contempt. "I see you've brought your minder with you. You can wait outside, Doreen, thank you. I'll authorise a cup of tea for you."

"I want her to stay," Ainsley said. "We've got something to talk to you about, haven't we Mrs Potts?"

"Well," he said, "what's to do?"

"Well, as you know, I am the father of my child and I want in future to become the husband of my wife."

"You've got that back to front," Arnold said, "but carry on."

"What I'd like to do," Ainsley said, a bit sheepish, "I'd like to fetch the babby round for you to look at. After all, you are his grand dad."

"Oh, it's a little lad is it?" Arnold said, softening a bit. "Well, at least with it being of the male gender there's a bit of a prospect of the Addison line being continued."

"Can we bring him round to see you?"

"We?" he said. "What, you mean that lass you're intent on marrying?"

"She is its mother, so she's entitled," Ainsley said.

Arnold looked at me. "This is all music to your ears, int'it, Doreen? Just what you wanted all along."

"I had nothing to do with it. It was your Ainsley's carnal desires that caused that baby to be conceived."

"He's shown no signs of carnal desires before," Arnold said. "Quite the reverse. He was addicted to painting by numbers until he was twenty-one."

"Well, now he's got big responsibilities another little life to look after," I said.

Arnold mulled it for a moment then said to Ainsley: "Your mother's coming round tomorrow, fetching me a Cornish pasty. I have to have top-ups, you see—they only give you concentration camp rations here. If you bring the babby round then, me and your mam can both inspect it. Then we'll see how we go on."

We then sat in silence for about five minutes, looking out of the window and then admiring the artwork on the wall. With nothing further to say to each other, Arnold said, "Well, you'd better be getting off then. I'll see you tomorrow. And if you can see your way to fetching me a quarter of liquorice torpedoes and, perhaps, a box of Maltesers, it would be greatly appreciated."

* * *

I got a call from a reporter on the *Advertiser* today. Apparently, Snark Productions have alerted them to the upcoming *Service with a Smile* TV programme. They wanted to do a story about it, given it has a local flavour and so they sent a photographer round to take accompanying pictures.

Stephanie had already told us not to give away any "spoilers". We were only to speak in general terms, not to say what the outcome had been, nor nothing about the riot.

Well, Iris was over the moon with all that, the realisation of her plan. She had us dolled up in our best uniforms, standing on the doorstep of the shop, holding a bag of chips each. They took a hell of a lot of pictures and I thought, if they print all that lot, there won't be room for nothing else in the *Advertiser*.

"This is just what we need," said Iris, "a bit of publicity that will make us stand out from the crowd. We need to become a destination fish and chip shop, like the Magpie in Whitby."

She instructed the photographer not to get any part of the Chips & More! shop in the photos. They'd muscled in on everything else, she said, they weren't going to steal our thunder as regards publicity.

* * *

Today me and Iris are going to take our Sylvia and her brood—and Ainsley, who sometimes feels like a third child—to introduce little Trystan to Mr and Mrs Addison.

When we got there and our Sylvia pulled the baby out of his pram, Irene Addison started blubbering.

"Oh, look," she said, "he's all wrapped up in swaddling clothes, just like baby Jesus on that very first Christmas."

Our Sylvia carefully handed the baby to Irene and she sobbed all over its little layette. Then she said to Ainsley: "I forgive you son for being a rampaging lustful beast what couldn't wait for his

191

wedding night. Your filthy behaviour has resulted in this marvellous little soul, so I shall have to let you off. What's he called?"

"This is your grandson, Trystan," I said proudly.

"No, this is not Trystan," our Sylvia says. "This is Theodore Arnold Addison. We thought we'd include Ainsley's dad's name."

Arnold seemed genuinely moved. "You've named the little babby after me?" he said. "Let's have a look, Irene, let me see if he's worthy of the name."

Irene reluctantly handed the child over to his grandfather. Arnold gazed down at him and—and this is one of the most amazing things I've ever seen in my life—he burst into tears.

"Oh, he's bonny," said Arnold when he'd collected himself. "And to think, he's got my jeans running through him. Although I don't think I've ever had blond hair."

He tenderly rocked the baby from side to side for a moment or two and then he said, in a very serious voice, to the assembled party:

"I've got summat to tell you. I've been keeping it to meself, but now, having seen this little nipper, this little fragment of meself, I feel I have to share it."

We were all goggle-eyed about what was coming.

"I've suffered a revelation," he said. "It was when I fell on that table and died, I had what they call a near-death experience. Although it wasn't really *near* death, I *was* dead. I was a certified goner until they arrived with that electric shock machine. But while I was dead, I saw a long tunnel with a bright light at the end of it, like you do. I could hear me mam calling, Arnold! Arnold! It isn't your time yet, love. You must go back for a while and make up for your cruelty and nastiness. You've been a right bugger and you've got to put things right. We'll all be waiting for you when your number comes up. Your uncle Jerry and auntie Colleen send best wishes. It's not bad here, you'll like it. But not yet."

There was a stunned silence in the room for a few moments. Then Irene Addison said: "Did your mother say anything about that dog they used to have, their Prince? Is he there with them? I hope so. Has he still got distemper in the hereafter?"

Arnold ignored her. "The point is," he said, "I've got some making up to do. I've got wrongs to put right. And just being in the company of this little tyke... what's he called, besides Arnold, did you say?"

"Theodore," our Sylvia said.

192

"Aye, well, we'll see about that," Arnold said. "But as soon as I laid eyes on him, I realised what me mother was on about. It's this little lad and, of course, me own little lad—our Ainsley—what matter…"

"And don't forget the little child's mother," Iris reminded him, indicating our Sylvia.

Arnold looked at her and reluctantly said: "Aye, her an'all…"

"And the mother's family," I said.

"Don't push your luck, Doreen. It's got to be one step at a time to kick off with. I can't be rushed. There's a lot of contemplating to do. You can't teach an old dog to change its spots overnight, but I'll get there, just give me time."

"So, can we get married, dad?" Ainsley said.

"Nay lad, I can't stop you, can I? You're a grown man now. Well… a man anyroad. But if you're asking if you've got my consent and approval, the answer is yes. We must get off to a better footing, the pair of us. And I shall expect you to produce more sprogs to join this one. We need an heir and a spare and you need summat to occupy your time."

Arnold looked around the room at everyone and said: "Now that I know they're waiting for me on t'other side, I've got to do everything I can to redeem myself before I'm called to join the great majority. I don't think I'll have long to wait."

"Oh, don't say that, Arnold," said Irene Addison, "you'll be a lot healthier when you're not so poorly. You've got months in you yet."

He looked down again at little Theodore and said: "And this babby will want for nowt. First thing though is that we've got to get him legitimised in the eyes of society. We don't want nobody calling him a nasty name, accurate though it might be. So, you'd better crack on and arrange the wedding—and don't spare no expense. I'm sure Doreen will help you make the arrangements, she's fond of spending other folks' money."

* * *

Well, the day of the TV broadcast came along, and we all settled down in the front room to watch it – me, Iris, Derek, Sylvia, Ainsley and our Sylvia. Beryl and Ulrika was invited, together with little Jean-Claude and our Charmaine Bernadette. Pride of place was given to Theo (that's what he's to be known as) in his little crib.

It was funny seeing the shop on the telly. It all looked familiar but at the same time not quite real. And seeing yourself from all different angles was a bit of a shock. I just wished I'd paid a visit to Maison Tracey's before we started, my hair looks like a rat's nest from behind.

They'd taken all the boring bits out and just left in all the arguing and nastiness. Iris came over like an old witch, tormenting poor Des, worrying at him like a dog with a biscuit, while I stood in the background watching it all happen, mouth ajar as though I were a bit touched.

"Oh, gran, I didn't know you were so awful," our Sylvia said. "I hope you're not going to be like that with our Theo."

"It were just play acting," says Iris. "I just put on a show for the cameras."

Derek was shocked. "I didn't know you could be such a bully, Mam," he said. "You're giving that poor chap a really bad time."

I took the opportunity to say, "Now you know what I've been complaining about all these years."

"Look, Derek, you've got to learn the difference between the real me and the part I'm playing to get the publicity for the shop," Iris said.

"I don't see any difference, meself," I said.

As the programme went on, it turned into the Des and Iris show. And because they'd edited out all the in-between bits, it just seemed like concentrated persecution of Des by Iris. Des, in return, gave the impression that he was putting up with all the insults and jibes because he was too polite to retaliate against a defenceless old lady.

"There's going to be hell to pay after this, mother" Derek said. "You're coming across as a right vicious old bag."

"They say the camera never lies," I said.

By the end of the first programme, Des was looking like a dog in need of the RSPCA. If he had a tail, it would have been between his legs.

As the credits rolled, the announcer was saying, "How much more can Des take before he flips? The next episode is at the same time tomorrow."

"There's never going to be more of it, is there?" Derek said, full of dismay. "Everybody's going to hate you, mother, if you keep carrying on like this."

"That'll be nothing new for her," I said.

The phone rang and when I answered it was Marje Bickerstaffe. "I'm surprised at you, Doreen," she said. "And as for Iris, I think it's a scandal. You both want locking up for subjecting poor Des to that."

"It's not as bad as it looks," I said.

"I hope he prosecutes the pair of you for human rights abuses. I don't know how he puts up with it."

As soon as I put the phone down it rang again. "You don't know me," a woman's voice said, "but I've just watched *Service with a Smile* and I'm scandalised. Who is that horrible old woman? If I was Des, I'd give her a smack in the mouth."

And then someone else came on, a man this time. "You want to watch yourselves, you two old cows. People have been murdered for less than what you're doing."

"Are you after having fish and chips?" I said. "If not, please go and jump off a cliff."

"Who was that?" Derek said.

"I think it might have been a semi-death threat. I've took the phone off the hook. I think the general public have took against you, Iris. You've unleashed a wave of hatred. I don't think I'm going into the shop tomorrow, there might be more threats."

"Well, I'm not bothered," Iris said. "They can say what they like, just so long as they buy their fish and chips from us rather than Chips & More!"

* * *

Well, we did open the shop the following day, although I had Derek's cricket bat under the counter in anticipation of any rampaging psychos that might turn up in search of fishcakes.

First in were these two young girls. They were giggling behind their hands and staring at Iris as though she were an exhibit in Madame Tussaud's. They bought fish and chips, though. They didn't say anything about the programme but that's obviously what brought them in.

They were followed by a bloke who ordered fish, chips and a can of Lucozade. He saw Iris hovering in the background and said: "Well, done, Mrs. I'm glad you gave that jumped up Des McIntyre a blasting. He's a right bighead."

"Oh, I don't think you'd think so if you met him," I said.

"He's too full of himself," this chap says, "He needed a bollocking like that woman gave him." He gave a little wave of acknowledgment to Iris. "I'm right looking forward to tonight's programme, Mrs. I hope you finished him off."

And so it went on, the pros and the antis came in one after another, all of them making known their opinion of Iris's behaviour. Nearly all of them bought something, though, just to be in the premises that they'd seen on the telly and to meet the people they'd either cheered on or booed at.

After the service was over, I locked the door, turned the sign over to "Closed", and Iris and me sat in the back having a cup of tea.

"Have you noticed how much we've taken today?" Iris said.

"About four times as much as previous," I said.

"That is the consequence of fame, Doreen," she said. "Wait until the whole thing has been shown, we'll be nationally known…"

"And hated," I said.

When we got home, Derek was waiting with his *Daily Mirror*. On page two it said: "Chip Shop Terrier Savages Des McIntyre." There was comment about the show, which the paper had had a preview copy of. Iris was portrayed as a vile, cantankerous old biddy who had run rings round Des McIntyre. She was the real star of the show, it said. "The new rottweiler granny who needs a visit from the social services." Accompanying this was a mock-up photo of a vicious dog on a chain with Iris's face superimposed on the top.

I said to Iris: "Now then—are you happy with this?"

"I'm over the moon, Doreen," she said. "I might be the new most-hated person in the country, but it's going to sell us an awful lot of chips."

The following morning, we had a visit from a film crew from *Look North*, the local evening programme on BBC, and they did an interview with us. It was going to be their 'light-hearted' closing item that evening. Iris was also booked for Sky News, but they cancelled her at the last minute in favour of a story about a lad being attacked by a mongoose. Apparently he was feeding it raisins when it suddenly went for him.

The next episode that evening, showed the riot that Stephanie herself had provoked. They had edited it in such a way as to make it look like Pearl Harbour and the storming of the Bastille rolled into one. And they'd added sound effects unlike anything that had been heard at the time. All it lacked was machine-gun fire and mortar bombs. Somehow Iris had blood running down her face. Our Sylvia said it was a special effect created with CGI, whatever the hell that is.

"You're packing that shop up," Derek said after he'd watched it. "It's too dangerous for me mother to be in such an environment. She could get lynched next."

"It wasn't nothing like that," I said to Derek. "People was annoyed, but they wasn't about to string us up from a lamp post. Throwing your mother about and manhandling her was just a bit of fun. Stephanie and her gang have boosted it up into something a lot more dramatic than it was. We've been in far greater danger than that, haven't we Iris?"

The phone calls started again, this time with people asking if we was OK, and commiserating, as though we'd had a narrow escape from the Russian revolution. That streak of phony blood they'd applied to Iris had altered everyone's opinion.

Marje Bickerstaffe had changed her tune. "Was Iris injured at all?" she asked.

"Unfortunately not," I said, "although I wouldn't have blamed Des if he'd stuck her head in the frier."

The customers in the shop next day were all very sympathetic and saying how frightening it must have been. The two girls who'd been there the day before came back for another look at the newly-minted local TV stars and to purchase another bag of chips and, on this occasion, one battered sausage between them.

I was enjoying the hero worship better than I had the hatred. Iris was just glad it was having the effect she'd aimed for, good or bad.

The third episode featured our scoring of Des and that retail guru who was trying to tell us what was wrong with the business and how we were going to change things.

"Bloody expert!" Iris said. "We didn't need no advice from him to get sales going."

"Yes, but how long will it last after this has finished?" I said. "People have very short memories. They'll soon start drifting back to Chips & More!"

And, unfortunately, I was right. The mad rush that resulted from *Service with a Smile* petered out within days. As our customer base dwindled, next door's started to grow again. While we sat twiddling our thumbs, Chips & More! had to order in extra supplies to filful demand.

But still, we had the wedding arrangements to distract us. I went to the vicarage to see about the service with our Sylvia and Ainsley. Iris wouldn't go because she said she was frightened by the size of the vicar's face. But despite this, he was most obliging and, as well as arranging the reading of the bands he fitted in an emergency christening for our Theodore Arnold.

Grandad Arnold (as we now had to call him) wasn't out of the clinic in time for that, but he swore that he would be ready, come hell or high water, to be best man for Ainsley at the wedding. I thought our Gary would have been a more suitable choice for that duty, but he refused point blank to do it.

"I will not collude with that oppressive and homophobic institution in any way whatsoever," he said. "Me and Bill will come to the reception, but you won't get me into a church, except perhaps with a packet of firelighters and a box of matches. Besides, it's all a farce. Our Sylvia's about as holy as a packet of Polo mints."

I think he feels quite strongly about it.

The reception was put in the hands of the Applegate Hotel. I'd been there to a couple of wedding receptions and a funeral wake. They was all very satisfactory, although I considered the chocolate fountain to be a death trap waiting to happen.

Then me and Iris had a lovely time rifling through the dresses at Dora Cooper's Wedding Requisites store and choosing one for our Sylvia. I didn't trust her choosing her own or it might have ended up being more of a clown show than solemn nuptials. I don't know if anybody makes a biker-style wedding gown but if they do, you can bet she'd find it.

She was that took up with the new baby that she was quite happy for us to rig her out in traditional fashion without protest.

"What flowers do you want for your bouquet?" I said.

"Oh, you choose, Mam," she said.

"Are you having a veil?"

"I don't know—you decide, Mam."

"What about bridesmaids, are you having any?"

"Whatever you think, Mam."

"And page boys? Page boys can be nice, so long as they're not little monkeys running riot."

"Whatever you say, Mam. I don't know nothing about page boys."

"Do you want a matron of honour?" I wish I hadn't said that because she went for Ulrika.

Well, she showed little interest so, in the end, it could have been my own wedding I was arranging as everything was to my taste. It's what I would have chosen for myself should I have been getting married at somebody else's expense.

It's all very simple when you've got money. You just tell other people what you want, and they do it.

It weren't like that at my wedding to Derek, all them years ago, we had it all to do for ourselves. The reception was in me mam's front parlour and consisted of a running buffy of cake, potted meat sandwiches, cheese sandwiches, egg sandwiches and assorted lettuce and tomato salads and crisps. After that, raspberry trifle was served. All home-made. Ale was on tap and a cheery knees-up followed the feasting. Later, to soak up the booze, there was cheese and pickled onions, with sherry for them as wanted it. The presents from family and friends consisted of, amongst other things, an alarm clock, a half canteen of cutlery, a framed picture of a little girl with a tear on her cheek and a set of loose covers for the settee. These were proudly displayed on the kitchen table for everyone to admire.

We were poor in them days, but we did have a lot of fun. You do when you're young, don't you? Anything amuses you when you're with your friends and the ale is flowing liberal. Like when one of our guests—John Price it were—went out into the back yard for a smoke, he got bitten about the face and neck by next door's Alsatian. Well, me and Marje Bickerstaffe nearly wet ourselves laughing. Me mother was annoyed and said we ought to be ashamed of ourselves, laughing at other folks' misfortunes. I said, "It wasn't that bad—he only needed four stitches."

I don't think the Applegate Hotel will be quite so much fun. It'll be all fancy tablecloths and balloons floating over the table and lasses dishing up seasonal vegetables with silver service to go with the roast pork. There'll be separate gravy boats no doubt. But Arnold's business associates were coming, so it had to be posh.

As our Sylvia changed the baby, I thought I'd better have a talk with her about a wife's duties. Not that there was much I could tell her about the...you know...the physical aspects. In fact, she could probably educate me in that department, being a much more experienced woman. No, I wanted to tell her about what day-to-day life would be like when you're chained to the same man for the rest of your life.

But then, I thought, maybe if I tell her how Derek and I have managed over the past thirty-two years, how it was at the beginning and how it is now, she'll probably cancel the nuptials forthwith. It's a marathon not a sprint, I said to her, and you're likely to get cramp at certain points in your lives together.

"Is there anything that's troubling you about the upcoming joining in holy matrimony?" I said to her. "Any advice you want me to give you?"

"No," she said.

"Well, anyroad," I said, "as far as the intimate side of things goes, you seem to have got that sorted out. It took me and your dad a while when we first started. He turned out to be important in the downstairs department. We had to go to the doctors about it."

"We haven't got that sorted out," she said.

"What... you mean, like... the messing about in the bedroom department?"

"No, we haven't managed it yet. Well, Ainsley hasn't anyway. He's still a virgin, as regards messing about."

I was a bit mystified.

"But... if you haven't messed about, I mean, properly messed about, how have you managed to produce little Theo?"

She looked down, a bit shamefaced.

"Don't tell me..." I said. "Don't tell me it isn't Ainsley's babby."

"Well, it is, in the sense that he's claimed it. I never said he was the father—it was everybody else."

"Who is the father, then?" I said.

"It dunt matter, Mam. Ainsley loves our Theo, so that's all that counts."

"You've had a very narrow escape, lady. Ainsley's dad was all for having a DNA test until he had that encounter with the supernatural. Now he's enamoured of our Theo."

I thought for a moment, then I said.

"Does Ainsley know he's rearing another man's son? Does he know he's got a cuckoo in the nest?"

"I've not said nothing about it to him, and he doesn't seem to know how babbies are made. He's ever so innocent. He thinks because we had a bit of a kiss and a cuddle in the nude, that was sufficient."

200

"I don't know who's more ignorant, him or you. So, who is the father, then? You must know."

"My lips are sealed, and I don't want you saying nothing, neither. It would break Ainsley's heart if he thought little Theo was not flesh of his flesh."

"I'll buy Ainsley a sex education book. But I'm not sure they do a Ladybird book of husbandly duties in the manking about department. He's got to be educated in the correct procedures. He's certainly got to be disabused of the idea that babbies are anything to do with storks or gooseberry bushes."

I'll be walking on eggshells now until that ring is on her finger and the vicar has pronounced their union to be concentrated in the eyes of the Lord, even though it is based on a lie.

* * *

Our Sylvia only went to one fitting of the wedding dress when two had been recommended, so when it came to her time to walk down the aisle on the arm of Derek, her proud father, her frock looked a bit like a work in progress. The sleeves were different lengths and there was a big bulge at the back. Our Gary said she looked like the Hunchback of Notre Dame. He can be right cruel when it comes to his sister.

Ainsley was rigged out in his Moss Bros dress suit, with matching floral waistcoat and dickie bow, which he kept pulling at and making faces that indicated he couldn't breathe. I whispered to him, "Be patient, you'll only have to put up with the choking until you get through the service, then you can take it off. Try to tolerate it unless you start to lose consciousness."

Grandad Arnold had his best man duties to perform. His girth was such that there was hardly room for anyone else near the altar. Irene was sitting on the front row having been given charge of Theo during the service. When the baby started crying—and he's got a good set of lungs on him— a woman tutted. Irene turned and glared at her.

Our Sylvia and Ainsley remembered what they had to do, which was a miracle in itself, and so the service didn't turn into the fiasco that I was dreading. Ainsley had a bit of trouble getting his "I dos" out due to the strangulating effect of his dickie bow. Iris spent the time closely studying the hymn book because she couldn't bear to look at the vicar. He was a real trigger for her big face syndrome.

I was too tense to have the crying do that is traditional for the bride's mother, so I had to pretend I was ruring and dabbed my eyes with my best silk handkerchief.

After the vicar pronounced them man and wife, he warned us against chucking confetti outside the church as it was against the rules. Rice could not be thrown neither because of the vermin risk.

We then all repaired to the Applegate Hotel, where mojito cocktails awaited our arrival. There was an element of socialising, which seemed to be strictly separated on lines of who had money and who didn't.

Our side of the family—together with Ulrika and Beryl—gathered at one end of the room and Arnold's business associates and their wives, expensively dressed and coiffed, gathered on the other. There were suspicious glances going both ways.

Then the gong was rung for us to proceed to the wedding feast. There were name tags for everyone telling you where you had to sit. Our family were at the far end, while Arnold's crowd were at the top. Of course, me and Derek, being father and mother of the bride, had to sit at the top table—even Arnold couldn't avoid that—and I parked myself next to Irene.

Then it was time for speeches. Arnold clinked a glass and stood up. His stomach caught on the table and it almost tipped over. He managed to save it, although his glass of champagne was tipped over.

"First off," he said, "I'm going to invite the father of the bride to have his say. So come on Derek, lad, make your speech."

Derek was mortified at the idea of speaking in front of all these business people but, knowing it was his duty and there was no escape, he got up and said, "I am very pleased for both the bride and groom who have both got married today. I hope they will enjoy their honeymoon and that it won't be too tiring for them—y'know what I mean?" He thought everyone was going to laugh at that, particularly as he accompanied it with a suggestive wink, but there was silence, so he didn't proceed with any more of the jokes he had planned and said, "I would like to thank Arnold and Irene here for their generous sponsorship of the wedding and for the waitresses who have served us lovely grub and given extra crackling for them as wanted it. I would also like to thank my wife Doreen for being the mother of the bride. Thank you."

With that, he sat down with his face flushed with embarrassment.

Then Arnold rose again, this time avoiding a collision between the table and his bulk.

"Now, before I speak, I'd like to say something," he announced. "As father of the groom and best man at these festivities it falls upon me to say a few words about the happy union what we are celebrating today. As you know, my son Ainsley has presented me with a bonny grandson. I say that without shame because these days nobody thinks nothing of giving birth outside of marriage, do they?"

Irene started to sob.

"But all the same, we want the child— our little Theo Arnold—to have all the advantages of legitimacy, which he will now have. But I now come to the changes that have occurred in my personality. I shan't go into detail because those who need to know already know how this has come about. There is no need for me to say any more about my near-death experience during which I encountered my late mother who told me to pull my socks up as regards my behaviour. And so, today, I would like to tell my mother—who I am sure is watching all this from her place in the heavenly firmament—that I'm going to make amends. I want to apologise to my new in-laws, the Potts family. I have treated them something abominable in the past. In fact, I will go so far as to say it was egregious what I did…"

Ainsley looked at our Sylvia for help in translating his father's words into a form he could understand. She was as lost as he was.

"And so," Arnold continued. "I want to put things right today in front of everybody here assembled and also those who have pre-deceased us. I want us to get off on another foot."

He looked down at me and smiled. I felt a bit sick, but I smiled back.

"Doreen and me have been at loggerheads in terms of our business dealings recently, haven't we Doreen?"

I nodded.

"I have sought to put the mockers on her dream, which I deeply regret. So now I want to put that right. In way of recompense, I am hereby relinquishing the Balaclava Street branch of Chips & More! It will be closed for business within the week."

203

I heard Iris let out a little yell of delight and she shouted, "Bloody hell!"—which got a bigger laugh than Derek's mucky suggestions had.

Arnold continued: "Henceforward Balaclava Street is the sole province—as regards chip shops at any rate—of Doreen and associates. Chips & More! will be removed to another location, far enough away so as not to offer competition. I hope this will give Doreen and her erstwhile partner, Iris, the opportunity to build up their own empire. They've definitely shown an aptitude for it. In many ways I wish they worked for me—they're a sight better than some of you lot."

Arnold's business associates laughed, but there was a definite nervousness about it.

Arnold looked up at the ceiling: "And I hope, Mam, that what I have done today will go some way to placating the powers-that-be up there and putting me in their good books." He looked back at the guests. "Well, that's it as regards the speeches. I would have read out the telegrams at this point, except there haven't been none. So, now we come to the toast. Please raise your glasses to the happy couple…" He noticed that his champagne glass was empty due to his tipping it up with his stomach. He signalled to the waitress to refill it, when this was done he raised the glass and said, "The happy couple!" We all raised our glasses. Then he said, "please enjoy the rest of your meal, which I believe consists of tiramisu, although I would have preferred jam roly-poly and custard meself—and then take to the dancefloor and have a boogie, as they say. The bar's all bought and paid for, so don't hold back on the boozing."

Iris came running over to me. "Did you hear that, Doreen?" she said, all excited.

"I could hardly not have heard it," I said. "He was bellowing in my ear."

"It's grand news, int'it?" She leaned over and gave me a little kiss on the cheek. I tried not to recoil but it was instinctive. I did share her excitement, though.

Then she turned to Arnold and gave him a kiss on the cheek, too. "Abolishing your chip shop on Balaclava Street is very generous of you, Arnold," she said. "It almost compensates for you trying to do us in that time."

Arnold harrumphed, looked away shame-faced and said, "Aye, well…".

Then the happy couple left for their honeymoon. Arnold had said to them that they could go anywhere they liked, even on a world cruise if they wanted but, in the end, they had chosen Camber Sands because (a) Ainsley had once vomited on a cross channel ferry and was therefore categorized by his mother as a 'poor sailor', and (b) because Ainsley knew Camber Sands from previous visits as a child, he was confident he would not get lost.

The two babbies were left in the care of the grandparents—Theo was given over to Arnold and Irene to look after and little Charmaine Bernadette was with me and Derek.

Derek had said he didn't want to stay at the reception any longer than necessary because he felt uncomfortable among posh people. But when he heard the bar was free, he changed his mind. And the evening progressed very satisfactory.

That is until our Gary came over to me and said, confidentially: "Young Theo has a grand head of hair, hasn't he, mam?"

"Oh, he has that. Luxurious, in't it? He'll be a gorgeous young man when he's grown up."

"You know he doesn't seem to resemble anyone in our family— or Arnold's as far as I can see. He certainly doesn't look anything like Ainsley, does he, or our Sylvia?"

I started to feel a bit uncomfortable. "Just a minute, Gary, what exactly are you saying? What's all this about? Do you know something I don't?" I lowered my voice, "Have you got knowledge about an alternative father?"

He wouldn't elaborate, and him and Bill went home at that point. But it has unsettled me. If they know, then others must have their suspicions. At the moment, though, Arnold seems satisfied with the finished product. I just hope whoever the blond father is, he keeps his peace and we don't end up with any custody battles.

* * *

True to his word, Arnold decommissioned the Chips & More! The fascia was taken down, the fittings removed, and the place was completely empty by the end of the day.

People were turning up for their Chips & More! supper, finding the shop closed, looking a bit traumatised, and then deciding to give us a try. It took only a few days after that for us to realise that, if this kept up, we would soon be generating enough money to eventually turn a profit.

More "For Sale" signs were going up on the housing estate, and after a few months it was clear that Iris's assessment of the new population as being yuppies and potential victims of anorexia proved wrong. Even these middle-class young folk liked fish and chips. And because so many of the women living there were working, there wasn't enough time or energy for them to be cooking elaborate meals when they got in. So, a fish and chip supper, available right on the doorstep, was just the ticket.

* * *

We had to have another re-relaunch, of course, and we invited Des McIntyre to come and do the honours. To our surprise he agreed, and not only that but he waved his fee which, I understand, is very substantial when he opens new supermarkets and that.

"I hope you've forgiven me for doing you over," said Iris. "You know I only partially meant all them insults."

Des laughed and said that on the basis of our encounter he had been signed up for several other reality shows. He was coining it on the back of *Service with a Smile*. We announced Des's presence in the paper and a good crowd turned out to see him on the day we re-re-opened Doreen's Ocean Breezes with a new sense of optimism.

Also present were Mr and Mrs Deans, who had journeyed from Heckmondwyke for the occasion. They told us the good news that Harbour Lights was in the process of being reconstructed and the opportunity had been taken to install luxury improvements in the bungalow, such as non-slip mats in the bath. The authorities had told them that the fire had been the consequence of natural causes—i.e. a lad putting a firework through the letterbox. So Arnold was off the hook as regards that bit of evil-doing.

Six months on and we are taking enough money to pay ourselves a wage. It's hard work because being open six days a week with just the two of us takes its toll. So we took the decision to employ another member of staff, namely Kathy Hornchurch, who used to run Kathy's Café till they pulled it down to make way for the new cycle-lane road widening scheme. "Bloody bicycles," she said, "they want banning." She's got plenty of catering experience and she's right nice with the customers. That helped relieve the pressure on us and even gives us the occasional night off.

My dream of becoming a businesswoman has been a bit of a nightmare at times, but I have, in the end, filfulled it.

Printed in Great Britain
by Amazon